# BONES IN THE DAM

Terrance Lane Millet

ISBN: 978-0-9971268-1-5 (sc)
ISBN: 978-0-9971268-0-8 (e)

Library of Congress Control Number: 2016905045

Publisher:
Terrance Lane Millet
3525 N.E. Canterbury Circle
Corvallis, OR 97330
Terrance Lane Millet

Lulu Publishing Services rev. date: 6/7/2016

# Contents

**Part Three**
**Interlude: What The Silence Said**

Notes

To Martha's Sons


A rough sea!
Stretched out over Sado–
The Milky Way!
~ Basho

# PART ONE

# Prelude: On The Little Abitibi

## CHAPTER ONE

# Stanstead, Quebec, 1940

What is the self?

~ Yedermann

The border is an incision, severing the streets, houses, and lives of Derby Line, Vermont, and Stanstead, Quebec, making one town two, bringing down the knife of nationality on the ties of family and history, but like the shapes of history, the border is neither geologic nor visible: it is the enforcement of an idea—the idea of place, which determines the human idea of self. Like all national borders, this one outlines the limits of perception, for beneath such temporal groundings of the moment, old urges and identities move with the drift of continents, and are shaped by them, and share their tectonics.

High on a hill above the streets, small movements tug the filaments of light and darkness. A man gazes up at the stars, and the woman he loves lies tight against him. She studies his profile, sees the moon reflected in his eyes, thinks of him left in the wake of his older brothers who enlisted in the Canadian forces. She sighs. She watches his lips form words, watches his even teeth bite off the syllables. She thinks about saying something to make him smile but lifts her hand instead and traces the outline of his profile. He sighs. She draws little tight circles around the dimple on his chin, runs her fingers over his chest, and he grunts softly.

A faint aura of "manly suffering" is in vogue; Humphrey Bogart and James Cagney have walked off the movie screens into life. It allows the man to talk tough about things he doesn't understand. This and his ironic self-deprecation make him a romantic figure in the eyes of the woman. His facial planes and surfaces are chiseled on her mind.

Tonight, he talks big about war and heroism and responsibility. He quotes Kipling. He embraces the Englishman's sentiment, yet calls the English "Limeys." His opinions stick to him like burrs stick to a dog running through a field, gathered thoughtlessly, clinging stubbornly.

"The Brits are the best shock troops in the world," he says. "They stay put until the last man dies, and never run. But," he continues, believing this to be a wonderful thing, "I don't want to be in a Limey unit all the same. I want to fight with the 2$^{nd}$ Infantry." And he quotes Kipling again and the woman feels goosebumps rise on his arm. "Though I flayed you and I slayed you, by the living God that made you/ You're a better man than I am, Ghunga Din!" he quotes.

He means to show that he harbors no prejudice, so he continues in the same breath to enumerate the virtues and the shortcomings of a host of other unhappy stereotypes. Only the fighting Irish escape a pejorative label. It is a thrilling sort of ignorance, a simple ignorance that will develop in later years to tough talk about "The Red Menace."

"The Yanks are unstoppable if they are winning, but they'll bog down under pressure," he says in the sort of heroic illusion that young men embrace before they go to war, believing that it is noble to die bravely and uselessly.

The woman's heart sings with his knowledge, and she wonders how he knows such things. "The Vingt-Deuxs are tough," he continues, "but they shoot everyone in sight, including their own men. Besides, you have to be French to join them." It is all nonsense. It is a time of nonsense bouyed up by the parroting of news squibs, of propaganda, of stories passed down from father to son.

"Do you have to go to the war?" the woman asks.

As the geography of the man's mind shifts for the woman, the ancient warrior in the hot blood stretches and wakes.

The man pictures the clash of tough-minded men on ravaged fields while nurses wait for the wounded with admiration in their eyes, and he sees the nurses patch them up with clean white bandages and send them back to the sport and the spoils of war while a grateful populace cheers with adulation. The soldiers never go soft and there are only a few romantic wounds and little life lost in his imaginings, and the fighter planes drone angrily overhead.

And he says through clenched teeth and narrowed eyes, "Sure I do! George is joining up tomorrow with Waterman."

He will enlist and get his uniform. He will, he imagines, return and tell stories about his pals in action; he will talk about the toughness of the Germans, and the tragedy of war.

It is the nonsense embraced by all times and by all warriors. It is the sort of thinking that will persuade the British to die in their thousands on front lines and spur tough-minded Canadians into wave after wave of annihilation on the beaches of Dieppe. He will be there on that stony beach. He will run through the enfilade of German machine guns in the fog. He will hear the chatter of the MG 34's spitting out 900 rounds per minute and feel the whine of the bullets and wear the wet screams of men.

"Will you come back to me?" she asks.

"Sure," he says, but he is dreaming of medals and wounds and the fight for country. She snuggles against the night's chill. She loves him for coming back, though he hasn't yet left, and she tries to imagine what he will be like, a seasoned veteran with new toughness and tragedy. A hero. Her hero. "Sure I will," he says.

When she moves her hand into his and asks him about having a family, his reverie is shattered. The notion startles him. It is too early to think about children. He has only just attained manhood, freedom, and there is much to do.

But he remembers a line from Cagney and says the right thing for the moment, and she nibbles his ear in gratitude. He calls her "Doll".

The woman and the man lie together in darkness. The scent of new-mown hay unrolls over the hill into the night. The grass is soft beneath them, the earth is cool, and the stars above are relentless.

The woman watches the man and pictures a house with a yard and flowers. She sees a husband coming through the gate after work, and her friends are envious.

The man squints at the stars and pictures a field of battle where heroes clash and the good survive and stare tragically into the distance. He sees a company of men.

Then he rolls towards her, kisses her hard on the mouth and pulls her close. His fingers cup the ribs beneath her blouse.

"Oh!" she says, "let's wait until the wedding. You won't be gone long. We have to wait! Let's! Oh, no one will ever believe we did! But we'll know." And she giggles in delight. He swallows his desire. It is a nascent wound.

The man holds the woman. They stare into the heavens, and a great stillness moves within them.

## CHAPTER TWO

# 1945

North Bay, Ontario: 1945

The Ontario Northland Railway Station

*Timestamp: 20:50*

A man stands on a wooden platform and waits for a train. It is January, and his breath is a frozen cloud. He murmurs names like Temískaming and Temágami and Abitíbi. The words are new to him, Cree and Anishinaabe words. They are the words of his wife's people. He stands on the snow and shifts from one leg to the other. The platform creaks with the cold. His ears sting with the frost, and he knows they will burn when they warm, so he pulls his collar tight around his neck and hunches down into it. He plans ahead. His feet are cold, but he knows the train will be warm, and after a few hours it will be hot and stuffy. Then he will walk to the junctions between the cars to cool down and think about fresh air. Cocooned in the sounds of wheels pounding and rails screeching, he will stand on the worn steel plates of the floor with his feet planted widely against the rough ride. He will imagine his wife waiting back in Quebec, where the little towns bead the border with old-world names like Derby Line, Rock Island, and Beebee.

As he looks south along the tracks now, the train comes coughing out of the darkness, clothed in the faint fall of the snow. The pistons muscle the big wheels around, and the earth trembles beneath them. The steam trumpet wails, and the headlamp cuts into the night, brightening the ice where the man stands. He thinks that of all the machines made, the steam locomotive is closest to having a soul. It coughs and wheezes with a deep and animal sorrow; its nakedness is its strength, and its call a lamentation.

He moves forward and leans on a baggage cart, rests a foot on the dented iron wheels, and lights a cigarette as the locomotive eases into the station. He coughs the smoke into the air, and when the train stops, he picks up his duffel and climbs aboard.

He turns right as he enters the car and right again to the first seat. The window faces the station. He drops his duffel on the outer seat and sits by the window and waits. As he looks out, the depot agent walks onto the platform with the conductor and lights a cigarette. After a few words, the conductor heads back to the caboose, and the agent glances first at the areas between the cars, then at the wheels, then at the windows, and then in through the window to him. The train jerks and begins to pull away, and the man watches the agent look back down to the tracks where the wheels squeal on the steel.

Then the train pulls past the station and from inside the Pullman the window affords no view but the dark. The man listens to the wheels sing as the rails carry them into the night, and he looks out the window trying to summon up the dark eyes of his wife.

"Michael, come back to me just as you are," she said when he left for the war. And then, two months after he returned: "Let's start a family."

"I've only been back two months," he said, "and have to live in the Abitibi staff house for the first year. No kids. That's the company policy for recruits. We have to get in line for a house." He looked at her. "You'll have to stay here for some time. Then we'll get a place in Timmins to get you close."

She laughed.

"Shall we name him Michael? When we start?"

"No damn way. I've never liked that name and always wanted to be named Finn. Or Paddy," he said.

"We could call him 'Mick'."

"Mick? God, think what you're saying."

"Oh."

"Finn. Finn MacBride. It has a ring to it."

"What if it's a girl?" she asked.

"God knows," he said. "What do you think?"

As the train gathers speed, the mind of the man reaches for the sound of the woman's words and the shape of her face, but his eyes and his ears neither hear nor see her. The window before him presents itself as a darkness containing only his image. Beyond the window, and beyond the man's seeing, wolves run through a clearing on a hill, heading north. They run through the spruce and over the frozen ponds where the banked snow is heaped against the deadfalls; they run into the darkness and leave the white trails empty under the wavering curtain of the Northern Lights.

The man's mind reaches out to these things, as though pulled.

*Timestamp: 20:40*

When he hears the passenger enter the waiting room, the depot agent pushes back from the typewriter, stands, and walks across his office to the telegraph desk under the windows. The windows afford him a view of the platform. He pulls down the green blinds, checks the telegraph, arranges some papers, and picks up a yellow, wooden pencil. He twirls it between his fingers and puts it down alongside the telegraph and parallel to its base. Then he turns, leans back, and glances at the passenger through the ticket window. Beside the window, the door opens to the waiting room, and to the right of the door, two train-order hoops hang on the wall. He slides his thumbs into the watch-pockets of his vest. Then he looks around the room, checking for tidiness.

The office is long and narrow and painted a light, spring green, with the wainscoting a shade darker than the walls above it. The ceiling is a shade between the two. A scarred, walnut roll-top desk sits against one wall beside the door to the baggage room, and above the desk, a Good Housekeeping award hangs on the wall. The depot agent rests his gaze a moment there and nods. He rubs his thumbs against his forefingers through the wool pockets of his vest and nods satisfied.

A movement catches his eyes and he looks through the pass-through window at the passenger who is walking through the exit and out onto the platform.

"Mmph," says the agent.

The depot agent walks to the door, pauses to run a finger along the mail hoop, and walks into the empty waiting room where he turns to face the platform. Outside, he sees the passenger lean against a baggage cart and light a cigarette.

When the train pulls in to the station and slows, the agent looks past the passenger to the locomotive, and the engineer lifts a hand. The passenger picks up his duffel bag and climbs aboard as soon as the train stops. The agent watches the man board, then he looks down the platform and sees the conductor step down from the caboose and come toward the depot doors.

"Quiet night," says the conductor as he enters the waiting room. "Only got a minute." A cold draft moves along the floor from the platform door being opened. The agent moves his thumbs back and forth in the pockets.

"Yep," he says.

"Just the one?" asks the conductor.

"Yep," says the agent again.

"How far? Cochrane?"

"The colony at Abitibi Canyon. Another Hydro man."

"Seems young."

"Most are. Another one just out of the war, likely."

"Don't look army to me," says the conductor. "Not enough swagger."

"Well," says the agent, "he had himself on a gold ring, so I figure he's not long married and is up here on his own." He rubs his thumb against his forefinger in the pocket of his vest.

The conductor looks down at the vest and raises an eyebrow.

"Shiny," says the depot agent, "and no wear on it."

"Mmph," says the conductor, and shrugs. "Not much to guess on, Sherlock."

"He had him an Army-issue duffel, with a insignia on it," the agent added, "and a wood rifle kit. Lee-Enfield. That would be a Scout's kit."

"Well then," says the conductor. He surveys the empty waiting room. "What insignia?"

"Queen's Own Rifles."

"Ah. You might have stayed at home tonight and let me do the tickets for all the busyness there was. I thought there'd be a rush of survey men for Moose Factory."

"Nope," says the agent.

"What was the name on the ticket?" the conductor asks.

"MacBride," says the agent. "Michael MacBride."

Then the two men turn and walk outside onto the platform and look up and down the tracks. The platform is empty. The conductor walks down the platform to the caboose, climbs the steps, and hangs on to the bar, leaning out so he can see the line of cars clearly. He waves the all clear to the engineer. The agent looks at the couplings linking the baggage car in front of him to the first of the passenger cars, then at the brake hoses between the cars and at the journaling boxes where the bearings are housed. He lights a cigarette and glances up to the windows. The faces of the passengers are turned toward him and the station, and he shifts his gaze over them to the front of the car, where the passenger from the station is turned to him, and he looks briefly into the soldier's eyes. The young man's gaze is on him, but the focus is far away, and the agent recognizes the look from his own war. Then the train lurches and begins to inch forward out of the station. The conductor leans out from the caboose steps to see that the platform stays clear, and nods to the agent.

The agent raises his hand, then drops his gaze to the steel wheels of the cars as they move past him, gaining speed, rolling north. He looks for any dragging equipment, or sticky brakes, or overheated journal boxes with the telltale sparks and smoke. If he sees a problem, he will flag the train as the caboose leaves the depot. Otherwise, he'll give the OK sign. Then he'll go back inside the depot and telegraph the dispatcher up the line what time the train passed his station and if anything is wrong.

*Timestamp: 21:10*

When the train leaves the station, the conductor opens the caboose door, stands in the junction and looks in through the window of the steel door to survey the car. He makes his way out of the caboose and down the aisle to collect the new ticket, punch it, verify destinations, and place the punched ticket in the slot over the window. The car is a Pullman sleeper, its high, mahogany seats upholstered with deep green velvet, and the seats are fixed, facing each other. The seat backs have white linen covers at the top to protect the velvet. He grabs the seat backs as he moves to keep steady in the rocking train, tossed now by the steel tracks heaved by the bitter frosts of winter. A few passengers are familiar to him, and he watches them refresh their memories by scanning the nameplate on his lapel. They speak his name, and he murmurs a greeting. Ahead, against the entrance wall, in the first seat to the right as the passengers board, he sees the new man against the window. His duffel bag is beside him on the seat. It is, the conductor knows, a sign that the man wants to sit alone, but when he approaches and looks into the man's face and takes the ticket, he sees something else in the young man's eyes, and since it is the last ticket on the train, he sits down and extends his hand.

"Sam Farmer," he says.

The younger man takes the hand. "MacBride," he says. "Michael MacBride."

Then the men lean back in their seats.

"First time on this route?" the conductor asks.

"Yes sir," says MacBride.

"Heading to the Fraserdale Station. That means the Colony at the generating station on the river. Abitibi."

"Right again," says MacBride.

"You'll need to ride the speeder from the station in to the Colony," says the conductor. "They know your arrival time?"

"I hope they do," says MacBride.

"We can telegraph the station agent there when we leave the Cochrane station and make sure," says the conductor. "It'll be a cold wait otherwise, and a colder ride on that little speeder."

"Thanks."

The conductor nods and looks out the window into the darkness. He breathes deeply, and then sighs.

"You getting back from war work?" he asks.

"That's right."

The conductor nods again.

"Where?"

"Dieppe, with the 2nd Infantry. Then north to the channel islands with the 1st and from there into Holland in '44."

"Thought so. Dieppe?"

"Yes sir."

"You at the battle of Scheldt too?"

"That's right."

"That was the fall of '44. You got home quick."

"I had some leave and the war ended."

The conductor looks out the window. There is nothing to see, and the frost has begun to creep out of the corners onto the glass.

"This is a good place to be," the conductor says, gesturing out the window. "The north country. There aren't many people here and plenty of room. Mainly, it's about those two things up here. There's quiet on the rivers."

"I've heard," says MacBride.

"There's only 130 people living where you're going, and two trains a week through the Fraserdale Station. Nearest place is Cochrane, some eighty miles away. You'll be left alone if you like in the Colony. The men there—and some of the women—did war work too and came up for their own reasons. I imagine you'll find what you need. They're a pretty tight bunch, I'm told."

MacBride thinks about a handful of men and women living where the unbroken trees roll over the horizon with the sounds of animals and birds and the water. The nattering of red squirrels will replace the machine guns' chatter, and there will be no tanks or divisions rolling over the hills, and no loss, and the skills he learned with the rifle will be useful and good. Then he thinks about another tight bunch of men.

*They called it "Operation Jubilee," but the naval support never came to soften up the town before they were ordered to take the sea wall, and the French double agents had warned the Germans of the landing, so he ran through the fog and tripped over the shingle as the German MG34's lay down their enfilade from the end of the beach. He couldn't tell how far ahead the guns were, but he was running blindly towards their line of fire. It would be like running into a wall of lead, he thought. Behind him, the engines of the small Churchill tanks and Dingo's revved high as they wallowed, mired in the deep shingle. Useless. Then he was in it and heard only the men around him curse and gasp, and the dull, wet thumping of lead on flesh, the sudden exhalation of breath, and then the screaming. He ran directly into a stone wall and was knocked on his back, then crawled along on his belly with the bullets whining inches above. When he came to a break in the wall he crawled onto it. It was a double stairway, choked with rusty barbed wire, and the only way up was under it. The sounds from behind were sickening, so he raised his rifle over the wall and squeezed off five rounds in the direction of the pillbox. Then he reloaded and forced his way under the wire a step at a time until he reached the street. When he got to the top step, there were a handful of the 2ⁿᵈ laying down fire at German positions along the street. God knows how they got there, he thought, but he didn't stop and crossed in a crouch to a doorway with a dead German on the threshold. He ran for the stairs to the second floor, made his way to a window with the intent of firing down on the enemy positions pinning down his company across the street. When he got to the window and looked down, the fog thinned enough to see they were all dead, but there were others coming up the access laying down enough fire to cover his as he went to work thinning out the German positions.*

*After watching the Canadians come up again and again from the beach and either being cut down in the street or working their way into the blind streets to the German infantry waiting for them, he realized there was nowhere to go but back and report what was happening further into the town. At that point, he was out of ammunition, and the only way back was the long way, down the road and around the far end of the pill box out of the line of fire, where the enemy would be massed.*

*He was disgusted with the whole operation.*
*It wasn't until he was on the beach talking with his CO*
*that he realized the blood on his jacket was his.*

"Dieppe was bad," says Sam Farmer.

"Yes," says MacBride. "It was. The Jerries were dug in, and our ships didn't soften them up before we landed. We went in with 5,000 men and lost more than half of them in six hours."

"I lost my son there," said the conductor, "that's why I ask. He was in the 2nd, same as you. I don't need the details. I know it was bad."

"I didn't know a man named Farmer there," says MacBride. "Not in my bunch. I'm sorry."

"He was with the Royal Regiment."

Wiped out, thinks MacBride. They sent five hundred men in with that regiment and six hours later, only fifty came back. He looks at the older man. "I'm sorry," he says.

Sam nods, then says, "You stayed with the Infantry."

"I got into the Scouting and Sniper Platoon after Scheldt," says MacBride, "and stayed in Holland. It made more sense than walking into machine gun fire."

"Not much intelligence on the Dieppe landing, was there?" Sam asks.

"Not a God-damned thing that helped us," says MacBride. "It was flanking fire all the way up the beach."

"That's what I'm told," says Sam.

"Sons-of-bitches," says MacBride. Then he looks down to the wedding ring on Sam Farmer's finger. The conductor follows his gaze. Then he sighs and turns to look out the window.

"Well, it's quiet up here, peaceful," the conductor says. "I took this run for that. It's harder on the Missus since I don't get home as much. But it's temporary. Mostly, I can keep busy with the tickets, and then watch the land go by. It helps settle me, thinking about my boy. And I see a number of you fellows coming north for the country." He looks back from the window to MacBride. "I think you'll like it. Come back to the caboose if you want some company. There's a pot of coffee on the stove."

"Sure," says MacBride. "Thanks," and he reaches out to shake the conductor's hand as the man stands and walks down the aisle. MacBride turns to look out the window. The conductor's words stay in his mind, and he thinks about the men and women who are already there in the settlement. Then he reaches into his duffel bag and takes out a large, manila envelope. He shakes out a letter, typed with a typewriter whose keys needed cleaning. The spaces of the 'D's", "C's", "O's" and "P's" are filled and smudged. It is a letter outlining the facts about the place he is about to reach. He looks at it as he would a mission briefing. It will apprise him of more than just where he is going. He has read the letter already more than once, and the facts are with him, but he goes over them again and again. They are the kind of facts that he loves, for they are dry and give him the nature of the land and the data that yields understanding and saves lives. They are the sort of facts that bore ordinary people, and this makes them even more interesting to MacBride because they calm him. There will be no ordinary people where he is going. They will know the habits of the land and the climate because their survival can depend on it, and when it comes to staying alive, MacBride has learned, no fact is too trivial for notice.

*September 5, 1944*

*Abitibi Canyon Data*
*Abitibi River - General Information*

*The Abitibi River has its source at Abitibi Lake and flows north for a distance of 210 miles into the Moose River at a point approx. 8 miles from tidewater level. The drop from source to outlet is approx. 878 feet and the drainage area south of Canyon is 8443 sq. miles. At a point 43 miles south of Canyon, the Abitibi River is joined by the Frederick House River which flows out of Frederick house and Night Hawk Lakes. The drainage area is 1091 square miles and the elevation of the lake is 902 ft.*

*Canyon Generating Station and colony are approx. 100 miles from tidewater. The average forebay elevation at*

Canyon is 641 feet and the average tail water level is 404 feet giving a drop of 237 feet. The colony is 680 feet above sea level.

The Indian word "Abitibi" has two interpretations (so I have heard). The more probable is "turbulent waters," which aptly describes its turbulent course over many rapids and low falls. All but one of these rapids south of Canyon have been flooded out by the four power developments. The other interpretation is "muddy water," which is descriptive of its dark brown color. The coloring matter is of a colloidal nature, being of finely divided clay particles which remain in suspension.

For domestic use we clear up the water by coagulation (using alum), filtering through sand, and chlorination.

The houses, staff house, store, recreation building, some service buildings, school, and ball park, occupy an area of 19 1/2 acres. It is serviced by a road in the shape of an ellipse which is approx. 3,200 ft. long. This area is located in a clearing of 350 acres, which area includes part of the fore bay. This clearing constitutes a fire guard for protection from forest fires.

All male employees other than operators are assigned positions on the hose and ladder brigade and storage tank valve. The operators handle the chemical extinguishers.

*Seasons*

As compared with Southern Ontario, Spring starts about April 30th; Summer about June 15th ; Fall about September 1st, and Winter about October 15th. There is appreciably longer daylight at Canyon during June and July and shorter during December and January than at Toronto. Canyon is at approximately latitude 50 degrees.

During the past ten years, the maximum temperature was 100 degrees on July 12th, 1936; the minimum temperature was –57 on February 8th, 1934. The mean temperature for the ten years was 30.9 degrees; the yearly mean ranging from 28 degrees to 32.7 degrees.

The heaviest snowfall was 132.2 inches for the winter of 1933-34; the lightest snowfall was 44.5 inches in 1941-2. The 11 year average snowfall was 77.3 inches.

## Victory Garden Produce

Potatoes, carrots, beets, cabbage, strawberries, raspberries, celery, peas, beans, chard, spinach, lettuce, salsify, onions, endive, parsley, parsnips, squash, vegetable marrow, etc.

Corn, tomatoes, and cucumber are grown but they come to maturity only in exceptional years.

3 acres in "Victory Gardens."

## Early History

The early history of the area is associated with the Hudson Bay Co. fur trade. The nearest company post, "New Post," was located six miles North of the Abitibi Canyon. The Hudson Bay Co headquarters for the district was at Moose Factory, located on an island in the delta of the Moose River, near James Bay. They traded along the Abitibi River inland to Abitibi Lake. Transportation was by boats and canoes.

Portages were made at the various rapids and falls by carrying the heavier boats by man power and dog teams. The cargo boats were 30 to 40 feet long, similar to the lumberman's pointer, the lumber for which was sawn by whip saws from logs of native timber.

There were no Indian villages in the vicinity of the Canyon. The Indians lived in temporary camps when trapping and hunting which they did during early winter and spring.

> *The T. & N.O. Railway reached Island Falls, 43 miles North of Cochrane in 1922. In 1922-3 surveys were continued north to Moosonee. Rail was extended to Mileage 68 in the fall of 1927, and on to Moosonee (Mileage 186) in 1931.*
>
> *Construction work started at the Canyon in 1930 and the hydraulic works were completed in 1932. Installation of the first two generating units was completed in 1933. The first unit was placed in service on May 24, 1933.*
>
> *The first residents in the vicinity (after the Hudson Bay Co.) were the family of John Reise who settled at New Post in 1923. They cultivated the land which was very fertile at this point.*

There is no signature to the letter, and MacBride wonders who wrote it. The style has the feel of a military man. He puts the letter aside and thinks about the Victory Garden and what John Reise fed his family. A lot of Moose and grouse and fish and duck. Maybe rabbit. MacBride had eaten rabbit in Belgium, and he wasn't enthusiastic about having it again, though it was better than mutton, which he had come to hate. No tomatoes with the vegetables. Canned goods shipped in on the train, maybe, but they would be prohibitive in cost. There was not much room for error in circumstances like those, especially at forty below, he thinks. The narrow margin of error is familiar and somehow comforts him.

## CHAPTER THREE

# Forty Below

M acBride wakes up cold the next morning and looks out at the icicles hanging from the eaves. They are lit by the lamplight from his room, some six feet long. Below, where they have fallen, their thick ends stab the snow like a picket fence.

He hears someone in the kitchen downstairs. Mrs. Mulligan, the woman he met last night, he thinks, making breakfast in the dark. He looks out at the night stars, hard and blinking. The dawn will not arrive for hours, so he pulls on his trousers and sweatshirt over the woolen longjohns, laces his boots, walks down the stairs, crosses the hall and walks up to the Underwood typewriter on the foyer desk outside the door to the dining hall.

This is what he had heard last night as he tried to sleep. It is the same sort of typewriter he used to type up his reports overseas. With this one, the black enamel has flaked off the frame and one of the supporting leather pegs on the front leg has slumped so that the machine cants like an old ship. MacBride runs his hand over the solid iron of the frame and rings the little bell on the carriage. It has a high, pure tone. He hits a couple of keys. They strike the bare roller with the clickety-clack of railway tracks and telegraphs–the soporific codes of rhythmic peace.

"What are you doing in there?" Mrs. Mulligan calls from the kitchen.

"Nothing," he says reflexively, and he runs his fingers over the machine as he looks at the window to the winter. There is nothing to see but the reflection of the room he stands in. Then he turns and walks to the kitchen where the cook works at the stove. She is stirring porridge in a pot and setting up the pans for frying eggs and bacon, managing it all like a symphony conductor.

"Coffee's ready," she says. "Help yourself." She looks at him over her shoulder and smiles. "Mr. MacBride."

"Thanks," he says. "Michael, please." He smiles back, thinking she reminds him of his aunt. Short, the same white hair pulled up into a bun on the back of her head, hair that when unloosed will flow down her back in the wonderful cascade of a woman wise and winsome in her power. She has the Irish face too, round with a wry mouth, a long upper lip, and the direct, blue eyes he knows he has himself.

"I'm not serving yet," she says turning back. "The oatmeal has to cook and the biscuits are just in the oven. It'll be the better part of an hour. You can eat when the shift arrives." MacBride feels her brogue settle over him like the soft touch of the peat fires his father made.

"That's fine," he says. "I'll nurse the coffee, and poke around."

But once he's back in the foyer, the coffee is not enough. He walks down the entrance hall to the front door and looks out across the road at the little houses hunkered down in their drifts. The winds have heaped the snow on the roofs and folded the little houses into the snow like soft meringues. He can glimpse through the windows a faint life stirring inside and looks at the thermometer outside attached to the window frame: forty below.

He puts down the mug and takes up his green parka from the closet. It is company issue and military design, given to him the previous night when he arrived. The lining of the coat is a thick, red wool, and he ties the lining loosely at the waist with the cincture and zips the parka up. The canvass feels good around him, as though it will last for years. Pulling the hood up over his head, he steps into the felt-lined boots and out through the door into the cold. He inhales the cold air laced with an ozone edge. Immediately, the small hairs in his nose freeze together and pinch.

He sets off north, following the road unrolling over the bumps of the frozen earth. A light sprinkling of snow squeaks beneath his feet, and, around him, the houses are cushioned with snow. Their windows frame bright, warm kitchens, and the people within lift their faces in the frames and nod as he passes.

The road loops right, around the last buildings, to the dam. At the point where the dam meets the earth, a concrete obelisk with a bronze plaque stands. MacBride has read about it, and it is, he realizes, a part of the reason for his morning walk.

He walks to the monument, a seven-foot structure with a brass plaque on each of the four sides, built to honor the men who perished building the dam. More than a dozen, he has been told, lost in the concrete, thrown into the wet mix and left there when a retaining wall collapsed. The poem on the plaque is one he knows and likes: Kipling's "Sons of Martha." He knows that when the summer comes, he will stand at the plinth before he takes the elevator down into the dam, and the summer sun will warm him, and he will read the verses of the poem and memorize them.

Fifty feet or more below the plaque, level with the dead, are the men he will work with. His shift is four to midnight, and soon he will meet the midnight crew when they leave for the staff house and banter over breakfast. Some he has already met, army men older than their twenty-five or thirty years, still calling each other by their last names, Beamish and Legris, Nichols and Brennan, Hoff and Byers and Grills and Fielder and Riddell and Mitchell. Now his name too. They will work in the belly of the dam, below the names on the monument. It seems terrible to MacBride that he has come all this way to escape the twisted forms of death only to have them suspended in the concrete around the place he will spend his days.

He looks away from the plaques. The road continues across the dam to the wilderness beyond, where someone long ago once built a cabin. The little homestead claims the river's edge where a drift of stunted pine huddles by the building, and the grove faintly rebuffs the wind and winter's scrutiny.

He walks to the middle of the dam and looks to his right, up the fore bay of Little Abitibi. A diving board holds vigil by a little island linked to the land by a log boom. Its platform is encased in ice. The frozen river stretches beyond it into the twilight. The dark line of the forest along the riverbank is an unrelenting edge, and far away, the white ribbon of the river disappears into the boreal gloom where the pine and spruce narrow the waters like a closing zipper. There is no movement upon the river, nor in the forest, nor on the snows, and the silence is a weight in his ears.

Then the wind picks up, and he thinks of the gelid water beneath the ice and lifts his face to the night, hoping to glimpse the last hard, bright stars overhead, but the snow is moving in and falling around him. He casts his mind through it and up past the clouds to the moon where the heavens are clear. He thinks of his wife and the sound of her laughter.

The snow floats down and the flakes melt on his face.

Then through his boots he feels the cold and steps away from the river and back to the road. He turns to the staff house where the biscuits are ready and the men will meet to eat together at the long tables.

## Chapter Four

# The Midnight Shift

Abitibi Canyon: August 1946

Midnights

*Timestamp: 06:00*

Near the end of his shift, MacBride walks from his desk past the banks of dials that indicate water flow and amperage towards the entrance of the inspection tunnel. The tunnel runs transversely through the dam from one bank to the other, affording a submerged glimpse of the deep state of the concrete, the health of the dam. This is not a job he likes. Today, he will inspect the east tunnel. He opens the door and stares into the gloom. A strand of bare light bulbs hangs from the ceiling as far as he can see, looped from hanger to hanger, casting harsh shadows on the walls. Two narrow wooden walkways cover the floor on either side of a central runnel that carries away the water leaking through the cracks in the walls. He closes the door behind him, and looks up. One hundred feet overhead stands the monument to the dead, and the dead are here too.

They are around him in the concrete. Twelve or twenty. Which? No one seems to know exactly. They are above and below him now, cocooned and contorted lacunae in the concrete where only the river weeps. They are forgotten men, missed and blamed and hated perhaps, for leaving their families, for vanishing. Now, only the waters know them, the water at his feet, dark from the Little Abitibi leaking through the deep fissures in the dam there, and there, and there. It moves over and under and through the men in the concrete who float in their terrible wombs. He puts his fingers against the wetness oozing from the walls of the inspection tunnel, and the wetness runs to the little runnel in the floor that is an open artery carrying away the minerals of memory. In this little river of souls, slow and thick through the fissures, the men move from their long dark sleep to the water, dissolving, called by time to the fish and the frogs and the eagles, to the things of the river that live in the sun.

Beneath one hundred feet of water, he walks among the bones of the dead, and the soldier in him listens. Faint and far away are the sounds of Dieppe. He begins the long walk to look for anything out of the ordinary, his breath visible before him, his footfalls faint in the cave.

He looks up. It is June outside, and the sun will be climbing when he finishes his shift and rides the elevator up to it. He has four days off and decides to take the boat and head up river to fish for a couple of days.

He walks on.

*Timestamp: 08:10*

When the shift is over, he takes the elevator up to the top of the dam where the utility road connects the settlement to the taiga. He stands against the railing by the water, looks out over the head-pond, lights a cigarette, then walks over to the observation tower and climbs twenty feet. Upriver, past the high, pale cliffs, the trees are stitched thickly to the shore and fingers of pink granite reach into the river where they break up into small, smooth islands. The water is taut beneath a whisper of fog, but by noon a breeze will pluck the surface of the river into a small chop that may tempt the walleye in spite of the daylight.

Overhead, small cumulus clouds brighten with the coming day. He climbs down and walks off the dam, past the staff-house, and along the road to the boathouse.

He is anxious to be in the boat and hopes the weather will last.

*Timestamp: 09:40*

A small anvil-head billows in the north-west threatening quick showers, but the rain will move on and may bring up the fish. He is not worried. He knows the river and opens the throttle. The boat cleaves the water and the small waves hammer brightly on the wooden hull.

A mile upriver, where the cliffs are high and covered with a thin, pungent carpet of leaf and loam, he pilots the boat to the shore. Pine and black spruce grow to the edge of the cliffs above him and lean out towards the river. Eventually, their roots will tear free of the earth and they will tumble into the water. The pale sand beneath the topsoil is soft and always eroding, falling away to form narrow beaches at the base of the cliffs that last until the spring melt washes the shores clean, mixing the fine sand into the water and carrying away the fallen trees. It is a constant process, and the trees, stripped of bark and foliage, wash up on the banks further downriver, silvered, and dried by the weather.

He steers the boat onto the beach, jumps down, pulls the prow up on the sand, then stretches out on a dry area and falls into a light sleep, letting the sun pull the darkness of the inspection tunnel out of him.

When he wakes, he pushes off and starts the motor, heading to the shore opposite the cliffs. Here, the trees come down to the river and the rocky outcroppings are spotted with moss. He heads for a break in the rocks where a stream runs quietly out of the forest, forming a tiny inlet. As he paddles the boat to a landing, he surveys the area for good fishing spots. Around the granite, the stream is fresh and clear and will excite the fish where it meets the muddy Abitibi.

Once he's ashore and dressed his tackle, he stretches his legs and looks at the water below him on the narrow beach. The sand underfoot gives slightly and bulges around his feet as he walks to the end of the inlet where the feeder stream enters the bay.

MacBride looks down as he walks. The water is lively over the rippled shallows, and bright little perch hug the banks, occasionally disappearing downstream into the muddy waters. He wonders if they navigate by what passes for smell, because they find their way back out of the murk and take up the same positions on the sandy bottom, their mouths into the current. They keep their place with only their ventral fins waving as they let the water flow over their gills. They are small things that defy an easy scrutiny and seem charged with potential as they move in bold concert here where the pickerel cannot get them.

The bigger fish stay in the weeds and the holes, and only an occasional flash of muted silver from a flank shows where they wait.

MacBride looks up, suddenly happy, steps out of the water onto the granite, and casts a lure far out into the river.

*Eventually, he dreams, when a house becomes available, he will take the train out to Kirkland Lake and bring his wife back to their first home where, he knows, she will want to raise a family.*

*If he has a son, he will bring him to these places when the boy is older and the pines drop their dry cones on the duff. He will rough up a little of the duff with his fingers and hold it lightly in his hand, releasing the clean scent of summer savory for the boy to smell. The sharp scent of spruce gum will fill the air where they sit, overlaying the soft balm of fern. The sparrows will swarm down around them in search of seeds as he and the boy lean their heads back against a tree, pulling in close, and they will stretch out their legs, tilt their faces into the warmth of the sun, and gaze up through the boughs of the tree, past the breeze moving through in the needles to the small, white clouds racing high above.*

*But for now, the river is his.*

## CHAPTER FIVE

# Letter to Eve

Sunday, September 6, 1946

Hello—

I just read your letter, and you mention the big house on Main Street and your visit there. That house always appeared impressive on the outside, a good house to look at, but your feeling that when you were on the inside looking out the view was changed and not very good struck me. The road and storefronts are not much to look at from a living room window.

We often live that way. You reminded me that we can spend a lot of time looking at things from the outside, having opinions and impressions, but if we go inside and look out, we can be surprised. You mentioned we sometimes do that with people. I'll have to spend a little time thinking about that. I think you are referring to my impatience with a few of the men here.

It can be hard talking to people who see the world in ways that we find upsetting. I'm running into a little of that. Many of the people here, especially the ones who weren't overseas, talk about the war in black and white. Maybe it's a matter of looking at life, of interpreting it and putting our own emphasis on what appears to us. Maybe that's why we're so understanding of friends and those we love—we take the time to look out their windows with them.

But the world exists outside our interpretations too, even outside our notion of times, and sometimes we're lucky enough to simply be there, to see it. Then we see the world with an honesty that stays with us and forms who and what we can be. Mostly, it takes a moment slow enough for us to let the "busy-ness" go, and be fully present where we find ourselves.

Life on the Little Abitibi is like that.

I think of the night trips home in the boat on the river here. I could have been doing any number of things—fishing, thinking about you on the smooth granite islands, spraying DDT on the mosquito streams—but often the sun has set by the time I'm done, and I boat home in the dark.

The stars are bright on the river here, and you can tell by their reflection on the water what is river and what is shore. The water is a shiny darkness bordered by the flat black of the trees. Their jagged tops show where the sky begins. From my point of view, navigating like this is a comforting process, built on knowledge that you pick up, and my trust in it is becoming absolute. Of course, I had to navigate by landmarks in the dark before I came back, but I feel safe here in ways I haven't for a long time, and that's something the place itself provides—a belief that the world can be a good place.

There are times when I sit on the small seat by the motor on these rides, and I imagine you here, our faces close as we look ahead into the night. Finally, my fingers go numb from the vibrating engine as I steer home, and I realize how far away you are. But the smell of the boat's varnish and wood and the wool blankets is strong, and the slap of the cedar hull on the small waves is good, and the musty oilskin tarp on the floorboards keep me dry in the meantime.

The sleep is good here. Soon you will be here too, and our little family will ride the river with the stars overhead mirrored in the waters beneath us, like a ribbon between heaven and earth.

It's a good place to be. When the lights on the dam appear in the night, you know you're home. At first, from a long way off, the lights look like distant beads on the dam thrown down on the fore bay. I want to tell you this is the view looking out from this place, and that's what I see when I look out the windows. I know the waters and the way here, and there is room for us, and we can steer our little family with love and peace over the dark and watery river under the sky. The small wave-tips will slap the boat, bearing us up as we head for the lights on the dam, and I can already hear you quietly say "Look—we're home."

When you are here and we return from such boat trips, once back at the boathouse we'll tie up, gather what we can, and walk up the hill to home and bed. The baby will sleep while I carry him, and we'll walk from the river to the house. It's a lovely little house they have reserved for us, small but cozy, with a bedroom for us and one for the baby. It's house number 7.

The summer nights are rich, rich with the thick cool air, and I look forward to sharing our home and the nights with the two of you.

Thank you for that hope.

Love, Michael

P.S.

I'm using an old typewriter here in the operations room. From the look of the letters, it's the one somebody used to type up the data on the settlement I told you about. I can see it's got me a bit wordy, and I think of those short notes to you I used to write by pencil when I was overseas, not knowing if my letters would ever reach you. I don't know which seems more like a dream—there then, or here now.

CHAPTER SIX

# The Shootist

He bought the rifle, a Marlin 32-40 1884, from a Schuetzen Competition shooter in Montreal who had re-bedded the barrel and zeroed it in. He fired it before the purchase to study the grouping, and when it had been less than an inch at 100 yards, he said he wanted it. The rifle had a short barrel for maneuverability with fold-down tang sights and a peep on the stock. It had good balance and a long strap that could be twisted around the wrist for steadiness. It was made for the bush. There were few long shots in the taiga, a fact that at first suited MacBride, for he liked the idea of standing up when he shot. He'd had enough of lying on the ground taking long shots at a thousand yards, and, besides, he thought, the ground around the Little Abitibi was always damp.

"You'll never hit that moose," says Mitchell beside him. "It's got to be 250 yards."

"Not quite," says MacBride. He knows the Winchesters the other men carry are good at 150 yards, but beyond that they are not dependable. They are factory-issue 30-30 rifles ordered from the Sears catalogue. But the 32-40 round has been around a long time and was prized for its accuracy by sharpshooters for more than fifty years.

The bullet has a velocity of only around 1500 fps, so as he stands on the river bank, MacBride thinks it will be a little like lobbing a rock across the water. He visualizes the arc the bullet will trace. It's a far cry, he thinks, from the Lee Enfield .303 he'd spent every day with for the past three years.

Now MacBride pops up the peep sight, twists the screw to raise the sight, and estimates the distance at 200 yards. He is used to a greater target range, but with a different rifle. He must take this into account. The 32-40 cartridge has a slower speed than the 30-30's the other men carry, but its heavier bullet will compensate and drop the moose if the shot is good. The soft-point will lose about eight inches as it moves across the river since the breeze is behind them.

The animal has picked up their scent but cannot see them at this distance. MacBride knows he can make the shot without the peep, but he plays it close in front of the others.

He raises the rifle and centers the spot just behind the ear of the animal, accounts for the windage, moves his finger to the trigger, and slowly squeezes off the shot.

As he finishes his breath, the animal drops.

MacBride looks to where the moose has fallen. He is still and quiet, and feels his focus move somewhere beyond the trees.

It's the first animal he has shot since he returned, and the sudden, dead-weight collapse of the kill sobers him with its familiarity.

Mitchell shakes his head. "Jesus!" he says, "talk about luck. Let's get over there and dress her and get her back to the colony. We'll butcher it there and split 'er up."

On the trip back downriver, MacBride thinks about the Lee Enfield he used in the 2nd. The rifle was standard issue, but the most accurate No. 4's were pulled from the inventory and shipped to Holland & Holland where they were fitted with scope pads, an extra swing swivel to grip and steady the rifle, and a screw-on wooden cheek-rest. Most important, the rifle was re-bedded to improve accuracy even further. Once the process was complete, the rifle was categorized as a No. 4 Mk.1 (T), and was considered to be the best sniper rifle in the war.

He slept with that piece of equipment more often that not, and he realizes his hands, as they rest in his lap, are curling around the empty shape like an absent woman.

"The wife will be here this winter, right?" Mitchell asks.

"That's right," says MacBride.

"Been a while," says Mitchell.

"Yep," says MacBride.

"We'll have a party for her," says Mitchell.

"Good," says MacBride.

"You still good for the fall goose hunt at Moosonee."

"Yes," says MacBride. "I thought I might go up on my own a little earlier, just to look around."

Mitchell glances at him sharply, then nods and looks down river. "The nurse is due to be in Moose Factory around then, isn't she?" he says.

"Oh?" says MacBride.

Mitchell nods again. "My Daddy told me that when you have kids, you have to kiss the early part of your life goodbye. You have a different mission. You may not feel ready, he told me, but you have kids and you have to think about that, like they need to be rescued. Like that. It's not just about you any more. It's about the mission." He takes out the makings and begins to roll a cigarette. "Just saying."

Something else to put aside, thinks MacBride. A soldier and a military nurse pushing away the memories of death with their whispers. Some things are too real for noncombatants to see, and the soldier in him knows the seeing will stretch like strings of winking lights through the darks of his dreams. He may assume the role of husband and father, but his heart will beat in boreal remoteness while his wife searches for the man before the war.

"Right," he says.

And he wonders if he is in fact alive, or if he died on the beaches of Dieppe, and, dead now, lies dreaming, the last moment of consciousness stretched to fill an eternity so that his mind might avoid extinction. And in this dream, he fears, he will live and eat and sleep quite normally, until one night, dreaming a dream of no dream, he does not wake.

## CHAPTER SEVEN

# The French Loaf

MacBride's manhood, uncircumcised and unstinting, called once "The Dirigible", and now, by the company nurse, "The French Loaf," is, for a season, a matter of tactical discretion and pride.

"He's hung, and he can shoot," says the nurse, "and any man who can bring home the moose like he does, is a catch. By God, his wife better hold tight to that one. Why is she waiting a year to join him?"

Though MacBride swims modestly and shoots sparingly, the nurse substantiates her theories. Like him, she did war work overseas and has the no-nonsense attitude common in those who know each day may be their last: carpe diem and no waiting. MacBride recognizes the attitude and knows the niceties of etiquette are no match for the demands of doom. It is the recognition of tribe, the sentiment of those alone in the world, the acceptance that every day is a precursor to extinction.

While he is camping alone at the Red Sucker confluence, the nurse boats upriver on the pretext of tending the sick at Crystal Falls settlement, the next dam south, but instead pulls into MacBride's campground at 6am.

The sound of the motor wakes him and he peers out from behind the tent flap, thinking it prudent to remain inside.

She beaches the boat and steps onto the duff. Tendrils of morning fog coil around her bare feet where the skin stretches thin over the ankle bone.

She crosses the clearing to the tent. Her hips rock smoothly as she walks, and her breasts sway to the movement of her legs. She lifts the door flap, and slides inside.

"This is unexpected," MacBride says.

"I'm on my way to Crystal," she says. "Move over."

"Anything wrong?" he says.

"No," she says, moving closer. Her scent is a tincture of woman and morning ozone as she slides her arms around him. She sighs deeply, and pulls close, pressing his nose to the hollow under her ear where the musk of her lingers.

"You smell like woodsmoke and leather," she says. "Mmmm."

She lies in his arms and holds him close. Briefly, he seeks the word for what he fears, but the fear is without form, and MacBride lets it lie in darkness lest out of the void within him a thing of substance come forth, a thing unknown. "Let it remain nameless," he prays, "for I will give it no voice." It is enough to have her face close while her lips speak. Her cheeks brush him, and she whispers about her work as though it were a secret between them. Then she tightens her arms and pulls his head down and holds him to her breasts.

There is too much happening, he thinks, and now, as he looks down at her, he remembers the fine threads of awareness quicken as he recognizes the shape of his life: the seamless sum of uncountable and apparently random components that are, in fact, a single gesture seen now in its entirety, because this particular moment is the one he inhabits more completely than any other, the only moment any of us inhabit fully, he thinks, the ephemeral, eternal moments before death, moments as immediate and blank and undeniable as the instant of orgasm, (and where does the mind go at such times, he wonders) so that finally he sees the pattern of life as clearly and completely as he previously recognized a circle on a page.

The sky brightens outside the tent. She speaks of the war and her own interior landscape and it is strange. He peers at the tent wall and pulls the blanket around his chin. He murmurs softly so she will think he is still listening. She nestles closer, but MacBride's mind moves back to the early days, and he is lost in thoughts of his own. Memories snake through his consciousness and catch at his insecurities. He is afraid of losing his wife, who he has not seen in months. He knows that. He looks at the morning light and sighs and pushes the thoughts away. Then he is aware of the silence.

"I have to leave now," she says. "I have to be at work."

"Yes," says MacBride.

"I don't want to leave," she says. Then she sighs and sits up. MacBride runs his hand up and down her back. She slides into her clothes and crawls out.

He watches her walk across the clearing to the boat. She turns and looks to his eyes and blows a kiss.

"So long, Sweetheart," she says.

"So long," he says and tosses off a tough little wave, like a salute. Then she is gone.

MacBride emerges from the tent and stokes the fire and feels the warmth on his skin. He takes an orange from his pack and begins to peel the fruit before the fire. He pries off small sections of rind, and the juice explodes in fine and tiny sprays with all the colors of the rainbow as the peelings hit the fire. He separates and eats the sections slowly, looking upriver.

After another visit, she comes to be known in MacBride's heart as "The Juicer". Striding her, building up to her climax, he rides her until she sings "Yes, oh God, fuck me, fuck me!" Her vagina contracts in a tight series of diminishing spasms around his cock, and MacBride believes he has made a breakthrough. He's had no experience with a screamer before. Is it the latitude? The clean, thin, ozone-laden air of the north? The native heritage, perhaps, summoning up the ancient call of the land, a call clearer with the diminished numbers of the White Man, whose name in Cree translates as "Fish Bellies"?

He hopes he has found a key to simpler nights with the scars of war behind him. For a time, he is happy by the river while the world lies waiting for winter on the Little Abitibi, when the river will freeze and the waters lock the seasons under its ice.

It pains MacBride to put the episode behind him in anticipation of his wife's arrival. Once she appears, he will be prepared, and she will at first be glad to be with him. Her demur love-making will be open for a while but will last but half a season. He knows this from their times together. He has little understanding of her reasons for giving it up, but give it up she does repeatedly and after the child is born he suspects it will be permanent, and he will be left to contemplate the lives of the celibates and worry about his prostate as he wanders the tundra cocooned in the silks of memory, thinking of the company nurse who has returned to Cochrane.

And so it is that his marriage comes in his mind to parallel the denouement of war: once immersed in the screams of battle and orgasm, ordinary life is dull indeed. In a very significant way, he feels it is over. The days slog by in a parade MacBride wants no part of. Nor does he want to be a sidelined spectator, so he once again relegates himself to scouting the margins of the human hive.

The taiga becomes his world: it is the thing that endures beyond the short spasms of human song. The animals, the seasons, the topography, the geology of the Boreal Shield and the Hudson Plain wire him into their filaments. He is a node in their vast network. He is of the world again, not merely in it. Finally, the habits of scouting through the forests of Germany cover his feet like moccasins and walk him through the trees where he fishes the waters of the lakes.

He puts aside the short-barreled Marlin 32.40, best for close encounters, and prowls high grounds that yield open vantage of the lands below. With him is his rifle, his beloved Lee-Enfield, through which he makes connection to the the world, to life, and to the endings of life. He camps on ridges and stares into the distance. He looks for movement a thousand yards out. He prowls the cliffs around the river and he follows Polaris. Thought and memory are his companions. Alone on the ridges, he is the silhouette of ancient man, alone with his weapon in a world rich with wordless articulation. The stars swing hard and bright around the Great Bear while MacBride wonders if he has gone far enough north.

The hunter is home.

Beneath the pole star and over the world spreads the Hudson Plain. The trees diminish and end, the earth is a flat saucer of small lakes rimmed by thin soil and green peat, and the lichenous stones afford no shelter from the pressing sky. The horizon is a sharp line seven miles out, and MacBride's line of sight sweeps unimpeded over the earth. He thinks of the geology and the books he read to learn the history and the lie of the land before he came north to breathe it. The pages of books unfurl their facts in a comforting litany before him.

"Between the Boreal Shield and the Arctic Archipelago lies the largest continuous wetland in the world, the "bog and fog" of Palaeozoic deposits overlaying bedrock. The Hudson Plain. An endless fen of peaty soil. Damp meadows, low and marshy. Known for its vast population of biting insects: provender for the migratory birds."

As the words roll through his mind, his dreams move north, beyond the horizon to where the ice begins, where only memory is green and white bears haunt the tranquil snows.

## Chapter Eight

# A Stop Along the Way

The bush is cleared fifty feet on either side of the track. Here and there, where the tamarack and black spruce are stitched together by the alder bushes, the taiga thins around a boggy meadow where an old beaver pond has filled in. The water in the ponds and streams is tea-colored with tannin, and drifts of mosquitoes waft over the peat.

MacBride watches through a window streaked with ash from the locomotive. The sills are sprinkled with fine coal grit that people inadvertently rub into their eyes, and the passenger car smells of soot and tobacco and children's dirty knickers. When the train slows in the middle of nowhere and the conductor passes by announcing that they will stop for a half-hour, the passengers quickly spill out onto the clearing and gaze around at a place that carries no sign of man other than the train and themselves.

Today, the weather is fine, and MacBride stands on the turf a little apart from the crowd. He rolls a cigarette and watches the women pick berries and laugh and spread blankets over the damp moss. Some drink home-brew to quench their thirst, some sip lemonade, and they all watch the children flock along the edge of the woods. A handful of men smoke on dry shoulders of pink granite risen from the earth. Some of them slouch with a hand in a pant pocket, but the military men, MacBride thinks, are those who are wide-stanced and alert, glancing reflexively towards the darkness in the trees.

It is the second such stop on the trip to Cochrane. Because the pauses are due to problems with the engine, each stop is new, and MacBride understands they will not stop at that particular place again.

This pleases him. He takes mental snapshots of each locale and files them away, like he did on the scouting missions in Europe. There, in Belgium and Holland, chances were good he would never see the places again, but if he did, knowing the features of the land could mean his life. Now, in the north, he uses the images to form a map of the terrain. When the train speeds past these places in the future, the passengers will not notice because they experienced them only once and the details will be folded up in their memories. But for MacBride, who paused and stepped fully into the places, each will remain especially vivid, and such spots become bright little meadows in his mind where the light is steady and where he will retreat when he needs to rest from the crowds around him. Then, he will search his memory for details there that he missed with his eyes.

When the conductor rounds them up, they board murmuring and find their seats as the engine whistles and the cars lurch into motion. The train pulls away, leaving behind a little bit of their lives in a glade by the tracks.

MacBride stubs out his cigarette and boards the train last. He thinks of Eve waiting in town. He has not seen her in months, but he has written letters. At first, he feels badly that he has not written down these little stops and episodes and sent them to his wife in the letters, that he has wasted the time needed to write them down and share them so she can picture him in these places.

He knows she loves the north, that the land holds the sorts of deep meanings she seldom mentions aloud, but he changes his mind about feeling badly and is content that they are written within him, contained like a rich treasure, for he owns the stories and will take them with him wherever he goes, and they do not have to be told to anyone else. It is enough that they happen. It is enough that they are his.

He has had the land to himself until now, and he is not sure he can give up his connection to it once his wife and son arrive. He is not sure how much of himself he can give to his wife. She peoples the land with her own history, embraces a hundred little local gods of place and passage—the manitu, and to the west, she has written, even a province is named after the manitu: Manitoba, Straights of The Great Spirit.

He looks out over the trees to where no tracks scar the taiga, where the only paths are streams and rivers, where the bogs feed the waters their brown and bitter tannins and undulating, thick mosses rim lakes like the irises of eyes void of any creature quickening their deeps. The lakes stare fixedly at firmaments where no small storms of living things dwell, and the waters remain hushed and yield no bounty but a cold and constant beauty.

And in the winter, the lakes sleep beneath their lids of ice, and the wind moves over the face of the land, and the land is a waste of snows.

## CHAPTER NINE

# The Cabin and Beyond

A man stretches his legs and looks up through the boughs of a spruce tree. The branches move with the wind, and overhead little white clouds run before a gathering shadow. He closes his eyes. They are cumulus clouds, he thinks, small and puffy.

The fire is out when he wakes. The wind is sharp and a heavy scud darkens the sky. He hurries to the canoe, cursing as the rain, laced with sleet, hits.

He tightens the scabbard on his back, snugging up the carbine, tosses the small pack onto the floorboards, and then pushes the canoe into the river and paddles fast, knowing the current will help him get back to the cabin quickly. He pulls into the drift and stabs the paddle into the water, feeling the deep muscles in his back bunch. The small wake hisses behind him as he enters the rapids, and he plunges the paddle again and again into the current.

He knows he is being reckless as he works up a light sweat to rebuff the wind coming along the river, but the trip will be over before the sweat begins to chill him.

The rain is in his eyes as he works the paddle relentlessly and the bunching muscles warm his back and arms.

Briefly, he thinks about the berry jerky outside the cabin in the rain. It will be wet and ruined, but he can scoop it into a bowl when he gets there and stir in some sugar and a little of the dry pectin he keeps. Then he will heat it on the stove and make it jammy, to be eaten on bread. It will not be wasted.

He brings his attention back to the river and the rapids ahead. He pulls toward the shore to avoid the rocks, thinking it is always trickier moving downstream with the current, especially when the water's low in autumn.

He blinks away the rain. Ahead, the river bulges where the rocks fight the current, and the water curls around them, leaving a trail of small eddies downstream. He sees the rocks now and pushes toward the shore, locking the paddle against the side of the canoe, holding it tight and using it as a rudder to steer. Then, the water bulges and a shadow moves to the surface. He brings the paddle up and over to redirect the canoe as a submerged log bobs up and slams into the canoe, flipping it.

When he pulls himself to the surface, the canoe is capsized, downstream, and moving away quickly. He hadn't tied down his duffel, so it will be gone. There is no point in trying to catch the canoe, so he strikes out for the shore.

He crawls up onto a low granite shelf and looks out at the river. A dark shape lifts just clear of the surface forty feet upstream, remains there for a few seconds, then disappears. A minute later it appears again, briefly. What he sees is not uncommon. A waterlogged trunk has floated downriver and its forward end snagged the bottom. The current pushes against the free end, setting up a rise and fall like a pendulum keeping its own time. The tip of the log will rise and sink, rise and sink, like clockwork until the log breaks free or becomes waterlogged and sinks.

He shakes his head to get the water out of his ears and takes stock. His supplies are gone with the canoe, but the small skinning-knife is still secure at his belt and the Marlin is still in its scabbard. He looks down at his hands, gnarled and brown, to check for shock. The fingers are trembling and a pallor lies under the tanned skin, so he feels his pockets for the pipe and matches. The matches are paraffin-tipped, but he will have to make a shelter and find dry kindling to use them. The sleet slices through his wet clothes, puckering the skin on his arms and legs.

"Damn," he says.

He'll have to start a fire in the storm to warm up and dry the rifle. He will have to stay warm through the night, swim the river in the morning, then make a run for the cabin which lies on the far shore.

He moves quickly into a stand of aspen and kicks the loose leaves on the forest floor into a pile on the leeward side of an old white pine. Then he cuts long saplings with his knife and shoves them into the ground one foot apart, fashioning a curved double wall five feet high and six feet long close to the lower branches of the spruce. He lines the windward side of the frame with boughs cut from the tree to contain the leaves, fills the framework with the driest leaves on the bottom, piles the stack four feet high, folds the saplings over the top, fastens them so they form a framed cover. Then he weighs them down with more boughs, layered from the bottom up to shed the water. When he is finished, he breaks off the dried twigs and branches of the tree and builds a small fire close enough to the lean-to to create a reflected heat but far enough to pose no chance of catching. Then he strips off the rifle scabbard and his outer clothes, empties the rifle, dries it, and begins the process of warming and mitigating the wet.

When his shirt is dry, he wraps the rifle and stows it in the dry leaves at the back of the shelter, moves his outer shirt close to the fire, and moves back into the middle of the leafy heap and hopes the rain lets up.

The tree stops the rain and the leaves are good insulation, but he is still cold. He curls into a tight ball and listens to the weather. The rain pelts the boughs, and its sound reminds him of the drumming on the cabin roof. Then he thinks of the potbelly stove in the middle of the cabin floor and a fire in the stove and the hot, dry smell of the cast iron when it glows red with heat. He imagines the pop and snap of the fire, the flames licking up from the red heart of the blaze. He thinks about the smell of wood when it burns, about each wood blazing differently with its own smell, and of the smoke curling up from a big, wasteful blaze.

The wind rattles the poplars, and he remembers the sun outside the cabin that morning, and how the weather and his mood made him careless.

That's it, he thinks, if I make it, no more running off into the bush by myself. Then he shifts to escape a trickle of water.

He wears wool shirts and pants because the cloth insulates even when wet, and he is warmer. He always wears wool for that reason.

When it is damp from a light rain, it lies pleasantly warm on his shoulders, but now the clothes are soaking and are slower to give up the chill of the rain. He listens through the storm and peers out into the darkness, thinking again about the berry jerky he left outside the cabin door that morning. It would be too late to make it into jam now; the rain will have washed it away by morning, leaving only a red stain on the drying-board.

He keeps his mind busy to delay sleep until he is warmer, and decides to recount all the events of the day, from the time he walked out of the cabin that morning until he reached the point where he is now. He does not want to think about leaving the woman and the boy in a foul mood, declaring that he needed time away from them to think. There has been too much of that, so he begins with sitting outside the cabin door telling himself he was ready for winter.

He leaned back against the doorjamb and watched the light dance between the poplars around the cabin; it skipped across the carpet of leaves past the little pines to the water's edge where it lit the reeds and sank into the water. Frogs croaked in the reeds. Further out, the sun lay puckered like silver flannel on the little lake, and the bright flakes of light had been sharp and painful.

Even then, he wondered if this would be his last year trapping, or playing at it, because he felt the winters more.

Then, he brought out the strips of berry jerky to dry in the sun. He knew the boy loved the wild berry jerky. He thought about the meadow and the Red Sucker emptying into the Abitibi where the woman loved to picnic. He thought how she loves the spot, how they go there for day-trips whenever they can, how he cleared a small area there for the tent.

Now, huddled in the leaves, he can't recall what he thought next, so he thinks instead about what he did.

He cleaned the cabin. It was something he did thoroughly on the days he visited the meadow, and he worked to maintain the cabin the way it looked when the woman and boy were with him. He scanned the interior for a last look round: the rafter poles were straight, the shingles fast, the chinking tight in the log walls, and a picture hung on the wall with a nail. A double bed stood beneath the picture with a blue gingham bedspread folded down at the pillows to show a red Hudson Bay blanket. A long shelf of books ran along the wall beside the bed. The floor was swept; the pine planks were smoothed and sealed and a fur rug rested by the bed. Across the room, a steel trap lay oiled and ready by his boots in a corner. Then he turned in the doorway toward the clearing and the lake beyond. He looked to the rill draining the lake through the trees. Above, the clouds were dappled and streamed to a single point south over the horizon.

He guided the canoe through the rill to the river and paddled into the current. Halfway to the Red Sucker he pulled into a little bay to stretch the cramps out of his legs. He smoked a pipe, then entered the current again and paddled north with the flow towards the Sucker and the rapids that girdled the river below it. Then he saw the eagle, and thought it was a good sign.

He thinks about where he is now, blanketed in the leaves. He wonders where the other eagle is. There has always been a pair of them at that point in the river. It hadn't occurred to him at the time. The leaves press in on him, so he pushes his thoughts deliberately back to the river with the sequin-like waves on the water earlier that day. He is very sleepy, and when he feels himself falling asleep, he thinks harder and reaches further back to remember the woman's dress and the first time he brought her to the cabin. The boy was an infant in her arms.

He reaches out and takes the warm shirt-jacket, puts it on, and closes his eyes in order to imagine the dress in more detail: warm gray that reminded him of the soft, gray feathers of a ruffled grouse, ringed by rich brown, and she said she would accent the dress with the same brown. He told her she was right, and he gazed at her in the dress she might wear two or three times, and he loved her, and then it was later in his dream and she said "Here," and handed him a book of poems by Rudyard Kipling, and she laughed at his expression and said, "You can read them over and over and never wear them out and they will last a lifetime, and in the meantime, you can read them to me at night."

"Yes," she repeated, "you can read to me at night. Now take us home."

44

There were one hundred and thirty poems in the book and he read a poem every night until he knew them pretty much by heart, and as his eyes close despite his will, he thinks of all the times he boated the three of them back to the settlement at Abitibi Canyon.

But he dreams about the cabin and sees the rafter poles twisted and the shingles cracked. Snow drifts through the rafters and dusts the bunk and the riven planks of the floor. A raspberry cane reaches up through a breach in the planks, balancing a yellow leaf in the cold air. Across the room, a steel trap lies rusted beside a boot in the corner. He turns and looks across the snowy clearing to the lake. The frozen stream winds through the trees and the tops of the trees stand white beneath a flat sky with heavy clouds that race toward a single point over the horizon, and it gives him such a shock that he wakes up.

He is cold. The leaves over his face smell like raw earth. He thrusts his head up, sucks in the cold morning air, and shakes his head to clear it. Then he stands up and walks to the river. It exhales a wispy vapor, but it is narrow where he stands, and he can make it across with his clothes. The cabin is three miles downriver. The current will carry him to within a half-mile of it if his timing is right, and then he'll have to make a run for the shelter. If the river carries him past the cabin, he will have been in the water too long and may be too cold and tired to double back. If he gets out of the river too soon, he will have to travel through the trees with no trail to the cabin half a mile inland.

He steps up to the water. He has swum it before, but he knows he shouldn't fool himself. The cold and wet and fear have worn him down, and he sees the first flakes of snow settle around him. He looks up. The opposite shore is fading in the whiteout, and if the flurries thicken he might not recognize where he is when he lands.

He strips, ties his clothes and moccasins in a tight ball with the moccasin thongs, then weaves his belt through the leather thongs and straps the bundle to the scabbard on his back. The wool will absorb water and become heavy and the scabbard will be cumbersome, but he knows it won't drag him down like it would if he wore it, and he won't leave the rifle behind.

He dives in, ignoring the sour knot in his stomach, and the current takes him. At first the water seems warm, but it is a trick of the cold air. The bundle on his back chafes and soon he can't see either shore. He focuses on his swimming, locking his thoughts on the memory of the clear lake that morning, and he holds his thoughts tightly against the image of the sun on the soft and translucent water. He kicks his legs slowly and steadily and reaches methodically over his head in a slow crawl, breathing once every other stroke. He concentrates on his arms reaching up and forward, his hands cupping the water and pulling it down behind him while his feet kick the water away. It is like climbing through a thick wind.

The woman has told him he is a beautiful swimmer, and the thought comforts him and gives him strength.

When he reaches land, he's not certain where he is at first, but the swim was easier than he feared and he thinks he is upriver, south of the cabin. He scrambles from the water and out of the wind to a small copse of poplars. He tears the bundle of clothes apart, wrings them hard, dresses quickly, and looks around. Low sand cliffs will start to line this stretch of the river, so he can't follow the shoreline, which is narrow and treacherous and snagged with fallen trees, but here at the copse the banks have broken for a stream. Knowing where he is now, he jogs directly inland along the stream for a quarter mile and turns north, into the wind, parallel to the river. If he wanders too far inland, he will miss the cabin. The snow thickens as he looks for a landmark. The snow is melting as it hits the ground and there is no ice yet. Still, the gusts cut through the wool of his shirt and he can only see forty feet to each side, less ahead into the wind and a little more behind him. The terrain is hilly but will flatten closer to the little lake, which he wants to skirt by staying close to the river.

He begins at a measured pace, squinting into the snow, looking at the ground to save his eyes. Branches lash him. He ignores them, concentrating on climbing up each rise and down each slope into the wind, always into the wind. He is moving well and breathing deeply, when his feet begin to numb. Then the bones in his fingers begin to throb, and he thinks it might be the wind that finishes him.

"Too much thinking," he says into the wind and pushes back the fear. He thinks about the woman, about the circle of smooth campfire stones he sat beside yesterday. It seems a long way away from where he is now.

"Too much thinking," he says again.

He moves faster to generate more heat, but the cold snatches it away quicker than he produces it, and he is making it worse by running into the gale. He has to take the chance. He runs quickly. His stomach churns, still sour. "Don't panic," he tells himself, "or you're finished." His heart hammers as he focuses on the pace and the direction of the wind and each single stride.

A split and leaning tamarack looms out of the blizzard on his right. He recognizes it. He is a half-mile southeast of the cabin and knows the trail. A half-mile is a long way wet and freezing, but he knows where he is and can make it, and if he does, he thinks, with the ice stiffening his clothes as he runs, he will sit in front of the fire and eat oranges and spit the pips into the fire. He will peel the oranges and pry off small pieces of the rinds, and he will see the juice in the rind explode in a fine and tiny spray with all the colors of the rainbow in it, and he will remember to think they were like tiny explosions on the sun that he read about once. Then, when he gets home, he will tell the boy about the oranges.

They called them solar flares in the book, and he thinks that it is a wonderful phrase and repeats it, and he tells himself he must notice these things from now on and always be attentive to the moment. He has not been grateful enough in his life. He was not grateful with the woman. He has not read enough to the boy. He knows what she will say about that at first, when he reads the Burgess stories about Buster Bear and Sammy Jay.

"He's too little to read to," she will say.

"It will sink in," he will answer. "He'll get accustomed to it, to the sounds of the words."

"Why don't you help him practice jumping instead?" she will ask. "Something useful."

"This is useful," he will answer, "and someday may save his life."

And he will roast chestnuts in the fire and when they are done and steamy he will take them away from the heat and crack them open and eat them very slowly so the flavor was not wasted. He has not roasted chestnuts since he courted the woman in Quebec before the war. He will tell the boy about that, too. He will look out the window where the frost traces its passage and leaves its lace on the glass and he will look out to where the snow falls cleanly and in banks and he will take down his Peterson pipe from the mantle, the curved golden yellow meerschaum pipe that is Irish and his favorite because the woman gave it to him when they were married, and he will fill it with the fragrant Erinmore Flake tobacco from the tin that he loves, and he will light the pipe and sit back in the soft chair and enjoy his luck, and he will taste the apricot in the tobacco and blow smoke rings and appreciate his wife and son. If he survives, he thinks, he will sit in the big chair before the fire with a steaming mug beside him filled to the brim with wine mulled with cinnamon, or hot chocolate with nutmeg, or strong black coffee straight, or warm eggnog heavy with the dark Jamaican rum that he likes and ground Jamaican allspice on top. He will sit by the fire and take it easy and let the winter come to him like a lover because he loves the snow and its quiet and he will not blame it or curse it if it takes him now. Beyond a certain point, he thinks, winter is white and pure and reaching out, enfolding, letting you sleep. She doesn't conspire, he thinks, and there are no games, and you go to her because you are foolish, or make a mistake, or because you are ready to go.

The large, soft flakes fall slowly and heavily and he thinks that it really is amazing how some glitter like sequins and toss off silver chips of bright light and he is surprised how slowly they fall around him because the wind has died down and it is warmer, warm as he runs for the cabin and he feels he really does understand the snow falling gently among the spruce that stand now like sentinels around him, their boughs weighted with white light, and he runs past the trees and smiles as they fade in the distance and he suddenly laughs. Whether he makes it or not, he thinks, it is very beautiful, and he is lucky to be alive.

PART TWO

# Fugue: The Windhover

CHAPTER TEN

# The Cast

When you kill your demons, you kill a part of yourself.

~Finn

July, 1980

>   *One particular child crosses the clearing regularly to visit him. She is small, perhaps six years old, and walks barefoot through the village in the afternoon. Her ears and her nose and her lips are translucent and very fine, her dark eyes unwavering. She stops a dozen feet away to gaze at him as he sits in the bamboo cage. Eventually her father appears, never speaking to the girl, never acknowledging Finn's presence, and takes her quietly by the hand. Then he leads her away.*

Finn has slept about three hours when he wakes, and Lara stirs beside him on the bed. He reaches out to move his hand to her waist and around to her belly, feeling the tight mound of the baby beneath the flesh. He lifts his hand to her shoulder, and then to her neck where his fingers flutter lightly before circling the nape, probing for the muscles and soft cords beneath the skin. He works the muscles, softening them, molding them, and feels her relax. In the front of the neck is the larynx, he thinks, a fragile box of cartilage that is the gateway to the lungs, the seat of her singing. Below that is the supersternal notch, the pulsating hollow in the throat where the heart beats softly. Finn flares his nostrils

51

reflexively, and, with short, sharp intakes of breath, pulls in the night air, pungent with the smell of summer. He lifts his head slightly to listen, peers over her shoulders to the window, and taps his fingers softly to the heartbeat in the valley of her voice. Two hearts throb within her flesh. Outside the room, faint cries rise from the town, overlayed with the braying of car horns. The wraithlike hum of tires on pavement drifts through the night like a pulse, thinning and thickening.

Beyond the window the sky is dark, and the lake is not separated from it. Its waters are one with the heavens and the moon casts its light down upon them. The light skips over the waves, and Finn stares at the line dividing the pool of the moon from the water. Around the lake is the land, and the temperature of the land and the lake are one, and the air is still, and a great calm lies upon the world.

Far out, the Manitou Islands lie flat and silent on the waters. He cannot see them, but he imagines them. For the first peoples, they are the resting place of the manitous, the spirits. For the geologists, they are the remnants of a volcanic pipe, the plugged vent of a deep supersonic eruption when the fires of earth broke through. The islands are the eroded remains. For the prospectors, they were the failed hopes for diamonds and uranium. For the fishermen, a place to spend a sunny day. For his father, something else. "Everything has its manitou, Finn," he's said over the years. "The spirit of a thing shows in its characteristics."

The thought of his father's voice is a perturbation on the night air, for although the old man is visiting Ireland with Finn's mother, his presence is married to the house. It is the house Finn grew up in.

"You're up again. What is it?" says Lara from the dark beside him.

"Nothing," Finn says, looking down to watch the moonlight on the surface of her eyes.

"Memories of the lake?" she asks.

"No. It's good to be back, even if it's only for a couple of weeks."

"Talk to me, then," she says. She holds her tongue lightly to the bottom of her upper teeth, and she pauses with her lips parted, a small, tense hesitation that indicates, has always indicated, that what she wants to say is deliberate, important.

"I can't sleep," he says. Lara turns her head to the window. Her brow is phosphorus under the moon, and the light of the lake moves over her face. Her hands slip over the sheet to her shoulder; she touches his fingers at her neck, and holds them there.

Finn hears the small waves on the beach, but he thinks of war. He thinks of the flat disk of the moon tattooing his skin with the shadows of a jungle stitched with high voices, thin music, and the rattle of gunboats on a river.

His words are quiet and his body is still, but his mind soars over the trees that are not the trees of home. He flies through the shadowed valleys in the low, dizzying flight of a dream. He scorches the earth and lights the world, then rolls high and away as the flames balloon up over the villages beneath him. His fires lick the underbelly of heaven.

It was something to see.

"It's stuffy as hell in here," he says now to Lara. "I can't breathe." The memories leak through his dreams and seep out of the darkness into his marriage.

And she sighs, "Okay, let's talk about it some more, from the beginning," and Finn knows she is still angry from the afternoon and the disclosures that had been a long time coming. He shunts his thoughts away from the quarrel, away from the memories of the dead, and back to the seminary and an April day before he'd known Lara, before the war. He had been happy then. He thinks about Gerard Manley Hopkins. He thinks about grass and spring. It had been Easter, when "weeds in wheels shoot long and lovely and lush."

He speaks to his wife from a dream.

> "What are you doing, Finn?" the priest asks.
>
> "Poetry," Finn says, looking up at his advisor.
>
> "So while the world is starving, you are contemplating your navel. We are Christ's soldiers, not his poets. Focus on your work and your calling. Life is a war in the world, and the warriors use politics, not poetry." He looks off into the distance, tilts his head as though he can see God about thirty yards away. Then he looks down, fixing Finn with his pale, dry eyes, and fluffs out the black plumage of his cassock.
>
> "And what are you reading?" he asks rhetorically. "Hopkins. A man who failed God and failed himself. A

*man-child. If it's poetry you want, read Eliot. 'We only live, only suspire, consumed by either fire, or fire.' You've got to learn to be of the world, not just in it … burn a little now, or burn later." His lips twist in thin amusement. "The Seminary is the beginning of a narrow path." Then he strolls away and calls over his shoulder, "Is it too narrow for you, Finn?"*

"Screw him," says Finn to his wife. "So I flew to Southeast Asia and kept my book of Hopkins." The Windhover had been his alpha and omega, his beginning, and his end. The Jesuit's poems had become fire, and the fire was the tongue of God, a Hebrew flame-script that encompassed the world.

Now, Finn says to Lara that Hopkins' life was as hard as his poetry, and his truth possibly worse in the finding. The poet's search was a flight into suffering and satori, into existence and extinction. His life was tortured, he says. Finn looks up and then out to the moonlight moving over the face of the lake like a ghost.

"You left your calling," she says "to fly a jet? I can't get my mind around that."

"A war-plane. I'm not sure why," he says slowly. "I was angry." He waits for the earth to cool, for the temperature of the land and the lake to diverge, for the air to rise over the land and call the breezes in from the waters. But the night is a great weight. "I admit it." He speaks, and Lara listens.

"Angry at the priest?"

"At what he represented."

His mission: to hurl himself down like a wolf on the fold, then roll up into the high blue heavens. It was something to see, looking back at his bright trail in the silent valley below, the fires gleaming like garnets in the green jungle. The tongues of curled and blistering flames eating the earth in his wake, and he laughed with the thrill of flying up and away. The truth is hard. He was happy in battle.

On short leave he stayed on the coast, swam to the sand spits on calm seas, stood there and watched jets rising from the horizon seven miles away.

He flew to Hawaii, visited the volcano, watched the earth's blood bubble and burp in the crack between the worlds where the earth was a molten sea, where beneath the waters of the oceans the earth flowed, and Finn rejoiced at the tenuous separations of the firmaments. Upon the lava floated the lands, and upon the lands floated the waters, and upon the waters floated the ice and the air and the heavens, and Finn thought of wheels within wheels, and his sleep was a chalky dust beneath them.

From the mountains he went back to the beaches, basked in reptilian dream and watched sunbathers on the sand drink icy Mai-Tais from their weeping glasses. The sleep was good by the sea, and for a time he could forget the planet was not a large place, that seven miles away its edge dropped into eternity, that time collapsed when a Phantom appeared over the edge of the earth at Mach 2.

"Words can't describe these things," he says. His eyes burned in a red rift of realities where flames clothed the world and met the sky, a cauldron of hell purer than ash, purer than poetry. The fires scorched and the lava flowed like the napalm dropped from his jet. It would take a poet to tell them in ways that Lara could understand, he knows, but his poetry is burnt and purged away.

"A few seconds, and hope to Christ the first salvo nails you," he says to Lara. "Twenty seconds to extinction, courtesy of the flyboys in the sweet blue sky … " turning green earth to boiling thunder 'and the fire that breaks from thee then, a billion times told lovelier … '"

"You," she says, "you bombed people."

"Me."

"Why?"

"I was higher than Hopkins' Windhover ever flew. God, it was sweet to roll up into the high blue sky, to leave it all behind," and the flames licked up from the jungle floor.

"A poet in a plane," says Lara, "burning the people below."

"That was my mission," he says.

"Flying a jet."

"An F-4 Phantom II," he says.

"What's the difference? A jet, a plane. And what makes what you did right?"

"You have to know the facts," says Finn. "Your life depends on them. You can't think. Facts are all you can count on. You repeat them like a litany. Then, what's done is done." Finn knows the facts. "The F-4 Phantom II is a multi-role fighter with a crew of two," he recites. "It's powered by two General Electric J79-GE-17A afterburning turbojets generating 17,900 pounds of thrust each. The aircraft has a wingspan of thirty-eight feet, eight inches, a length of sixty-three feet, a height of sixteen feet six inches. Its weight is 41,487 pounds empty, 61,795 pounds maximum at take off. It has a ceiling of 58,750 feet, a speed of 1,430 miles per hour, a range of 2,597 miles, (And God, he thinks, the hurl and gliding of the thing.) Its armament consists of one 20 millimeter M61A1 Vulcan six-barrel cannon with 640 rounds, plus up to 16,000 pounds including ASMs, AAMs, cluster bombs, free fall bombs, laser-guided bombs, nuclear weapons, ECM pods, and drop tanks on nine external points. I used it mainly for cluster bombs and napalm." The facts unscroll before Finn's eyes.

"Napalm?" says Lara.

More facts. "'Napalm is a sticky thixotropic gel, firm at rest but flowing freely through a nozzle; it sticks to whatever it touches until it burns itself out at 1250 degrees Fahrenheit. When powdered magnesium and sodium nitrate are added, the mixture burns hotter than sticky gas, at 1800 degrees.' That's the manual, Lara. But the quality of fire," says Finn to the woman who is his wife, "is compelling. The types of the flame, the classes and descriptions, the soundless thunder on the ground. Beautiful in its way," he says as the poet's words sing in his ear: "*Then off, off forth on swing as a skate's heel sweeps smooth on a bow-bend rolling on the underneath him steady air striding high there rung upon the wimpling wing in his ecstasy.*" Then came the last day, looking back to the bright trail of a missile, flickering and nearing as the napalm billowed below.

"You were like death," she says.

Finn looks to Lara now, and he feels the chasm of his open mouth. "If there was ever an angel of death," he says, "it was the priest. He was the devil himself."

"No," she says, "no, it was you who rained down death, and the priest didn't drive you there."

"His heart was a lump of ice."

"Yours was a terrible fire."

"I was shot down," he says. "Maybe I paid for it. It was hell."

The SAM locked on his exhaust, he tells her, its eye fixed on the heat of the Phantom's trail. He rolled and dropped, but the missile brightened and closed until he punched the eject button, hurtling from the cockpit as the jet erupted below. He soared alone and wingless, and his co-pilot vanished. "Goddam," his mouth screamed into the empty sky but a part of his mind was cold and calm as the poetry rolled through it: *Brute beauty and valor and act, oh, air, pride, plume, here Buckle and the fire that breaks from thee then, a billion Times told lovelier, more dangerous, O my chevalier.* God, it was something to see, falling with the coffin of his body flightless over the boiling thunder floating down like a seed into the waiting arms of a jungle he'd lit up minutes before, and praying *O Jesus have mercy upon me O lamb that taketh away the sins of the world hear my prayer O lamb of God that taketh away the sins of the world ... Oh morning, at the brown brink eastward, springs O Holy Ghost over the bent World brooding with warm breast and with ah! bright wings* as his scriptures married in the synaptic fires of his brain.

He should have been bracing for impact, ready for whatever waited on the ground below. He needed to be combat-ready. But this wasn't what happened. Instead, he was tumbling between life and death, aware that he was between two states, afloat in the moment between the breezy beats of wings, having escaped death above and chancing with death below. The alchemy of satori outweighed the adrenaline's chemical rush of danger. There were no facts for this. Suddenly, the space between life and death was more compelling than mere danger and risk-taking. It was a crack between the worlds.

His body's push for action was stalled by the needs of the brain. It was stasis.

"You told me you were in Greece," says Lara in the night. "You told me about white beaches and dry heat, about the smell of new bread in the village streets as the sun came up, the sunlight spreading thick and gold around your toes like honey on the dusty roads. Your words. I fell in love with your poetry: 'Seahorses hovering like tiny dragons in clear seas, their fires quenched,' you wrote. 'Greece holds the bones of the planet,' you wrote, 'bleached and pure.' You made it sound beautiful."

"It was beautiful," he says.

"What?"

"I never told anyone about the details of my tour. I tell people I was living in Europe for those years. Not just you. I don't need to be damned by the people who weren't there. It's easy to judge, but you have to be in a thing before you can talk about it, and then you don't talk. Not when you know. Why open yourself up to that?" He knows the war has been his retreat, his seminary, and so he guards it. "And when we met," he says, "you agreed to live in the present. You said the past was dead. 'That's all we need,' you said, 'all that matters.' What would be, what we created. That was enough for you once."

"You showed me an Orthodox cross and a dried seahorse you got when you were there," she says. "I still have them. They were precious to me and now they're a lie." He watches her eyes now, open and unmoving. He knows she is looking into a past she only imagines.

"Not a lie, exactly," he says. "I gave them to you because they were important to me. I believed in them."

"You never said you were anywhere else."

"Not exactly lies," he says again. "I was everywhere. Honolulu and Anderson, Clark, Saigon, Tan Son Nhut. But I was in Greece, too. During the war. That's true too."

"My God," says Lara in the dark. "My God. Why did you lie to me?" Finn sees that her eyes are fixed on the unblinking moon. She is as cold as its light, he thinks, but she is his wife and he knows how to bring her back. He talks. It is not clear which are words and which are memories, but he tries to speak them plainly.

She reaches out to touch him. "You," she says, and Finn hears the sorrow in her voice. "I know it's hard for you. But I feel as though I don't know you anymore."

Finn's laugh is a brutal bark. "I am who I am. What does it matter who I was?"

"What if I can't handle *not* knowing who you were?"

"What if *I* can't handle it?"

"Talk to me," she says. "What was it like? What's so special about Hopkins' poetry?"

"His poems contain the presence of God in storms and dawns and in the green fires of foliage. He describes a world 'flashing like shook foil,'" he says. Then he resumes the story.

"When I was shot down, I landed in the river, tangled in the chute, and couldn't stay afloat. I sank, lost consciousness and thought I died. I said goodbye to everything, but someone pulled me out and got me breathing again. I didn't know where I was." And floating like an embryo in those waters, just as the dark moth of his vision fluttered away, the colors, he'd thought, dear God the colors! They shone naked and beckoning before him. Before the hands of men could grab his slack shoulders and pull him from that blooming landscape, he slipped into an inner light, a flood of cold, bright knowings with the hard angles and soft curves of new meaning. Ecstasy or extinction: it was like nothing he'd ever known. A joy beyond the joy of flying.

He had felt the facts slipping away, bringing fluidity as the satori kicked in. He felt the tightness of his mind and the lock of his words slipping away. He knew he was dying, and it was a flight of freedom.

"A patrol?"

"No. Priests. Buddhists. When I saw the priests, I thought I'd died. They didn't seem real. I mean I didn't recognize the world. I saw things. Under the water. And then the world was different. Is different. Both more and less real. They brought me back and took me to their temple. I stayed there and never tried to leave. I was supposed get back to the base, but those men weren't my people anymore. The priests were."

He watched the endless variety of God in the greenery; he slept in the shadows; he moved only when the moon rolled over the trees; he dreamed of the fire … *shine blue bleak embers, ah, my dear, fall, gall themselves and gash gold vermilion* … he'd wandered aimlessly around the monastery in the jungle where the Buddhists welcomed him with ample rice and few words. But some among them had eventually wanted his story too. It was the price that wanderers pay–the tale of their world.

To unsepulcher the truth based on too much talk, on the sum of innumerable small lies coiled within a big one, he'd told them of Gerard Manley Hopkins, who'd written poems of a fearful God he saw in storms and dawns, in fires bright as suns, in wheels of weeds and cries of birds, of stars so hard and bright at night they hurt the eyes, only to have his poems and his God rejected by fellow priests. The Buddhists laughed gently at Finn's hero, and for a time his sleep was good again. Surprisingly, it felt like where he belonged. Here were holy men who taught that the opposite of Truth was, at times not falsehood, but another truth.

Finn liked to think of that, of truth spinning like a wheel inside what seemed to be its opposite, but eventually the Phantoms came. The eyes of war locked upon him, and its engines found his sanctuary, and the flames fell from above. *Never shall they hunger or thirst again; neither the sun nor scorching wind will ever plague them,* breathed the fire. The napalm unfurled its carpet and the saffron robes of the monks curled up like bright petals before its wrath, and Finn fled into the trees.

A world away waves lick the quiet shores. Their ripples melt into the sand, and Finn's despair merges with Hopkins'. Here, now, with Lara, the poet lives. *'See banks and breaks now leavèd, how thick! Lacèd they are …'*

"I see things," he says. He glances at the nascent collection of Lara's bonecraft on the headboard, little skulls she's picked up on the beach, bleached by time and tide. This is something she's just begun on this trip to Lake Nipissing. The moonlight coats them like phosphorescent honey, but the sharp lines of their beaks and teeth are unforgiving, and Finn looks away. They are the hard things inside our mortality, he thinks.

Finn looks out a window to waters he cannot see. Their realty is an inference of sound and smell. Upon this void a carpet floats: the pool of the moon's bright eye. This is the moon that tracked cobweb shadows across the skin of a man in a jungle. This moon painted his flesh like a crazed and lunar porcelain inside a cage wherein he'd willed himself to shatter. This eye of night once washed his dreams in a chalky ash. It is the arbiter of emptiness, empress of that hour between midnight and dawn, when the air is hushed and sleep impossible, when the breeze has ceased and the earth is breathless, when the cricket waits and the salamander lies still as death. *O fire that burns away the attachment to* the world, hear my prayer, O fire that taketh away the sins of the world, have mercy upon me …

After several minutes, Finn says, "There was a child, and I never mentioned her." He thinks of her often; he thinks of himself staring out of a bamboo cage as she looks in. Small white butterflies flit erratically around her in the afternoon, and she sings to them. Finn knows the words: *Butterfly, butterfly, alight on me; white butterfly, tiger butterfly, come fly to me.*

The girl haunts him. He came down upon her people clothed in ruin, and in the midst of desolation she remained still and fragile and perfect.

"What girl?" Lara asks.

"Let me tell you," he says. "After a week in country, after they bombed the monastery, I was taken prisoner by the VC. They took me to a village and kept me in a bamboo cage. A tiger cage. Three feet wide by four feet high. Not enough room to stand up; just enough to turn; enough to lie down. You stoop and squat all day, and your muscles scream to stretch, to move, as you crawl back and forth like an animal. They look at you like an animal, and your humanity is washed away in tears and rain and the sores festering. What do you do all day? Squeeze pus from infected mosquito bites and scabs and jungle rot, and you try to remember what you read once and what the reading made you think about. Things like 'What is the measure of a man? Where was he when the foundations were laid?'"

"I lived there in the middle of the village for almost a year. In my own latrine. I lost track of time. I stank. I became something that didn't recognize itself. Or worse … sometimes I did. They made me into the demon they saw me as. The animal that I was.

"One little girl crossed the clearing to visit my cage every day. She was perfect. Small, maybe six years old, and walked through the village in a pair of loose, square trousers. She'd stop a dozen feet away to stare at me. Her ears and her nose and her lips were like porcelain, small and flawless. She stared at me for a long time, like she could see me when I could not. Sometimes she sang a song about butterflies, about white butterflies, and the dark ones like monarchs that they called tiger butterflies there, with orange and black wings. Then her father would come and take her home. He never talked to her or looked at me."

"She must have thought you were some sort of devil," Lara says bitterly. She glances away and presses her lips tightly together. "Oh, Finn. I wish I'd known this earlier."

Finn sighs. "You asked me to tell you, and I'm telling you." There is a danger that Lara will make this about herself, so he presses on. "She was afraid. I could see that. But she didn't judge me. You do. Now. You are judging things you don't understand. Other people here do. They never get around to themselves. Civvies. With their fucking apple pie. They never get to know about what they are, or have to kill their demons." He looks out the window to the lake. "They never have to look into their own souls like it's a matter of life and death. When you kill your demons, you kill a part of who you are," he says. "How can ordinary people judge that?" he says. "There are no demons in apple pie."

"Why did you wait so long?" she asks. "Why haven't you talked about it before?"

"That's not what guys do," Finn says. "And it changes you. It puts you in a different place."

If Lara judges him, he thinks, it is perhaps because she believes he is still human. "There's never a good time to talk about these things," he goes on. "They come out when they do," he says. But Finn saw what he thought was love in the little girl's eyes, and it kept him alive. He saw what he still believes to be *filio*, the love he is supposed to feel for his fellow man, and he cannot talk about it because he cannot account for it having been there, in that little girl's eyes, when it was never in his own. Even now.

And high above that small face for a time, and times, and half a time, he looked up to watch the jets swoop down like the Abyssinian on the enemy and drop their payload and miss the village where he waited in a cage praying for deliverance in the fire. The jets shrank to soundless dots in the sky as napalm roared and air rolled and fire ballooned up beyond the village, distant flames gnashing at heaven. Sonic booms split the valley and hot winds sucked the air from his lungs into the belly of the burn, and always the words were with him: *through the echoing timber does so rinse and wring the ear, it strikes like lightnings to hear him sing.*

He'd hated the sloppiness of the men in the jets who streaked past time and sound towards a hot meal and Johnny Walker Red on their bunks, leaving him unpurged in his tiny hell.

Some of them may have been friends.

"It was something to see," he says, something that he still sees when he dreams of his last day in the village when the jets screamed and the flames unfurled their thick carpet as he waited for the end and the village emptied. But the girl ran back and opened the door and scampered off to her father. Finn crawled out of the cage, suddenly greedy for life as he stood in the eye of the fire.

But he did not go far. There was nowhere urgent to go. The marines would come and find him or they would not. They would come after the napalm to mop up and the villagers had known it, so the village deflated without a breath. Finn was cloaked in a void as he'd walked away from the village and memory, away from caring, away from the empty eyes of villagers and gun barrels, and once more into the trees where the nights were an isotope of sound and smell, where his flight was an alchemy of dreams. He walked the earth, and the soles of his feet spoke to the paths in the shadows of death. His hopes rode on the heavy perfumes of flowers under the moon, and his fears married the night.

"But you escaped," she says. "You survived."

"I was lost," he says. "But when I was flying, that was me. That was who I am, and at night sometimes the dreams take me back to who I am, to that level, and what I do now in the daytime is something else. Something not true. I'm changing into something that's not me."

## CHAPTER ELEVEN

# The Catch

*He sleeps the night away close to the charred huts, and a
rush of marines rancid with fear and red meat come with the
dawn. Their hands are clammy as they hold him, their eyes
quick and wide. They pull him to his feet.*

*"Who are you?" they whisper.*

I t was a long way back to the base, to questions, to inquisitions. To
the Colonel in his plumage.

"What's your name, soldier? What's your number?" said the colonel
debriefing him. "How long were you out there?" he said. "We want to
help," he said. "What's your name?" Finn thought of Father Callaghan
and his relentless demands. Priests and colonels.

"Who are you?" the colonel asked. A faint aura of "manly suffering"
is in vogue; John Wayne and Kirk Douglas have walked off the movie
screen into life, and it seemed to Finn that there is a bit of Hollywood
in the colonel's words.

Finn could no longer remember when that question had not been
asked. Meaning and fact had fled into the jungle on separate paths,
dancing to the strange, soft music of the land. Sometime in the village,
truth had soaked into the red earth with the rains and leaked into the
trees where it multiplied and grew into something as ripe and rich as
the jungle. Truths lay curled inside leaves that trembled in the night
breezes. They oozed down the veins of the leaves and fruited in the
small, white butterflies that danced in the morning sun. Truths were

in the world, but not of it, and the colonel was a seedless fruit on the withered tree of Finn's past.

"Kestrel," he said to the colonel.

"What? Don't be stupid."

"My call name," Finn said.

"What?"

"Kestrel," he said. "The Windhover." Finn enjoyed playing dumb. He'd learned that people in command had no difficulty believing that their acolytes were stupid, and he enjoyed the time it gave him when the colonel extended him the benefit of that particular doubt.

"Windhover?" the colonel said. "What did you see?"

Finn looked past the colonel's head. He'd seen the dragon. He'd seen its fire. Dry, wet, quick, lingering, clean, choking. Sharp lightning and rolling boils. Seen napalm from above and below, from inside and out: aluminum soap, fatty acids, petroleum.

Who would have guessed?

Soap and fatty acid.

The stuff we're made of. The human body. The periodic table of hell.

"I saw dragons and saints," he said. "I saw heaven and hell."

"What can you remember?" the colonel asked. "Where the hell are your tags?"

He'd seen Buddhist monks robed in flame and turned to ash. The images of his mind separated themselves from the chaos and formed words, and he began to talk. He talked of starvation and the bare feet of children, of wide spaces between thick toes in a shoeless world; he spoke of toenails yellowed and cracked as though they were equal in the eyes of God to the sweep of rivers and the shadow of death. He described hands and fingers and gun barrels. He spoke of a fall.

The colonel thirsted for the memories of a man, and Finn remembered the man for him.

He remembered turning his face from hands and the barrels of AK-47's and staring at the dirt of a bamboo cage where the ants wrangled rubbish from the jungle floor. He remembered reaching out to crush the ants, forging a link between the imminent acts of extinction and himself, between being and not being, between doing and being done to, hearing the everlasting sibilance of soft laughter and the susurration of bare feet, waiting for the white blow of a bullet in his head, faster than sound, quicker than pain.

He remembered the specifics.

For almost a year the child slipped away from her hut to stand for a time staring at him in the cage. Was it every day?

"I flew. I piloted a jet," he said to the colonel.

"A Flyboy," the colonel said, leaning back. "We're getting somewhere," he said. "You're home now, son. You were gone a long time. Where in Christ's name have you been?"

"In a Phantom," Finn said.

"What was your last mission," the colonel asked.

"Cambodia. China. Wherever they sent me."

"Of course, we were never officially there," Finn says to Lara by the dark lake. "In Cambodia. China. But hell, we were everywhere. We read about our missions in the "Times" and the articles claimed we were in North Vietnam, but we were in Cambodia. And everyone back home believed it. The dopes. The people who know nothing and believe everything."

"We weren't there," the colonel said. "Officially," he said. "Not there."

Finn laughed. Lies, naturally. Finn had flown north into China on December 25th, dropping booze and chocolate to marines in hidden camps and free-fall bombs on Chinese soldiers on his way out. He'd laughed as they'd fallen.

He laughed again at the colonel. Officially.

"Talk to me," the colonel asked the second day. He waved a manila folder triumphantly. "Your file says you're a hotshot pilot and a hotshot on facts. Give me the facts."

Finn knew facts. "The F-4 Phantom II is a multi-role fighter with a crew of two," he said. "It's powered by two General Electric J79-GE-17A afterburning turbojets generating 17,900 pounds of thrust each."

"What else do you remember, son," the colonel said.

"I flew them," he said. He described the sorties north, the facts the colonel denied and the facts he wanted. Three times he had walked into the trees, and the facts had begun to move from memory to dream.

Sitting in that small room with the colonel, he wondered if those facts would ever move back out into the light of day.

"Tell us what you know," the colonel said, "what you learned."

"I learned that Napalm sticks to whatever it touches until it burns itself out at 1250 degrees Fahrenheit."

"You were shot down," the colonel said. "You were listed as missing. You've been MIA for a year. What do you remember?" the colonel asked.

"I was lost," he said. A bird that can't fly is only feathered meat and a bottomless black eye.

"Well," said the colonel, "remember."

The villagers had wanted his memory too. First, the military had wanted to use him for it, and then the enemy had wanted to strip him of it. He knew layouts, targets, villages, hills, gun placements. He knew maps. He knew facts. The friendlies would have killed him if he'd leaked what he knew. They would know where the information had been coming from, that he was still alive somewhere in the trees, and Finn had known that if the napalm did not get him, a special company of marines would be sent to stop him from talking. His missions had been unofficial and his co-pilot had not survived. He had become clever with lies.

He talked to the colonel but he did not separate the realities. Like the enemy. Like Father Callaghan. You have to be clever, he thought, you have to be nimble or you'll be judged, and that was a different thing than being evaluated.

Fact. Paper burns at 451 degrees fahrenheit.

He had stared out at ragged clumps of children, their black eyes fixed on him in the cage, at what he'd become. Someone who knew too much for either side to leave alone.

"Try to remember, son," the colonel said. "You're safe now."

A man and a woman look out on a lake. It is the same night, and the woman is Lara, and the man is a memory, and the memory speaks. Does he remember the village? Does he imagine the pungent jungle nights? The hot shrimp in Saigon? Are they memories or dreams? Oh, the mind, the mind has mountains …

"Gerard Manley Hopkins was a poet who became a Jesuit priest," Finn says very deliberately, fitting the words into his own ears. The words are solid and dependable. "He flew, and few understood his flight, or that he flew at all. When he decided to join the priesthood, he burned his poems. He turned the things he loved to ash to placate his God.

"He died of diphtheria, poor and unknown. While he lived, the Jesuits did not know what to do with him. He was difficult, but attractive. He was extreme. He fasted. He burned what he loved. Dying, his last words were 'I am happy. I am very, very, happy.'" says Finn.

"My name is Finn MacBride, and I feel like hell," Finn said to the colonel. And the colonel laughed.

"Welcome back," he said. "We'll keep you close to home. How do you feel about flying Hueys for a while? I see you're qualified for more than fixed-wing birds. We're short on chopper pilots and that will keep you closer to the ground where we can use what you've seen." Then he said, "First, we'll get you some R&R. A long one. Away from the debriefings here. Take the time you need. Say a couple of months. I think Hawaii would be best. Then some training."

Finn looked past the colonel and up to the clouds floating high and far away.

"You can take the chopper experience with you when you leave." said the colonel. "Are you planning to stay in long term?"

"No," said Finn. "Maybe one more tour. I need to think about it."

"There you are," the colonel said. "It's a good way to finish up here and stay in the air when you get back home."

And that was the third day.

## CHAPTER TWELVE

# The Return

*A distant speck moves over the grass. He is a man in the dream. It takes time for his movement to become recognizable, time for the silhouette to become an identity, and time again for the forming of the face.*

*"Finn," the man calls, "Where were you when your life was made? Tell me! Who stretched the lines that laid you out and shaped you? Who set the corner stone?"*

*The man is close and his eyes are hot. There is a twist to his lips, and the lips move. "What can you bear and remain a man?" they ask. "Will you know the meaning of your life? And knowing it, will you become devil or angel?"*

*Then the sound of his mouth ceases. His black robes billow in the wind, and the cassock lifts and balloons and covers the dreamer in darkness, and the darkness is void with no light and no Word.*

*In the darkness, the dreamer knows his demons have been dismissed as animal consequences, his hopes as the nesting of birds. When the darkness lifts, a man is gone and the grass is withered. Small vortices move over the grass and gather the yellow leaves. The dreamer calls into the whirlwind, saying that he needs his demons to remain a man, for a demon is a memory. Without it, some human part of him will be lost. He asks the wind what the wind cannot answer: "Who puts these things in the human heart? Who gives the mind such wings?" His humanity is a wound, and*

> *the thin wind whispers: "What is the knowing of a man?" and*
> *the blown leaves reply: "Remembrance."*

The quiet always wakes him.

"It's like the earth is breathing, and I'm stuck in the space between the breaths, suffocating."

And Lara speaks from the darkness. "What happened to the girl?"

If he is not careful, she will go into the bathroom and lock the door. She will take a hot bath, and that will be the end of the talking for a while.

"What about her?" he asks.

"She was different."

"A village girl."

"No," she says. "She was different."

"No," he says. Finn thinks about the ants in the cage, about the chain of actions, about the actors and acted on. Yes, he thinks, she was different, but he denies it for the third time.

"No."

"You did things," she says. "Terrible things."

"Terrible things were done to me. It was war."

"Those things were done to you after you began it. You were exactly where you put yourself, Finn. You went there. You weren't even drafted."

"I know that. I wanted to make a difference. Let's go back to sleep," he says.

"You're not telling me something," she says. "And I still can't believe you *liked* what you did. And your reasons for going there, dear God, weren't even political. You did it out of–what? Self-pity, out of weakness, anger at a priest? What? You ran away, for God's sake, and from what? From becoming a priest yourself? That's just too much to believe."

Finn mumbles.

"What?" she asks.

"I'm saying that part of me wishes I was still there," he says.

Something in him doesn't care anymore, wants it out. How often must he be angry at his fathers? "To hell with it, then," he says. "I liked it. Flying like that. There's nothing like it. Maybe I was looking for God. It was transcendent, all the destructive power. At my fingertips.

Concussion bombs and jellied gas. Cannon that could shoot lead so big and so fast it would turn an NVA patrol into hamburger with the press of a finger. Fuck them. They were the enemy. To be called in because a recon patrol was pinned down, would have been sacrificed, and to swoop in with the Snake and Nape, a first run to drop the snake bombs on the NVA and clear the area, then again with the napalm. To finish it. But I paid for liking it, and I paid for the looking. The looking's over."

"Then *you* sleep," she says, "if it's over."

"The paying isn't over," he says softly. "But I saved our troops. That's what mattered."

"Are you trying to be stupid? If you can't let it go," she says, "then go back to your damned church and ask for absolution."

Finn grunts. "I own my acts. I know that. I can't give them away. I've got to pay for them, in kind. It's not punishment, just payment. Then there's balance again, but the world is never the way it was before the act. That's what loss of innocence means. The world has changed and it's a sadder place. There may be forgiveness of sorts and pardons and absolutions, but there's still loss, and the re-establishment of balance can't make it up."

"That's just crap, Finn. How could you lie to me?"

"Do you know how many times people turn against you when you tell them you were there? People who've known you and think you're something else when they find out? Hate you on the spot? Call you baby-killer, and worse? Just like that. As though everything else they know about you doesn't count for a fucking thing. Suddenly, all you are is two years of your life out of twenty or thirty. Sure, we're who we were, but who we were is not who we are."

"I don't want to be one of those people, Finn, but you should have told me. Trusted me."

"And lost you? Seriously? How many times do you think this has happened? How many times do you think I've seen it happen to the guys who made it back? And to those who didn't, who died over there and still get hated? Screw the people who do that. They deserve what they get, and a little lie is the least of it. They don't get to put a target on my back whenever their little goody-two-shoes fucking do-nothing attitude prompts them."

"That's hard, Finn."

"No, dammit. I'll tell you what's hard. To stuff the guts back into your friend who's just triggered a land mine when you're nineteen, and then to do it again. And again. And hope to Christ it doesn't happen to you. To lose half your friends to bullets and bombs and shit-covered punji sticks and lose them in one year while the pussies back here sit on their asses and judge your life and your worth, and when you make it back won't let you forget it. Screw them, Lara, screw them. The enemy had more honor in battle than that. Why do you think so many vets go back into it? It's the only home left to some of them. If people can't handle the truth back here, then they don't deserve to get it. Don't blame me for that, or for wanting you enough to lie about it."

"But you were in a plane, Finn, dropping bombs."

"And I was on the ground for more than a year, in a cage, for a lot of it, and running for some of it, sometimes alone, sometimes with the unit that pulled me out. And how may of those marines do you think made it out with me? How many, Lara? And how many didn't, and how do think they died on the way out? Let me ask you something. Who were the lucky ones? The ones who screamed or cried as they died, or the ones who died instantly and had no time to scream or know their life was over? What would you want for yourself? Right. You never thought about that. And what a fucking luxury that is, not to have to think about it."

Finn realizes he's been shouting. He breathes. One breath in, one breath out. He thinks of the movement of the air over the land, moving with the night and the day, the long exhalations of the land and the lake, in and out, in and out.

"Sorry. And it was a jet, not a plane," he says. "You see what I mean? People know nothing about it. They just left us over there and they keep doing it. The question is, were those people worth it? The number of guys who made it back and wouldn't enlist again would shock you."

"Except for their patriotism, Finn."

"No. Except for their adrenaline, Lara. That's what becomes the reality. Not ordinary life back here."

"Finn, I'm smart enough to have understood all that if you'd told me. You know that. If you'd given me the chance to know this before we got married. It should have been our decision."

"Yes," he says, "I've heard that before, and I still lied. I know that. It was tactical. I'm sorry for it, and I'm not. What you wouldn't have gotten behind is how much I loved flying over there. The fact that it's where I'd be, if I could. I dream about it. The flying. The power and the flying. All that ordinance and technology from the most powerful country in history right there, an unending supply of it. I rode it all. It all flowed through me, through my fingertips. I loved it. I lit up entire fucking hillsides swarming with NVA. Fire and speed and cannon enough to have brought down a castle. And now I'm going to push chalk in a classroom and talk about metaphors to kids who think Hopkins was a pedophile because he was a priest. Jesus. The complacency and the boredom! This is a whole separate layer of hell."

Finn looks up and sees the horror in his wife's eyes.

"You loved it," she says flatly.

"I loved my job, doing it. Piloting a warplane is a high, Lara. It's your flying dreams on steroids."

"But the fire. What did you know about what it did? You dropped your bombs and flew away. Like now. You fly away from the carnage."

"The fire? When I was on the ground, I saw it. The trees burnt bare and the sap boiling out of the trunks, everything smelling of chemical, and the thick soot that choked you. Everything charred, trees, bodies, huts. And the jokes, the sick humor that kept you sane, kept you removed, the ground reports like 'Area cleared, except for some crispy critters. We'll take it from here.' I heard that a lot after a run, and it was good to hear. You do what you have to do, and if you cry, you don't cry until a long time after.

"But that's not in your mind when you fly. When you fly it's the enemy below, and your job is to kill the enemy and to minimize your own losses on the ground, and you have to be one with your machine, and you're angry most of the time. It's an extension of your body, and if it's not, you'll never be any good and your men will die because of you. I was good. I loved what I did. The enemy were easy to hate. They were down there crapping on bamboo stakes to infect our guys, and I carried the might of America on my back. And there was always risk. You had to fly low through the automatic fire and the SAMS and the hills that you couldn't see through the mist in the monsoon season. You never knew if you'd come back. And a lot of us didn't."

Finn thinks of the air balanced in the night outside, of its suffocating balance, and he knows that the movement only begins when there is no balance. The moment hangs in the heavens like a guillotine.

"When I got back, that's when I saw the pictures in newspapers and Life magazine of kids running down the road after a Napalm drop, burned and naked and terrified. What do you do with that?"

"I don't know," she says.

"Who does? If the people you fight for can't tell you that, what the hell can they tell you?"

"They can tell you about how hard it is to answer questions like that," she says.

"They weren't there. What the hell do they know? 'Difficulties.' That's horseshit."

"People have to get on with their lives," Lara says.

"I'm trying."

"You're too hard on yourself to make it work. And you work too hard on your anguish and your secrecy. And you're too hard on me." She pauses. "What would the monks say about it?"

"The Buddhists? That karma can be a nasty thing."

"What about the priests at the seminary?"

"They'd want confession and penance."

"Well? Would that free you from all this?"

"Confession? Jesus, Lara, a spiritual enema isn't going to fix it."

"What about forgiveness?"

Finn looks up and out the window. "Let me tell you something. That would take more than a confession. Pardon and forgiveness have nothing to do with each other." He thinks: A pardon is a legal, external document that allowed one to function physically in society. It has little bearing on the landscape of the soul. That is the realm of absolution and forgiveness. Absolution that issues from the confessional is nothing more than words. Only the victims can give it, and then only if they are willing and alive. Forgiveness is something else entirely. If others say that they forgive you, they give you absolution in their mind, but true forgiveness can only be self-given, and you have no right to forgive yourself on behalf of the people you harm. So forgiveness is impossible and absolution a lie. *Oh, the mind has mountains …* and he knows he is thinking like the priest he would have become. And it would take a priest to say these things, but those words have been burnt and purged from him as well.

"Maybe," he says. "I'll think about it." And if you run away from one lie, he thinks, you can run into another. There is only waiting and sleeplessness. "Maybe you've just got to say to hell with it. Maybe you've just got to accept the devils," he says, "and learn to sleep with them."

"How do you do that?"

"By sleeping with yourself," Finn says.

"I don't want your ghosts in our bed," she says. "All this talk about demons and monstrous acts just guarantees that you're haunted by the past. It's a self-perpetuated torment. You've been wounded, that's all, and there's a poison in the wound. Get the poison out and the wound will heal."

"How? That's simplistic."

"Talk about it. You defuse it. You get it into the open and deal with it–and yes, that means allowing others to deal with it, and it means you deal with them too. Own it. Get beyond it. Let me tell *you* something: you're hurt, not possessed."

He sits, gazing into the night. Pop psychology won't help, he thinks. His hand moves under the sheets and his fingers gently circle her wrist. The pulse beneath her skin comforts him. He speaks aloud and gives her reasons that the stillness comes in the night. These are good facts, and they never change, and they are a comfort.

"The sun heats the earth all day and the air over the earth rises," he says to her. He tells her the facts. "It pulls the cool air in from the surface of the water. The wind moves over the water and across the hills carrying voices from the boats far into the fields." And though Finn is home now, visiting his father's house on the lake where the hollow knock of an oar on a gunwale is a good sound that only briefly lifts the lid of a sunbather's eye, he is suddenly fearful. "That's what the afternoon breezes are. That's why you can hear people out on the lake so clearly in the afternoon."

"But at night the land cools," he says, "and the temperature of the land and the water balance, and the air doesn't move." Finn looks out the window and up into the night sky. A great stillness hovers over the earth pressing down on his heart and lungs, compressing the darkness there like a hand with no mercy. But he knows that it is no hand: it is the weight of remembrance, and there is no forgiveness in it.

"What in God's name are you talking about?" she says. She pulls her wrist from his hand. "You sound like a sermon. I don't care about the air over the lake." Lara is becoming a stranger in the bed beside him, and that pushes Finn deeper into the old story. The story of the beginning. "I want you," she says, "I want all of you."

"The atmosphere stays balanced for about an hour," he continues slowly and deliberately. "Then the land becomes colder than the water, and the warm air over the water rises, pulling the night air back from the fields and hills over the beaches and out over the waves. The land and the sea become equivalent. Everything becomes equivalent eventually; everything evens out." It is the litany from the cage. It has always worked.

"Finn," says Lara, "tell me about the beginning. Tell me what happened."

Finn looks up over the lake. "I was twenty-three when I left," he says. He wants her near and tangible and pulls her close, but she is hot to the touch. Then he thinks about the seminary, its books and the grass in April, and suddenly it seems like a place where he'd like to be again. It seems to him now that he'd fled a man, not a place, and the place calls and he wants to know it again in its beginning, perhaps for the first time, and he thinks of Eliot who writes about that, and he thinks of the priest who loved Eliot. It seems to him now that Father Callaghan and his poet were just two men with broken hearts.

"'Breeding lilacs out of the dead land'," he says.

"What?"

"Was it a mistake to tell you?"

"No," she says. She takes a deep breath. "It takes a little time."

"It takes forever," he says.

"No."

"It takes a life," he says.

"No," she says. "Life can change in a moment."

"It might take more time than we have."

"No."

"Well," says Finn, "We're both right."

And though he is very tired, Finn thinks about the butterflies he'd seen floating through sunbeams in jungle trees, about a child's song he'd learned from a girl in a village, and the words flutter through his mind with the image; "Butterfly, Butterfly, come land on me; tiger butterfly, white butterfly, don't fly away." It is a bright place in his mind. But it is his last image of the girl he cannot carry.

"Be still, sweetheart," he says, and gets up to walk to the window. "It's only me," he says, "it's Finn," and he hopes it is true. He looks out towards the lake where the air will soon begin to move. "God, I want to sleep." But he is not sleeping; he is standing by a window, looking out into the night and he knows he is not sleeping, but he is not sure that he is not dreaming. The old priest had been right. His difficulty has always been thinking he knows what he wants. It comes to him now, and suddenly something is very clear. He does not want to sleep. He wants to wake. Now he only knows in part. What is the shape of knowing even as he is known: psychosis, or wisdom? He looks into the distance.

> *It is as though the light is always behind the girl. He knows it is not so, that it is a trick of his mind. He wants her to see him in an entirety that precludes judgment, as he longs to see and to be seen. But he knows that this can never be.*
>
> *She seems to him like living porcelain formed from pure fire. Perhaps she does not judge him because he is not recognizably human. Now he will never know. He has never seen himself as monstrous, but he cannot deny the fact that he has acted monstrously.*
>
> *As he leaves the village in the confusion, he passes her lying limp in the old man's arms. She is wearing the same*

*trousers, burned now, and her skin is raw. The old man is*
*holding her, gently rocking back and forth.*

> *There are others still in the village that he'd come to know*
> *while he was in the cage. Some lie twisted and burned by*
> *their huts. Others seem untouched, as though the life in them*
> *simply left. These images enter his eyes through a will of their*
> *own, though he tries to keep his eyes fixed and rigid on the*
> *path to the trees. It is the second time Finn has been close to*
> *the receiving end of the fires he'd rained down from the skies.*

Finn looks into the night. Voices lift from the town through the darkness; the far-off trumpeting of car horns call and the O-o-o-o-m of tires on pavement soothe him. The sounds ride the winds to places roads will never be.

Behind him, Lara moves by the bed. The sheets rustle and the noise is a breathing that fills the room. Then she is behind him again, sliding her arm around his chest and resting her chin on his shoulder. He feels her throat on his shoulder blade. Her pregnant belly presses against his back. The cool draft of air he's been awaiting comes in the window. It is the beginning of the day, and the air moves over the waters toward the land, and the small waves quicken on the sands. He looks into the circle where the moon pools on the face of the lake. It floats upon the void, ephemeral, eternal, and Finn thinks that this is not a paradox at all, that disappearance is not absence, that a moment is, by its nature, eternal. Where he is, is what he is. He hears Lara's sharp intake of breath at his neck.

"Look at the moonlight along the wave tips," she says, and the heat of her breath moves along his jaw and meets the cool air at his chin and he breathes it, he breathes it all and the moon is coming down through the window and its light is like laughter upon the waters, like a promise and *Yes* it says *yes*. He is light-headed with looking as the light resolves itself again and again, "As though the moon is carving the waves out of the darkness," she says, and she says, "It's beautiful, Finn."

## CHAPTER THIRTEEN

# The Release

The fog lifts early the next morning, and Finn feels garrulous and lightheaded. His behavior is a lie covering the man inside. He chats idly before getting out of bed, and Lara looks at him skeptically.

"Let's make it a good day," he says.

"Okay," says Lara.

"The water's calm."

"Yes," she says.

"Shall I make a brunch? I'll bring you some coffee. You can have it in bed."

"You're very chatty this morning," she says. "But I'm still not all right with last night."

"Okay," says Finn. "I'll go make breakfast," and he leaves the room. He feels false to the admissions of the night and the daylight feels trivial. He knows Lara will move to make a claim on these revelations, to own them in some small part, and push for resolutions. A small knot of anger forms in his gut, but he retains the bright persona like a suit of ill-fitting clothes and patters about the kitchen. It is, he realizes, a thing he's learned from his father, another loner nursing the long, slow toothache of a foreign war.

He feels strange, as though an important part of him has been let out. Secret things that made him who he was. He's lost ownership of facts that now live in Lara's mind too. What she does with them is out of his hands, but she will do it by day. Some things are too true to ever speak out loud, he thinks. Life is shallower by day, and we are kept afloat on the surface of our deeps like waterbugs buoyed by surface tension on a pond. If the tension fails and we sink, all hell breaks loose.

By ten, the sun is high, and the trees throw down their likeness on the lake. The leaves lie red and gold upon small waves as Finn looks through the window, his father's window, the place where, in the quiets of night, the older man looks out to the Manitou Islands.

The house is gravid with familiarities. His father will be haunting the old paths of Dublin, showing them to Finn's mother, who will reveal her delight and her surprise at the new places, but hide her sadness at being so close to where a young man was shot down over Normandy in the war his father calls his. She will secrete the loss like she has hidden the letter by that young man, a letter professing a love that Finn discovered in the bureau drawer he emptied for Lara, a letter referring to Finn's father as a friend. She will stand behind her stoicism and denial, something she learned, Finn thinks, from her own mother, whose stock reaction to tragedy and loss was to say simply: "These things happen to people."

His mother has a quiet and stolid detachment that Finn finds only while flying. He's uneasy about what he said to Lara last night, and he's nervous about discovering the secrets of his mother, whose details he does not want to know. He needs to get out on the lake. If not in the air, then on the water, he thinks, as a small wave of awareness laps up on his consciousness: his mother, too, is one for living a hidden life, and he owes more to her than he's imagined. He looks across the waters to the islands whose manitous his mother never speaks of. It is his father who has adopted them. Perhaps she simply lives them in the strange, deep places she keeps and has no need for words.

Everyone has their secrets, Finn thinks, and they are invisible engines that drive more than we want to admit.

"Lara," he calls.

"Coming."

"Brunch is ready." He hears her splashing in the tub.

"I'll be right there."

Finn walks from the living room to the kitchen and the table. He wants colors. He wants them bold and simple, and he wants them in place before Lara can get to the table. He's filled the fruit bowl with the colors of apples and oranges and bananas. Beside the bowl are servings of white feta cheese, yoghurt, and amber honey. Beside these things is a plate of sliced tomatoes sprinkled with basil.

He hopes she will take the food and forget how bad the night has been. He's worried. She's been moody and piqued. Maybe the long autumn rains are getting to her. No, he thinks, she's pregnant.

"It's all set," he calls and walks back to the living room window to look at the lake again. He's been observing himself all morning, talkative, and feels as though he's watching someone else. It's a curious, detached thing. He looks out into the day, determined to shake off his broodiness.

The lake is alight with trees and sky. The world moves upon the waters, but he glimpses the darkness below. He strains to see into the deeps where the shadows are, but when he throws his focus beyond the surface, he sees instead reflections of the sky and clouds.

He turns and walks down the hall to the bathroom and opens the door. Lara is in the bath.

"You're still in the tub," he says.

"And you're still brooding," she says.

"Sorry," he says.

"I'll be right there." The tip of her tongue presses against her upper teeth, and she laughs. She pauses with her mouth open. "I want you to be with me no matter what," she says. "Always," she finishes. "Never leave me."

Her words surprise him. The steam carries the scent of bath oil to him, mingled and changed with her chemistry. He breathes it and thinks, smell is the old sense that runs deepest and lasts longest. He stays at the door and looks. Her flesh is flushed from the heat, her lips parted slightly as though in astonishment. Her long legs repose half out of the water, the tight taper of her thighs utterly relaxed, he can see, loosely cradling the dark triangle of her mons, then the soft mound of her belly dimpling above it into the navel and the plexus rising over the ribs, her smooth skin a living tent topped by her breasts and their ruddy puckers. Finally, the skin dips into the hollow of her throat and her neck to her head which is crowned with the filaments of her long, dark hair fanned out like sea coral in the water. Finn fights to stay present.

"Me too," he says.

Then he walks to the tub and squats beside her. In the hollow of her throat, a small pool of water pulses with her beating heart. She takes his hand and rests it on her belly. He feels for the heart within, the hidden life.

"Lotion me later?" she asks.

"Yes," he says.

With his other hand, he strokes her hair. He stares at his other hand, resting on the mound that conceals within the liquid darkness–their child. She is full of life, more than pregnant with it. It is everywhere over her. She floats in a series of circles: a sea within a sea, like Ezekiel's wheels: the tub, the tiny sea within with its own tides and rhythms suspended in the waters.

There is a sleeping face within her deeps that will be his son.

Lara draws her legs up and attempts to get out of the water.

"Careful,' he says. He reaches out and steadies her waist. Then Finn steps back and leaves the room to her.

"I'm hungry," she says.

"We have an hour and a half to get there," he says. "It's a good day for the lake. The food is on the table."

Inside, Finn feels the urge to shout, to lash out. Something has been left in the night, something more palpable than the polite intercourse of the day. The words of our mouths, he thinks.

After they eat, he waits in the car until she comes down the pathway to him. Once she's settled in the seat, he pulls out of the driveway. It's a short trip along the curves of the lake where the light lies gently on the maple trees and on small cabins with green-shingles and log walls and then through the town park where the grass runs down to the water's edge. Lara is quiet. He feels words welling up in him. The bright light on the lake pulls at him through the breaks in the trees.

"It's a good day," he says.

"Winter's just around the corner," Lara says.

"But we have today," says Finn.

Lara sits beside him with her hands on her belly.

"Is he moving?" Finn asks.

"Not yet," she laughs.

A small shiver runs down Finn's neck and arms. "When?"

"Soon."

Finn begins to imagine arms and legs forming up within, then changes his mind. Under water, he thinks, in the dark. Breathing it in and out. The thought hurts.

"Good," he says. He looks to the road ahead.

When they get to the wharf, he pulls up to the lot and parks, pointing the car to the lake. The ship is a good three hundred feet away. "It's a little walk," he says. "Are you good with that?"

"It will be good to stretch," she says.

Finn gets out of the car, walks around and opens the door for Lara. They turn towards the wharf and stop, looking down the length of the wooden docking to the boat waiting, The Chief Commanda, a ninety-eight-foot steel vessel built in 1954 for lake cruises, with a new coat of paint.

"It's getting pretty beat up," she says.

"It was built in the fifties," he says, "and this is its last cruise. They'll dock it and put the new one into service next year. Bigger, but the same name with a "II" after it. I've sailed on this old tub since I was a kid."

Lara takes his hand. "Let's go," she says. "Don't be sad." But the words that float between them are meaningless and maddening, empty noises in the air.

On the ship, they find a spot on the deck where they can be alone. As they look over the railing, Finn rests one hand on the small mound of Lara's belly. He can't get the thought out of his mind: she floats with the ship on the lake and their child floats within her. He sees these concentric circles, their own lives suspended in the waters. He knows he is being obsessive, but he imagines limbs crossed in a lightless lotus within the dark waters of his wife. The air around them is moist, touched with the scent of her perfume. The spray thrown up by the prow carries her perfume as the scent mingles with her chemistry, just like it did that morning in the bath's steam, changed and unique now, and he says, "Smell is the oldest of the senses and runs deepest and lasts longest." His wife is alchemy incarnate, changing invisibly before him. She is pregnant, more full of life than he can fathom. He brings a handful of her hair up to his face and breathes through it.

He rattles off more details, watching himself babble, and leans over to kiss her. She steps up onto the bottom railing and leans into the wind.

"Careful," he says. He puts a hand on her belly and steadies her. Like a fish in water, he thinks.

He looks away to the lake. The deep beat of the engine throbs through the steel and he thinks of the gunboats in Vietnam, with their throaty motors and the stink of diesel in the heat, the air a humid soup of sweat and fuel and fear.

But here, now, eight feet below, the prow slices the clean water and the lake is cool. It heaves like a living thing. Seas are like that, he believes, and big rivers if they are clean, and mountains. Primordial, with a slumbering presence. Enormities seem complex enough to house such mysteries. Big lakes, big rivers, the seas, seem almost to contain volition. He repeats these things aloud, to Lara.

"Yes," she says.

He takes his hand from her waist and, with the sweep of his arms, he encompasses the world. He speaks of Jung and the deep symbols of water and the unconscious and the unknowable, the tectonics of life and the planet. The primordial, pervasive smell of seaweed and water. The smells of birth. He looks at her. She smiles at him. For the moment, there is only the moment.

"These are the things that build our lives, like continents. And we're heading towards the Manitou Islands," he says. "Where the Ojibwa believed that the spirits gather."

"Yes," she says.

"They believed even small animals have spirits, and insects, called manidoowish and manidoowan." Finn realizes it is a body of facts he can plunge into and stop the thinking. He watches himself babble. "It changes how you see things, when you think of it like that. That's what medicine was: the gathered effect of a plant's manitou applied to sickness. And the spirits under the water, the manituw, had to be appeased every time you crossed the lake. That's what Dad told me. He pretty much lived it when he came back from the war, even when he was with with my mother, after I was born. He spent a lot of time alone, in the bush along the Little Abitibi. God, I'd love to know what that was like. Him alone living off the land for weeks at a time. It's almost neolithic."

She is looking back, her lips parted in a smile.

"Sweetheart," she says. "Your father is such a mystic." She reaches out and puts her hand on his arm. "And you, when you're not brooding," she finishes.

"These are important ideas," he says. "Everything has its own Manitou. Every plant and every stone." Somehow, his eyes are hot. He's preaching, but can't help it. Facts are an incantation to sanity. "Even machines," he says. "And ships and jets. The Phantom I flew. It felt alive at times. These things were different in Vietnam. Unrecognizable, but there. Now, shit … nothing."

"There is the world of ideas, and the world of reality," she says. "It's complicated. I know. I know."

"It's hard to know what works in the real world until you go through it," says Finn, "and then it can surprise you. I keep telling myself that."

"I know," she says, "but don't overthink it. Not today."

Finn sees something from the corner of his eye—a seagull swooping close. He hears Lara catch her breath. One moment she is standing next to him, listening, and then she reaches out to snatch a seagull feather carried on the wind, and is gone. She pitches over the top rail and falls towards the waves of the lake, her face tilted up toward him. He thinks, oddly, as he watches, it is his own face looking back at him.

He almost laughs, so incongruous it seems, so silly, not real. But then she hits the water, and that is real. The descent will be slow for her, cloaked as warmly as she is. He knows that immediately. He runs to stay abreast of her before he dives but his action is paralleled by thought: her eyes will focus on a surface that mirrors nothing so much as her own dismay that this most inevitable of things, her own death, should arrive so ordinarily. That it should be now, she may think, like this, looking up at her husband through the water, just as he looked up at the faces of the priests as they reached down to him. But these are his thoughts, not hers, he knows, but on some perverse level he is loathe to interrupt her experience.

For an instant he envies her descent, wants suddenly, impossibly, to switch places with her and ride the smooth folds down to the calm interface between the worlds, a place where *is* and *is not* flows imperceptibly together. It isn't that he desires extinction: it's the moment of enlightenment he craves, the feeling of bliss, of freedom, of letting go that comes in that instant of fading consciousness. He sees more completely then than ever before, and the instant lasts, becomes permanent; he owns his life fully then, recognizes its wholeness, is satisfied with it as though it were, after all, an object he himself, quite consciously on some fundamental level, has created.

He lifts his hand to a pressure in his chest. The time between the beats of his heart grows. He runs along the boat's rail watching her, the cold metal clutched stupidly in his hands. His body's push to move is stalled by the old bugling in the brain.

He knows too much of this, how the moments before death elongate and crease, for beneath the surface of this memory, he's hung in the old moment of his near-drowning as a boy. He'd jumped in the river with his boots on, and they pulled him down as he watched the surface of the water receding above him. He had not been afraid, not fully present as he'd observed it happening, until arms thrust through the water to grab him and pull him to the surface. His father's arms.

And then the war. It all floats into his vision as time folds like a piece of paper touching the edges of past and present, edges that should never touch, and he fights free of the moments of his own deaths, sinking, fading, faces above looking down in dim disbelief.

Below him, Lara is treading water, sinking slowly. His gaze is locked on her sea-green and unblinking eyes, on her hair fanned out in the water.

He steps over the railing and leaps, watching her watching him. Then he is in the water, her face close. There is no altered state of perception as the sharp edges of action pour into him.

Her lips part, but she does not speak. She looks at him and he watches her lips and feels something very deep inside him shift. The tip of her tongue moves slightly beyond her upper teeth. He does not want to lose that, that pause with her mouth open, a small, tense hesitation that indicates, has always indicated, that what she wants to say is deliberate, important, and this is a habit of hers that he loves very much and wants never to lose.

# The Melody at Night

January 1981

Tonight, Finn is thorough as he washes the diaper. His life is no longer wholly his own. His hands burn from the chafing, but once, he had not been thorough—a minute skipped in the washing, the water tepid, too little bleach—and a diaper rash had opened small patches of his son's skin, giving the flesh an angry, moth-eaten look that medication would not cover.

So now the air is thick and the water splashes over the cords of his hands, and he kneels against the curled rim of the tub and his knees ache. He bangs his feet against the washstand legs behind him when he shifts. Just a part of it, he thinks, on your knees every night, cleaning diapers in an attitude of prayer. He stops and listens. The night is quiet.

But the tub presses into his chest, and he squeezes the cotton under the hot water, swirling it beneath the thick layer of suds. Six cloth diapers swirl in the brew. He stops again and listens. He visualizes the little curled form of his son in the crib, the small, impossibly detailed fingers, and the toes perfectly formed.

He leans forward and pulls the plug. The waters rush down the drain. He twists the faucet, squeezes cotton under the stream, shakes the diapers apart, holds each under the icy stream separately as he wrings them hard, then tosses them onto the rim of the tub. Once they're squeezed, he spins the hot faucet, inserts the plug, pours in a cup of bleach, waits until the water is six inches high, and swirls the cloth into the mix. His hands are slippery now from the chlorine; the sweet, cloying fumes claw his throat and eyes.

Almost done, he thinks. He shifts to relieve the pressure on his knees, bangs his feet against the vanity again, and leans past the pain and into the porcelain. He blinks in the glare of the bulb hanging bare from the ceiling, then drains the tub, wrings the diapers a third time, rinses them in cold water, then in hot water to speed their drying and warm his hands. He snaps each cotton square with a clean smartness and hangs it overlapping its neighbor on the shower rod circling the tub.

He dries his arms and looks up at his work gleaming like a corona beneath the naked light above. At morning light, he will fold the clothing cleanly, and the seventh diaper, the one the infant wears as he sleeps, will have done its job. He raises his arms and spreads them wide, moving the palms of his hands on the face of the cloth.

He turns off the light and steps out of the bathroom into the kitchen. Guided by the soft glow of the nightlight over the counter, he walks gingerly to the sink, opens the cupboard door, takes down the coffee, a paper filter, and fills the coffee machine. He presses the red light of the switch. The little machine gurgles, and Finn grasps two mugs by their handles in the cupboard, slides them forward on the shelf and hesitates. He pushes one mug back and sets the other very carefully on the counter.

Lara is gone. She left the day the washing machine broke. Post partum depression, the doctor said. Finn raises his hand to his chin, cups it, and squeezes. She wanted to spend two weeks with friends, Phil and his wife Debbie, and has called only twice, once to say she needed more time and wanted to spend a week at the lake with Finn's parents.

"Take the time you need," Finn said. "But why with Phil and Debbie? Why not just go to the lake?"

"It's what I need," she said. "They're good friends, and I can't talk with your parents the same way."

"Is it helping?" Finn asked. "Debbie never struck me as being too deep."

"Phil has taken two weeks off to be home. So it's good."

"Phil took two weeks off work?" Finn asked. "Debbie too?"

"No'" said Laura. "Deb is still working, but she's home at night."

"I see," said Finn. "So you're alone with Phil."

"How's the baby?" Laura asked.

Finn is restless. The dreams have called him again when the night air is hushed and heavy. He quiets his thoughts with the clean-up. He waits, stares at the mug on the shelf, listens to the coffee's quiet splash, then fills his cup and walks across the room to the crib. He stands against the rails of the bed, nurses the hot coffee, and stretches his hand to the face of his son.

The baby sleeps on his stomach, his head turned to rest on his cheek. Finn cups his hand on the curled warmth of the baby's back. He rubs his thumb gently over the tiny muscles there, soft and relaxed upon the small bones of the shoulders.

The baby's legs are tucked up under its belly, lifting his bottom in the air, and Finn moves his hand down along the back to the padded, clean diaper and pats it gently.

He leans forward and inhales deeply, taking in the smell of his son's skin and the small clouds of infant breath, all of it sweet and yeasty and new in the world. The smell of the coffee and the scent of his son take the caustic sting out of his chest, and the sound of the baby's laughter tumbles faintly through his mind. He stretches down and nestles his nose into the neck and shoulder and behind the ears where the smooth skin sleeps and meets the hair.

"How do we forgive our fathers?" Finn whispers.

> *How do we address the words of our mouths? Do we call them lies when they say nothing of who we are? What do we say to the words that pretend that we live in the day when the truths that we keep, we keep in the night? How do we forgive the movements of our bodies when their moves smooth the lives of our loves but are false to our selves?*
>
> *How do we pardon ourselves? How do we live the days as the days come, and preserve the night and when it is time, to take the life of the night and put it away?*

The work of the baby's breathing rises around him. Finn hears his own chest work. He straightens to look across the room and face the dark. He looks north through the window over the land to where Lake Nipissing lies some three hundred miles north, where the light of the moon is a shimmering quilt on the waves by the shore, and where, further out, the Manitous lie cloaked. Finn shuts his eyes and listens. The little song of the baby's breath dances around the notes of his own lungs, and the sound of their breathing is clear in the deeps of the night.

## CHAPTER FIFTEEN

# The Darkness in the Trees

May 1981

> *He's pretending to be someone else, he can feel it, he can hear it, the public self, the dissociated observation of the social lie, the fabrication to make those around him comfortable. More and more his days will be a pretense, his character a cloak of affectations to meet the demands of circumstance. He will watch his own machinations. He will feel less and less. His moods will be overlaid with the mundane, his insights and inhabitations covered with words. In the deep fissures of identity, the windhover will be put to sleep, and then put out of memory.*

"Finn?"

"Yes?"

"Phil invited us over for a drink tonight. He's down in the dumps.'

"Great. That sounds like fun," says Finn. "What's his problem?"

"Don't be sarcastic. Debbie won't be back for another week."

"Debbie's gone?"

"For a while."

"Why?"

"I don't know."

"She's your friend, Lara. You don't know? How come you don't know what's going on with her, but you do with the husband?"

"Phil said she just needed a few more days."

"'Phil said.' What the hell? When?"

Finn looks up from his book and out the window. It's spring, and the snow is almost gone. He wonders why the woman needed a break. He knows things have been bumpy there since Lara stayed with them for two weeks after little Michael was born. Phil is one man he can't crack. He wonders if it's because Phil never went into combat. For Finn, that makes it hard to trust him. What can such a man know of his own heart? But he doesn't seem any good on his own, and Finn does not respect that. Plus, he seems to be needy and calls Lara more often that Finn likes. He feels sorrier for the wife.

"What time?" Finn asks.

"In two hours," says Lara. "Finish what you're doing and start to get ready."

"I don't need two hours to get ready to visit Phil," he says, wondering why she does, and returns to his book.

Once they get to Phil's, the three of them sit in a circle and talk. Phil has put out a little spread of bread and cheese, a pathetic effort to Finn's way of thinking and evidence that the man needs his wife. Or a mother. A man with no color and no panache. But then he sees Phil run his gaze over Lara's rump as she reaches over the coffee table for wine, a long, deliberate look that slides liquidly over her hips and thighs and comes to rest on her crotch as she turns back to the sofa. Then Phil glances over towards Finn and jumps when he realizes Finn is watching him. His face goes blank and a flush rises to his cheeks. Finn smiles tightly and says, "Nice, isn't it?," but he thinks, What the hell? Phil's eyes widen. Finn feels a pleasure at being so blunt, but he wants no nonsense, and he wants Phil to know that he is not too upset, that there is a recognition of the attraction, an acknowledgment, that it is understandable, but there is to be no nonsense of action or attitude. Lara is his wife, and the look was inappropriate but Finn wants to be past it. To look is human. To persist is trouble. Then he begins to talk as though nothing has happened in an attempt to make the younger man relax. As he talks, Phil looks to his eyes, and Finn can see confusion there, as though Phil were unsure what he is doing, not trusting the situation or Finn's reaction. Good, thinks Finn, because now he really doesn't trust Phil. Phil has a lot to learn.

Then, to make matters worse, Phil turns the talk to sex and how the possession that people feel is limiting and irrational. Finn looks over to Lara. Lara watches Phil. Finn is suddenly keenly aware Lara is Phil's age. Phil argues that people should not be exclusive and that sex with other partners should not be a deal-breaker. Lara looks at Finn, blinks twice and looks away. Finn sits up straighter, on the alert. He has heard it all before, has even argued for the points that are being argued now, but it was a long time ago when he was single. And it was in the abstract. Few things have been abstract since the war. He does not have the energy to argue with Phil because Phil has no right to pretend to be single at this point. Finn does not want to reason with him, and he doesn't want to joust for his own wife.

A great wave of tiredness washes from one side of his ribs and over his heart to the other. He thinks of the period of time when Laura left him and the baby alone to spend time with Phil and Debbie, only Debbie was at work all day and Phil took the time off. The PPD. Shit, he thinks. He wonders if this has something to do with Debbie's absence, but he doesn't want to jump to conclusions.

There is the world of ideas, he thinks, and the world of reality. "It's complicated," he says. "It's hard to know what works in the real world until you go through it. Then it surprises you," he says, looking at Phil. These are the words Finn uses in the classroom, but he sees that is not what Phil wants to hear, and the man fidgets impatiently.

Phil leans forward, trying to say what is in his heart. Finn sees what's coming and wants no part of it. Phil struggles to get it out as though he were trying to give birth to a hurt he carries, to get it out in the open in the hope that maybe then someone can do or say something to help. But he looks down at the rug as they sit in the circle and he says, "I'm looking and looking, and I see … I see … everybody's feet. All I see is everybody's feet." Finn wants to laugh. He looks down. It's true. At least Phil got that right. "And then," Phil says, "I see nothing. Nothing between the feet." A profound utterance has somehow gone amiss, leaving the words like crumbs from a feast.

Lara pours more wine into the glasses and will not meet Finn's eye. Suddenly Finn does not trust Lara, either.

The three of them sit in the circle and drink wine and eat wafers as the room darkens. They speak of flesh and spirit and how people become trapped by the demands of their bodies. Phil laments how physical relationships should be free and joyful and open. Dusk creeps in through the windows until Finn can not see Phil's face. Only the dark shape of his head is clear against the windows, like a shadow, and Phil speaks out of the shadow.

Finn studies Phil. He wants to memorize what a man who makes this kind of pitch in front of another man's wife looks like.

Then Finn watches Lara as Lara watches Phil. He wants to say "What the fuck, Lara?" but he only says that he agrees with none of it. It's nonsense, he tells them reasonably, a result of the Cartesian mind/body duality, a notion that causes no end of grief and rubbish between men and women, who cohabit a sufficiently perilous no-man's land in the best of times, and even though they may have not heard of it, he says, Phil is pushing the same unsound philosophy, and Lara, he says, is listening.

He looks at Lara hard, feels his stomach knot and, because she seems to stare at Phil like a deer in lights, he decides to bring out more heavy weaponry: academic jargon. Screw this, he thinks, time to go in for the kill. Polysyllabification with Phil will be like carpet bombing: his brain is as smooth as a baby's ass—not a convolution in sight. Finn feels his fingernails biting into his palms as his fists tighten, but he takes a deep breath and smiles. He's the devil citing scripture. He tells them he's heard it from a lot of people like Phil. He drops the word "Phil" a full note. The idea lasts a few years, he says, unless you're on the make, and he's sick of listening to it because he believes that the mind and the body are not separate. The body, he says, is a part of the mind with its own patterns of behavior, and its thinking is at times far more subtle and powerful than the thinking of the brain, which is just a part of the whole. Finn lines up the words: "The brain has its rarified ideals and the body has its hard-won patterns. This is one of them."

Lara fidgets. Finn holds up a finger and deliberately looks at her the way he looks at the students in his class. He is suddenly pissed at everything–Phil, Lara, his buttoned-down classrooms, his demons locked in a box. "The arena of love is not a rarified place," he says. "It is not lofty, despite the heights it takes you to. No, it is carnage and ecstasy; it is ruin and salvation. It is perilous and absolute," he says, "and it is of a different order of rationality." He feels his finger pull at an imaginary trigger. Phil looks at him blankly. Finn goes in for the kill shot: "Phil, you have to learn to accept more than you can understand. And if you do not, the arena can shift very quickly from the Cartesian duality, an idea, to the field of the Fisher King where the heart and spirit are wounded and will not heal. Or worse. Some son-of-a-bitch will get violent. That's where you are now, Phil," Finn says, "right about where some mother-fucker gets violent." Finn leans back in the chair, and he can feel the muscles in his thigh twitching.

Lara moves closer on the couch and puts her hand on Finn's knee. Phil sees the gesture and looks away. Finn sees the gesture and ignores it. He wants to get in a jet and bomb the shit out of something.

Finn watches Phil roll his head to the right and look out the window. Only his profile is visible, and his left eye, but that is enough to see that it is stricken. The eye is a combination of darkness and light, of focus and evasion, of the points of light picked out of the crepuscular room by the white orb in a man's skull. It is something raw. Phil's eye is like that. It is unfocused, but looking for something. It is unusually transparent in the cornea, with more of the white exposed around it, and it seems larger than usual. It holds the light that comes from the outside and from the inside, and the darkness too, from the world inside Phil and from the world outside. It is the eye of a dying man, and Finn recognizes it.

Fascinated, he looks past Phil and out the windows into the darkness gathering in the trees, to the trees that are solid and real, and then back to Lara's friend. The rest of Phil's face has not changed that much; the change is all in the one eye. It is as though the man's desperation, what haunted his human heart, what is in many ways impossible to articulate or discern or comprehend, is penetratingly written on an organ designed to see out with, not in through. But Finn looks hungrily into it though he knows the look will haunt him for a while. It is an old haunting, but he knows what fathered the look that is born in the eye will haunt Phil even longer.

After the talk, Finn gets into the car and drives Lara home. He has been a son-of-a-bitch but is content because it is still *their* home. He looks north to where Lake Nipissing lies three hundred and eleven miles away, and his father's house, and the Manitous, and the forests that made him.

It is a long drive home along the Thames River, and the waters flow quietly between the banks. The last light is a living thing on the river. Black maple and willow trees line the shores, and they pass by Huron University and the old seminary as they drive, and a small park where barley once grew. Finn does not speak, and Lara is still. Words are shapeless and without form on his tongue. It feels as though time has gotten up and run away. He is driving through another place than the one they lived in only hours before, and he looks out of the car windows to the water, and the face of the river is smooth. An occasional ripple dances where something lies below. There is no sense of time along the road as he drives.

When they are home, Finn pays the sitter. Lara goes upstairs to check on the baby. Finn walks the young woman to the car and on the way back, his legs feel like dancing, but not the kind of dancing on a dance floor: the kind of dancing a man does in a boxing ring.

Then he walks upstairs to join Lara. They look down on little Michael sleeping. Lara reaches out and takes Finn's hand in her own.

"I love you," she says.

He kisses Lara. Lara kisses him back. They go to their room and Lara pulls Finn down beside her on the bed. He undresses her slowly, then rolls her onto her side and draws up her right leg. He begins that way, building up to a steady intensity, and he watches as she lies her head on the pillow and arches her neck. The more he moves, the more languid Lara's head becomes on the pillow. It is as though she is swooning, as though the bones in her neck are softening. Once, she lifts her head slightly with what seems a great effort and looks into Finn's eyes. Her eyes are wide and questioning and her cheeks are flushed. Then her head falls back to the pillow. She begins to moan softly and small tremors run down her arms.

Later, the wind is high and the trees shake in the darkness. They rattle and clack against the house as Finn lies in bed, so he gets up to fetch the old khaki coat that smells of sweet woodsmoke and kitchen, and he leaves through the back door. Outside, from the veranda, the sounds of the trees are musical and resonant, the solid knock of living wood. He walks out over the grass and stands beneath the leaves and presses his hand to the trunk of the biggest maple. Then he leans his brow into the tree and sobs once. It is a long night, and the trees move in the darkness.

## CHAPTER SIXTEEN

# Fahrenheit I: The Fire Tetrahedron

June 1990

They fly a DC-3 Otter floatplane from London to Petawawa, then up the Ottawa River and over the trees to the harbor at New Liskeard. Finn enjoys the flight, and he never tires of it, though he does it every summer. Flying is never routine. He looks eastward for the tors and massifs of Quebec where the tectonics of the Canadian Shield left its mark on the land, but west of the river, the hills flatten towards the Hudson Plain and the clouds hang close to the earth.

Don Anderson pilots the aircraft. A bush pilot, he grew up with Finn on the Little Abitibi and has never left the North. Finn sits in the passenger seat and studies the old rift valley that cradles the river, the failed arm of the ancient Ieptus Sea. The headwaters of the Ottawa fill old seabed with the fresh water of Lake Temiskaming. The west bank of the lake is English, and the east is French, and the fires of old rivalries still smolder over the waters where the little towns hug the shores and the northern lights rain down their dance on the winter snows.

The area was active with mining before Finn had been born, and the town of Cobalt was the largest silver mine in the country. It was hard rock mining then, when the ore lay close to the surface and the miners learned their craft with pick, shovel, and dynamite as they burrowed deeper into the crust. The tailings are still visible from the air, and the rock retains its scars. From Cobalt, the men spread north to the gold fields of Kirkland Lake and Timmins, where Finn was born when it was among the world's largest gold mines.

Don circles the lake once, heads the plane into the wind, and lays the pontoons down smoothly on the lake. Then they pull into the harbor, climb out and secure the craft.

"Mary Beamish is still here," Don says. "Bob's been gone since last fall, but she's hanging on to the house for a bit longer. The kids don't want it and moved to B.C. Sick of the winters here. I know she'd like to see you. It's been a couple of years, hasn't it? And if she follows the kids out west this could be the last time you see her."

"Good," says Finn. "That would be good." Bob worked with Finn's father in the settlement on the Little Abitibi and engineered the speeder and the train to the nearest connecting station.

"Then, you can check into the Firehall," says Don.

After the visit with Mary, Finn takes the bus to the base, and he and Don part company for another year, for although Finn treasures this flight north with his friend, he loves the solo trip south on the train, secure in a berth alone, reliving the trips to southern Quebec he took with his mother every summer when he was boy.

There is a routine to be followed when arriving at the base. After checking in with the crew and mechanics, Finn enters the hanger and spends two hours going over the Bell 204 he will fly this summer. The metal of the modified Huey feels good under his hands, and Finn maintains an almost unbroken physical connection with the machine as he walks around it. He feels the tension drain out of him. Soon he will be in the air.

Supper in the canteen is desultory as the crews check in with one another, giving the long, probing looks that mark an awareness that not everyone may make it out. It is too much thinking for Finn. As soon as he can, he leaves for his barracks and calls Lara.

"It's me," he says.

"Are you settled in?" Lara asks.

"Pretty much. How's Michael?"

"He misses you. He's driving me crazy with his talk of helicopters. Where does he get all that information?" Finn chuckles. "Have you committed to stay just the one month?" she asks.

"Pretty much."

"Finn, we need you here," she says. "Every July and August you're away. You're addicted. This is Michael's ninth summer."

"Lara, they need me here too. It's only for two months. I know it's every summer. I know it's hard. But this is important."

"But it's every summer. Michael wants to learn how to do certain things, like fish. He wants you to teach him."

"I know. When I was his age I was trapping and hunting on my own. He'll pick it up. I'll get to it. Stop babying him."

"And who taught you to do those things? Where have you been when you could have been here doing for him what your father did for you? Are you ever going to get it? Finn, when are we going to get you back? I mean all of you."

"Well," said Finn, "okay. You're right. I've been thinking about it. I said I would. I'll cut my time here down to a month." At times, fighting the flames in the bush seems more manageable than the fires at home.

"I'll be careful," he says, listening to his own words. "And I'll phase it out. For you and Michael." His father's advice comes back to him: "There comes a point, Finn, when the early part of your life has to be over." But Finn wonders what would be left. And the words of our mouths that leave out who we are, he thinks. What can we say of the words in the day? What can we tell to the truths that keep to the night?

Later, the wind changes, and a stillness hangs over the base. Finn walks to the window of his room and looks out to the fire glow beyond the trees. The trees are untouched between him and the flames, and there is a darkness in them that calls him. Tomorrow, the endless variety in the greenery will unfold itself before he gets to the burn. That's what he wants to save as he stands in the shadows. That's his mission now: not to sow, but to stop the fires. He looks up. A smoky moon rolls balefully over the trees. Finn thinks of the fire's bleak embers and the gold vermilion of the hot coals as he wanders out of his room and around the base to the nearest trees.

At the base of the trees, the earth is etched with the shadows from the moon overhead. The shapes are old and familiar to Finn, like the crazed finish on pottery, and they bring back the nights of his wandering in Vietnam between a sleep and a sleep, and he moves among the shadows quietly. The night wind pulls at the pines above.

He hates wrangling with Lara. Her words stay in his head more and more and interfere with the words of instruction that appear before his eyes when he needs not to think. He knows she's right, but something in him always pushes back. Her voice keeps him awake in ways contemplating action never does. They repeat in his head. He thinks of a line from Blake: "The tigers of wrath are wiser than the horses of instruction." There is no room for wrath in his life other than here, where he contends with the flames, when the fire in his belly is at one with the burning world.

Then he walks back to the hanger and checks the helicopter again. The Bell 204 is ideal to fly in and drop the team, and the model is familiar: a modified Huey. For Finn, piloting it is a dance with the winds, and the flames now take the place of small arms fire from the enemy. It is as routine as a need can be.

He leans against the craft as he looks northwest through the hangar doors towards the fires. Above the trees, the horizon glows like false dawn. The stars are hidden and his arm is up over his head, and his fingers press tightly against the metal skin.

The smoke rises over the trees in the morning, and from where Finn sits in the canteen at his breakfast, the sky is dirty and the sun is pink. The fire is downwind and west over the horizon, and Finn watches the distant pyrocumulus clouds as he lingers over his bacon and eggs. If the clouds move closer to where his team will be putting fire breaks, he will have to deal with stack effects should he fly too close. The heat has created strong updrafts and thermal columns that will buffet the helicopter. Finn feels himself smile. It is not enemy munitions, but it will do. So long as he is in the air, so long as there is action. The conditions in the distance are extreme, and there will be fire whirls moving up to fifty miles per hour. Tornado winds.

Even flying closer to the base, the flying will be dicey. As he sips the sour canteen coffee, he watches the mechanics on the runway. The chief mechanic, Doug Hoff, has his head in the engine cowling, and two other figures in orange overalls are checking the rotor blades on the tail. It takes them twenty minutes, more time than Finn thinks they need. Finally, the lead mechanic turns to the canteen window and raises a thumbs-up. The helicopter is ready to go. Finn leaves his cup on the table, puts on his aviator sunglasses, and walks out to the runway. Before his Rapattack team arrives, he wants to run through the routine himself, work the pedals, the collective, and run his fingers over the instrument panel. As he goes through the ritual, he thinks through the day ahead. Two drops, one pick-up. The second team, set down later in the day, will work through the evening for a late pickup.

Finn eases into the pilot's seat, sighs, begins to whistle 'California Dreaming,' and relaxes.

Then his headphones crackle. "Finn?"

"Right," says Finn.

"Are you all set to go?" Finn recognizes the voice of the team leader.

"Ready," says Finn.

"We're on our way. They're calling for the winds to pick up later. That could bring the main burn close in sooner than we expected."

"I'll get you in and out," says Finn.

If the winds are predicted to kick up, he will stay clear of the extremes and drop the team safely in front of the fire's path to set up the breaks. He'll take the forward rate of spread into account when he drops them. Even a slow burn in these woods can move faster than a firefighter can walk.

Once he is in the air, the old calmness kicks in. He feels his head start to move in time to a tune, and he whistles "Light My Fire" by the Doors. He is amped. The crew behind him is watchful. They note to one another that in this area the flames are three to six feet high, and that's a good thing. He listens to the talk, and with their words come the echoes he waits for. When he flies, there is always another company of men. He pilots the friends who were lost to the war and the years, closest now when he is in the air. Their voices fall faintly and far away upon him as the signature *whump-whump-whump* of the Huey's rotors resurrect the haunted jungles of Vietnam.

Finn is comfortable flying in both worlds at once. He thinks of them as overlays. He believes that his reflexes now come from that duality, that the speed and the edge of his youth flow from the past into the present, that without that very particular simultaneity he would be a poorer pilot and his men would be at greater risk.

He uses those skills now as he lifts the craft to gain a vantage of the fire's layout. The task on this arm of the burn is to limit the advance and contain the destruction. As the helicopter climbs, Finn and the crew scan the topography to get the big picture. Knowing what's happening and where will help on the ground when vision is limited. The elements of the fire change, but every advantage counts. From this height, the crew can see where backburns will cut off access to the fuel-rich stands of pine and spruce, and where the smaller burns can be directed to wet areas that will naturally slow down the rate of spread.

Finn turns to the crew and nods. The nearest fires are small and should be easily stopped. Once on the ground, the team leader will hash out the details and radio them to Finn as he flies back to the base.

He directs the Huey to a point mid-way between two stands of spruce, thickly laced with underbrush.

Finn fights to keep the chopper steady as the team rappels down the ropes to the forest floor. He pushes the limits. The flames can be contained and the spread halted if the firebreaks are timely. If the winds pick up later, before the smaller fires are halted and the fuel exhausted, the flames could reach one thousand feet. He will still have to fly them out. He swoops in as close to the fire as he can get, fighting the winds pulled in by the heat to feed the blaze. He gauges the increasing strength of the wind, feeling for any change in direction, keeps the craft from stalling or moving into a downdraft, talks over the radio with the base to let them know what's happening and his ETA to pick up the second team.

In the meantime, he feels the heat of the fire through the plexiglass windshield. He's accounted for the proximity and picked the appropriate fuel to allow for it. The JP5 has a higher flash point than the JetA he prefers, and it's safer from the heat, but he'll have to work with the slower response time to get the bird up and away safely. For Finn, there is always time. He can cut it a bit closer.

"Move, move, move!" he yells at the team. But they are moving without the need of his urging and he knows he is shouting for his own benefit.

Then they are down, and the winds pull at the chopper. He talks to the men on the ground. He decides against fighting the winds and opts instead to go with them, riding them towards the fire as he pulls up sharply to gain the speed and the height he needs to spiral back away from the flames that further off reach more than a hundred feet in the air. Finn tilts the craft forward and up. He looks towards the fire and smiles as he rises, looking over the terrain from this vantage, then calls the men on the ground again to tell them about obstacles they can't see but would hamper their progress.

The fire could move tangentially to the main front to form a flanking front and trap the men below. Finn scours the landscape to spot any signs of jumping or spotting, or vertical convention columns carrying firebrand to the trees behind the men. At this point, there is nothing to see, but later in the day the temperature will rise and the winds will pick up.

He radios the team on the ground. "Nothing to report," he says.

The headphones crackle and the team lead answers, "Thanks. Let's hope it stays stable. See you on the pick-up."

"Roger that." A sudden wind buffets the helicopter, tugging the craft towards the main burn. He compensates and increases altitude for a better view. The center of the fire front, some three miles away, shows higher flames and whiter colors.

The pages of the manual loom before Finn's vision: "Fire is the exothermic chemical process of combustion." The words move from his mind to his tongue and roll resonantly from his mouth. It is poetry to him. It is a litany.

There is more. The ground is dry for miles around. Finn runs through the specifics of what he is battling. It is warfare of a different kind. Fires spread quickly and unpredictably. Torching in tree canopies cause spot fires as hot embers and firebrands light up fuels downwind five miles away. If those winds drove sparks to distant stands of resinous spruce, the temperature could soar to six-hundred degrees. Heat like that could cause sudden and explosive spontaneous combustion in the dry forest, catching the Huey in fatal heat or turbulence. Worse, the resulting flashover could move faster than a running man, and this is the main danger to Finn's teams. This is what worries Finn most: his people on the ground. He looks hard for the perils. So much depends on the type of tree and the weather and wind factors. There are hidden dangers too: a valley, a rift, or a hill could funnel flames and heat upwards. At the moment, the fire burns predictably, but a firestorm could be coming.

Finn feels alive again. His mind is jammed and he is pumped, but calm. Lives depend on his skill and timing, on his mastery of the facts and the air. He feels the turbulence hitting the craft like soft fists and, pulling for lift, gains some altitude.

Although the fire on the forest floor at the drop has flames reaching three feet in height now, high winds could push temperatures to 1,472°F. Finn runs through the possibilities. When that happens, the fire could produce 10,000 kilowatts or more per yard of fire front and flame heights of fifty yards. The electrical potential of the flames would be affected by the fire itself, and the trees would become electrically charged. The flame on these trees would create a minor plasma ball that could jump thirty feet to other charged trees. Such balls of flame might ignite behind the lines of firefighters and trap them. Finn searches for signs of electrical discharge at the edges of the fire that would indicate these dangers. Unstable conditions in the air would be perilous on the ground.

For the first time in a year, Finn feels that what he is doing matters. Such flames are cooler than napalm or the fires of hell, but they will do.

After the drop, Finn flies back out to the command area and pilots the helicopter in close to the hangar for the landing. He's whistling again, this time "People are Strange." The mechanics wave him in for the landing. The chief, Doug, waits for Finn to step down.

Doug looks him over. "Any problems?" he asks.

Finn nods. "The collective is a little stiff," he says. "Twist and lift aren't as smooth as they could be."

"Could be the cables," says Doug. "I'll check." He looks over the helicopter for a few minutes, and then looks up at at Finn. "You're getting a little close to the heat in this thing," he says.

"It's fine,' says Finn.

"You're taking chances," says Doug. Finn looks steadily into the older man's eyes. The mechanic doesn't blink. "I'm saying that the skin on this bird heats up pretty quick," he says. "It can affect things, like cables."

"I don't think that's the problem," says Finn. "And we're flying with JT5, so the flashpoint is high enough not to be a problem."

Doug nods. "All right. But this isn't Nam, Finn, and it's no place for old hot-shot pilots. You're taking risks with the men and with my bird."

"There are lives at stake on the ground," says Finn, "that hasn't changed, and I know what I'm doing."

"So do I," says Doug. He nods slowly. "And my job is to keep this thing in the air. It's no good to anybody on the ground. I'll get her ready for you," he says. "Next mission is at fifteen hundred. And stay the hell away from the burn. It can be as hot as napalm, and you damn well know it."

"Right," says Finn, and he begins to walk away. "A bird that can't fly is only feathered meat and a bottomless black eye," he says to himself. Then he stops and turns back. The mechanic is still watching him. Finn raises his hand. He feels like dancing.

"You're right," he says again and walks to the canteen while the mechanics check the helicopter for the second deployment. Finn buys a cup of bad coffee at the counter and moves to the window to watch the mechanics. He thinks of the manual in his room and the print in it laying out the facts, and he goes through the list of the fire tetrahedron. The words to the facts move comfortably across his vision, and his mind slides into the chemistry of the fire, into the crack between the worlds where the salamander, creature of fire, lives. So said the Buddhist priests in Vietnam.

"Fire starts when a flammable material in combination with oxygen is exposed to a source of heat above the flash point of the fuel and oxidizer mix and is able to sustain a chain reaction. This is called the fire tetrahedron. Fire cannot exist without all of these elements in place.

The tetrehydron is paramount. Once ignited, a chain reaction must occur allowing the fires to sustain their heat by releasing more heat energy in the process of combustion. Thus does the fire propagate." Finn hears himself saying the words aloud. He knows it might sound a little crazy, so he lowers his voice.

"Fire can be extinguished by removing any of the elements of the Tetrahedron. The application of water removes heat from the fire faster than the fire can produce it, and so the chain reaction is not maintained." Finn goes through the words like beads on a rosary. Like a prayer. And it is, he knows, a prayer to the Fire Triangle, the trinity of his youth. The word Tetrahydron sounds like the name of an ancient god. It is spirit and animation.

And then he sees the second Rapattack team heading from the barracks to the runway, ready for the next flight. They will have to wait until he has gone through his briefing.

An hour later, the helicopter is checked, refueled, and ready for another run. Finn is back in the pilot seat and the team is secured behind him. He will drop this team off and pick up the first and bring them back. The crews are ready for the routine, but find it hard to be on long shifts every day. For Finn, the pace is fine. In the war, he sometimes flew Hueys for ten or more hours a day, one after the other. Three flights were low key, though the pace could pick up if the fire reached the level of a firestorm.

As he flies the crew to the drop over the same ground covered that morning, Finn is conscious of the repetitive atmosphere in the hold behind him. The crew are watchful, scanning the ground below for the positives and negatives of laying down the fire breaks: a rift here, a hill there, a thick stand of spruce atop a high point able to toss a firebrand miles downwind. They look for points of access and egress should the fire leap through the canopy to a point behind them, a point where Finn could not land the Huey.

The watchfulness betokens an immediacy that Finn has not experienced in crews since the war, except here, among firefighters whose lives are at risk every time they deploy.

They are in the moment, as is Finn, and in such moments the rest of the world fades away. It simply does not matter. What matters is staying alive. What matters is a question of wit and luck and trust.

The talk of the team behind him is an echo of the morning. It echoes the comments uttered by men thirty years before on the drops in the jungles of Vietnam. They are the timeless words of men and women on their way to confront forces that could well overwhelm them. They are, to Finn, the most meaningful words in the world. They underlie the businesses of daily human life, just as the tectonic plates of the earth underlie the ephemeral tangle of greenery rooted in the thin topsoil of day. Beneath these superficial layers lie the moments and the magnitudes that shape the planet and the human lives that dance above like long-legged spiders on a lake.

Soon, the secondary smoke marks the backburns where the first team has done its work. Finn pilots for the point north of the smoke where the breaks have been placed to intercept the fire's path. The team will be there, waiting for him and waiting for the new crew to relieve them. The winds move towards the breaks, and Finn rides them. The center of the forest fire sucks in the air, ballooning the oxygen level, shooting the temperature up, and feeding the blaze. Finn rides the winds like a fish in a current. His skin is the Huey's. The presence of the crew behind him fades until only he and the winds are real.

When his headphones activate, he expects it. He sees the crew on the ground before they see him. He calculates his approach and his landing, his deployment, his pick-up, and his flight out before they are even aware he is there, and even then, they will hear the whumping of the Huey's rotors before they pick him out in the sky. Finn sees the before and the after of the mission. The vectors are set in his head. He creates the sequence, and he saves men. He battles the blaze.

He knows how the team behind him will jump into action. He knows the high-fives that will mark the passage of men and women, one to the other. He knows the shape of the conversations that will take place in the cabin behind him as he flies one team back from the shadow of death to a torpid canteen at a way station in the Canadian north.

When he lands the first team back at the base, Finn debriefs, checks over the helicopter, and talks to the mechanics as they work. The Rappattack team is exhausted and sooty, but they circle Finn and the mechanics to talk about the day and pay homage to the machine that got them there and back safely. Finn insists on the ritual gathering. He eats a baloney and mustard sandwich as he talks. Then he thinks about calling home.

He feels good about the work and there have been no problems. The first units got in and out and the fire barriers are in place. There have been no injuries and no losses. Now he will wait to see what the winds will do. It's a good time to call Lara and check in. He wants to leave the tension on the other side of the fire.

He enters his room, picks up the phone, hits the speed dial, and hears the ringing.

"Hello?"

"It's me," says Finn.

"Good," says Lara.

"We had a good day. A couple of close ones when the winds shifted, but we got one unit out and back and the other dropped."

"Good," says Lara.

"How's Michael?" Finn asks.

"He's fine."

"And you?" he asks.

"Fine," she says.

Finn hears a voice in the background. "Who's there?" he asks.

"Oh, it's only Phil," she says.

Finn is still for a moment. "What's Phil doing there?" he asks.

"He's just helping out around the house, Finn. Some yardwork. Caulking the windows."

"Caulking?" asks Finn.

"Yep," says Lara, "they're calling for rain." She sounds flippant.

"I don't like it," he snaps.

"Well, where are you? Gone. You're gone. You put yourself at risk. What about Michael? What about your son? How many times have I said this? He needs you. I need you. We're all at risk. You're addicted, Finn, and not to us." Finn can hear her winding up.

"No," he says. "Let's not quarrel."

"Something could happen, Finn, and we'd lose you. In the meantime, Phil is helping out while you're gone. He wants to teach Michel to fish."

"Like hell! I'm going to do that."

"You're not here."

"I'll be back in three weeks. Take Michael to Mom and Dad's for the summer. To the lake. I'll meet you there. I'll be damned if Phil is going to teach my son to fish."

"Well, maybe to start."

"Lara, this is not negotiable. All right, you're being clever, but if that son-of-a-bitch touches my fishing rod, there will be hell to pay. Keep him away from my son. And from you. I mean, what the hell is going on there? I'm going to send Wayne by to check up on things."

"We don't need your Vet buddies dropping by."

"I'm calling Wayne. And Dave. I won't have the enemy in my home base. I'll send the whole goddamned platoon there if anything's fishy."

"You're over-reacting."

"Where's Phil's wife?"

"They're separated again."

"Why didn't I hear about that?"

"I thought I told you."

"God dammit, Lara, send Michael to the lake, and you follow, and I don't want Phil around there. I'll do the caulking, by God." He realizes he's pronounced the word like 'cocking.'

"Calm down, Finn."

"I'll fly this goddamned helicopter down there right now if I hear anything's screwy."

"Finn …"

"Lara, I'm serious. God damn it, I need you to cover my back."

Finn gets off the phone at once and calls his father. Before he can say anything more than "Hello," Finn rushes on.

"Dad, I want Lara and Michael to come up to the lake now. I'll meet them there when this tour is done in a month. Will that work?" Finn feels a little short of breath.

"They're as welcome as the flowers in May, son. You know that. Is anything wrong?"

"No," lies Finn, "but I worry about them on their own in London, and a month on the lake will be good for them. Especially Michael. I want to teach him to fish when I get there."

"Terrific," says Finn's father, and then after a pause says, "Michael called just the other day, and I think he's ready for the lake. He said his uncle Phil was going to teach him to cast."

"Oh?" says Finn. He tries to play it down.

"Who the hell is Phil?" his father asks anyway.

"Someone we know. He was married to a friend of Lara's."

"Was?" says his father. And Finn realizes the old man is already out in front of him.

"Let's get them both up there asap," says Finn.

"Roger that," says his father, "and you hightail it here as soon as you can. I'll get the boy started and ready for the boat. And Finn?" he says.

"Yes?" says Finn.

"What the hell?" says his father.

"I've got to make another call," says Finn, and hangs up. But before he can make the call to Wayne, he hears the squawker and his heart races. It's not his pick-up, so someone must be in trouble. Maybe the wind has changed. Maybe the fire has jumped the back-burns and is heading in a new direction. A crew could be cut off. He moves to the window and looks out. Lightnings flash in the distance at the edge of the fires and the flames soar over the horizon. They mark the electrical discharge of a major conflagration. The trees themselves will be charged and act as dipolar antennas, throwing fireballs of plasma for miles. The winds have changed, and the fire is running towards the teams Finn and the other pilots dropped off earlier that day. Below the window, Doug and his crew are rushing to the hangar. Finn grabs his gear and runs. It's back to the air.

The night has not yet cloaked the hills and hidden the teams on the ground, but it is coming, and with it, flames a thousand feet high.

As Finn reaches the helicopter, Doug grabs his arm.

"Two crews, cut off," he says. "Fireballs landed downwind from them. Six personnel. Yours. You know where you put them down, know the topography. You're their best hope."

111

"Got it," says Finn. "I'll go for the crew furthest in first, nearest the main burn, then pick up the second crew on the way out. He slides into the pilot seat, lifts the chopper and heads into the fire.

The winds buffet the craft as Finn nears the point where he dropped the crews off earlier. He sees, he hears, he feels. In the distance, the sullen reds of the fire have turned white, and lightning flickers on the horizon. Riding the winds, he sees the new fire line a half mile from the main one, U-shaped and cupping in the crews. At this point, the fire is beginning to create its own weather, and, like a firestorm, the winds are rushing in from the perimeters, pulling the flashover back toward the main line of the big fire. The crews are trapped.

He lifts the Huey over the flames and spots the first team heading for the mid point between the fires, high ground, with enough clearance and distance from the turbulence for a helicopter to get down close enough for a pick-up. It's the team furthest from the main line, and Finn changes tactics: he'll have to pick them up now and only then head for the team in the greater danger.

"Damn," he says. Then he hears Mick, the team lead, over the radio. "We see you."

"Make it quick," says Finn. "We've got the other crew further in."

"You didn't get them first?" Mick asks.

"I just got here," says Finn. "I'm not going to touch ground, so run like hell and jump in." He moves in over the rise and drops the Huey straight down, pulling up three feet from the ground. "Go! Go! Go!" he yells into the mike. The three men run full tilt to the chopper and even as Finn feels the thumps of their bodies landing on the floor behind him, he is pulling back on the collective and lifting into the air.

"Jesus!" says Mick. "You took the wind out of me."

Once he is up, Finn turns to Mick. "Where's the other crew?" he asks.

"Over that rise, one o'clock, between us and the main burn, from the last radio contact from Cal. Cut off," says Mick.

"You were all cut off," says Finn. "The flashover had you ringed in."

He brings the Huey around and makes for the area Mick indicated. The flames are higher and hotter and the smoke thicker, but soon he sees the crew on the ground. The winds pull at the craft.

"Jesus," he says. "This won't be easy."

"Shit," he hears Mick say behind him. "We can't get down there. They didn't have time to clear an area. They're in a depression. That brush could go up any minute." He looks harder. "They must have figured they'd have to ride it out and left the high ground."

"I should have come for them first," says Finn.

"It wouldn't have made any difference," says Mick. "It took maybe four minutes for us to get aboard. They wouldn't have made it to high ground in that time."

Finn looks around but the smoke is too thick to see far. There is no time to wait for another craft to get near enough to drop retardant. There are no holes in the fire line, and it is too late for another chopper to stop the flames with buckets of belly tanks.

As Finn fights for altitude, his gaze is fixed on the upturned faces of the three crew on the ground, pale ovals in the shadows. The faces are small with distance and the eyes of the faces are fixed on the windshield. They are looks of warriors giving their last looks to what they have known. They are the looks of leaving. The crew, a woman, a medical student at her college, the other two young men working their way through college, doing what mattered, putting themselves in harm's way, stand firm on the ground, their legs apart at shoulder width, solid with knowing. Then, the woman and one of the men start to dig in and unroll their portable shelters as Finn fights the winds. They have a chance, Finn knows, but a slim one. The heat will be too great to bear unless the burn jumps over the shallow depression where they are making their stand. Even then, he knows, the fire will take the oxygen away. The fire will unfurl over the land and roll the living things up in a carpet of ash. He shudders. As he looks at the one man standing, waving Finn away, it is Finn on the ground, looking up at the F-16's that soared unreachable and away.

Then two figures disappear under their shelters. The oldest of the crew, Cal, the team leader and a military reservist, raises his hand again to wave Finn back, and points to the north end of the burn. He will make his run in that direction. Finn points the Huey in that direction, hoping to spot an area good enough to get down and close, but they have not had time to clear the brush back to allow either a landing or an approach low enough to throw down the rappelling gear to get anyone off the ground.

Finn realizes that alone, without the crew behind him, he would go down to save the crew on the ground. He would sacrifice himself to that effort, and, doing so, would leave Michael orphaned and Lara widowed. He sees clearly now that he can't be trusted on his own. The old pull to satori has merged with recklessness. It is more than a matter of numbers, of weighing lives in the balance, and the shouting of the crew is a clamor behind him.

He risks igniting the chopper and everyone aboard.

A fireball arcs over the trees to his left and Finn veers and fights for height.

Mick raps Finn's helmet to get his attention. "It's time to get the hell out of here!" he says.

"We still have crew on the ground," yells Finn.

"They're gone. We can't get down to them."

"We have to keep trying. Cal is making a run for the high point."

"Frying our asses isn't going to save him!" Mick yells back. "There are some things you just can't do, Finn! Let's get out of here."

"We can't leave him behind," Finn yells.

"It's numbers, you stupid son-of-bitch," Mick yells back. "You've got a crew here depending on you. Get them the hell out of here!"

Words from twenty years earlier explode in his head, words crackling over the radio, repetitions he'd pushed back into the cloudy mixtures of memory, young men yelling that a Phantom was minutes away with a payload of fire and death: snake and nape. And always the panicked reaction: "Let's get the fuck out of here." Finn stares into the fire, then ahead, and as he pulls up and away he feels his face contort in a rictus of grief and rage.

The next morning, Finn calls Lara. He is still in bed when he makes the call, exhausted and dispirited.

"It's me," he says. He can hear the plea in his own voice.

114

"Sweetheart, what's wrong? What happened? Are you all right?" she says.

"We lost some people," he says. For a moment, he can't get more words out. "A flashover cut off three crew." He blows out hard to settle the shaking in his gut.

"Oh, God, Finn. Are you all right?"

"Yeah," he says.

"Tell me about it," she says. "Give me the facts, Finn." He says nothing.

"Finn," she says again, "settle down and focus on the facts. Tell me the facts."

And Finn settles into the posture that began with Father Callaghan and a Colonel half a world away. Now, he suddenly sees, it is the ears of his wife that listen; it is this woman's hand that smooths the thin varnish of details over his soul. It has been this way for a long time. Finn is glad for the realization, for although it is an insight as small as the moment, its mass is tectonic. He watches the awareness of this particular fact move to the surface of his mind like a small island in the sea that, even though it may subside again, declares itself implacably.

As Finn leans into his story of battle and loss, he accepts suddenly and keenly that Lara's ears are open and listening, that it has been so since their first nights on the lake. It is clear to him at this moment that the priest's ears were always closed to his confessions and the priest's heart deaf to his hurts, but the heart of the woman is open. It has been he, Finn, who has played the priest, remote and clad in darkness, constantly out of reach. The moment for him is as the space between the breezy beat of wings, and Finn moves into the space.

## CHAPTER SEVENTEEN

# On Little Long Rapids

July, 1990

Hi Sweetheart,

Don called from New Liskard, and since I had a few days off I met him there and we flew up to Little Long Rapids. We spent the afternoon there and then flew here to Abitibi Canyon and are staying at the Staff House (the only building left) tonight, then fly back tomorrow. There's something to be said for these little bush planes. They can land wherever there's water. I can understand why Don stayed up here. You can go where you want.

Today, we took the elevator down to the operations room where Dad used to work in the dam. It's automated now, and the room is empty, but there was an old Hydro coffee mug hanging on a peg in the lunch room and a note pad on the table listing some items to repair. Been there for years.

They have an old Underwood (same vintage Mom used) here in the Staff-House that's in working order, but the ribbon is dry, so I'm using their IBM. Mother used to write her letters at night using her old manual, and the clickety-clack would lull me to sleep, but I can't sleep tonight, so I'll put down some thoughts and send them off to you. I don't know if it's the mosquitoes whining outside the window screen, or the frogs singing, but I can't stay in bed.

So, I'm up here on the Little Long Rapids and the Little Abitibi where I worked in the summer to put myself through college, building the dam there—and here, where I lived as a kid. You know some of the story. It's funny being back, and I remember you asked about working in the camps, but I realize now the reason I didn't say much was because it somehow got blurred in with the military after college. I don't know why.

Little Long is a ghost town now, like the settlement here at Abitibi Canyon. It's odd to have the places where I lived fade away so fast. Both places have been leveled. It makes me feel like I have no connection with place and home in the old sense. I suppose on some level I always thought that houses were supposed to last longer than the inhabitants. But permanence is a thing for monuments.

When I worked at Little Long building the dam, we were brought in by train on a two-hour ride from Kapuskasing. It was a big camp with a supplies station, a cafeteria, and bunkhouses for the men. There was a recreation hall with a pool table, and we ordered our beer by the case from town. Waiting for that and putting in the time on the job was all there was to do besides watching whoever tried to date the girl in the cafeteria.

Yes, there was one woman who worked in the cafeteria, and looking at her and talking about her was something a lot of men did. After four months in the camp, it seemed like she was the only woman left in the world.

We had seven hundred men in the camp and the job never shut down. There were three eight-hour shifts every day but Sunday, and the machines worked that way too. The work was all about the big machines, the Euclid trucks and earth-movers with tires taller than a man, and the cranes that sat two hundred feet above those of us who worked below. The eleven-ton hoppers were filled with concrete high above the canyon floor where the crane operators, who were artists for the most part, lowered the hoppers at a phenomenal speed, seamless and smooth, and stopped them suddenly just short of the ground. The long cables stretched with the load as the brakes caught and it took your breath away to see them come down so smooth and fast because sometimes they came down in the wrong place or the operator misjudged the timing and the big hoppers slammed into the ground and, sometimes, onto a man beneath them.

It didn't happen that way often, but the sight never left you, and you thought about it years after you left the camp and believed you had forgotten about it. At night, you remember the noise of the machines and the men who worked the machines—the rest of us were worked by them, trying to keep up. You'd hear the noise and shouting and dynamite especially at night, and men were hurt and lost their lives. We'd hear that a man was gone and you would remember seeing him around the camp and on the job, and then he wasn't there any more, and the work went on. He would have a family somewhere, but you didn't want to think about that because it was bad luck and could happen to you, and except for a few remarks to make the thing bearable and deny the danger, you didn't talk about it.

That's the way it was in Little Long Rapids on the Mattágami River when the dam was going up in 1962.

You never knew when it was going to happen, and sometimes it wasn't accidental (I told you about two attempts on my life there by rival crews), but it rarely happened in numbers the way it used to when Dad worked the dams, the way it happened in 1932 here on the Abitibi Canyon project. A crew of men fell into the wet concrete here, in the middle of a pour, and were left because they couldn't be recovered without dismantling the project. The dam was completed with those men encased in the structure. The bosses didn't know who all of the lost were, and so a few simply disappeared as far as family and friends were concerned. Dad never talked about it. Now that I think about it, there's a lot he's never talked about.

That's the kind of work we did in the work camps—okay, I'm going to say it—while a thousand miles away and fifty years later people turn on a light or kitchen appliance and never know about the men and the work and the death that made their city living easy, and they never think the heat in their homes comes from a place where dead men are twisted in the concrete around the generators that spin out the electricity. The dam is a tomb that generates electricity for places like New York City.

As kids, we used to walk across it to the woods and think about those bodies hung in the concrete all around where our fathers were working. The bones of working men are in all the places where big things have been built, the bridges and the dams, but the middle class don't know much about it, though they should. You can say people outside the camps are not expected to know or care about this sacrifice and hardship, but their ignorance gives an edge and an anger to the men who work the camps, and it means those outside the camps are in no position to judge those working men, though they do.

Back in the woods by the old lakes and rivers that have no roads to them, where the mills and dams and camps are crumbling and deserted, you can find the graves on the hillsides where no-one goes, and the stones on the graves read "Unknown" or give a first name and an unknown origin and the day the man died on the project. You will read things like: "Unknown Worker, Fell, August 5, 1931," and you know some poor son-of-a-bitch fell one hundred feet from a scaffold to the concrete below, and nobody knew where he came from, only where he went, and even that was soon forgotten.

Here, where I am now, there's a concrete monument on the top of the dam to honor the dead men, naming most of those who lie in the cement below, and on that brass plaque there is a poem that calls them the "Sons of Martha," meaning they're the men who worked and built and were killed and forgotten. It's a poem by Rudyard Kipling that cites a verse in scripture that pretty much sets up and justifies a world of haves and have-nots. Kipling seems pretty pissed about it. I guess I am too.

Even for us, a generation later on the Little Long project, death was always a surprise but always present. I guess it always is. And I see now that's why you worry and have your own anger about me flying Hueys to the fires.

That's enough for tonight. I'll sign off and get this to you tomorrow, but I'll talk with you then too and catch up on how you are, and how Michael is doing.

Love-<br>Finn

PS.
Well, I'm up again. It's 3am, and there's no breeze. I can't go outside and wander around or I'll be eaten alive by the damned mosquitoes. I don't remember them as a kid at all.

Also, my mind's going a mile a minute, thinking about some things I mentioned earlier. I know I'm ranting, but it reminds me of being stereotyped and dismissed as a laborer here, then as a seminary student in London, and again as a veteran.

At Little Long, some of us worked double shifts and overtime to escape the hours of waiting because sleep was not a rest. A stupor settled on everything and spread to the work and only the beer would thin it, so even in our own eyes we became cyphers in a story that was no longer ours, though it is the working man's story and always has been. That's what I'm thinking about, and wondering where those men are now, men who would have risked their lives for me and me for them.

They matter because the men who came afterwards to operate the projects came with their wives and their families and their careers, and for a while they enjoyed the workmanlike quality of the place when the term still had meaning and had not become a foolish thing to say. The Operators identified with it because the blood spent making it pervaded the physical elements of the plant and was still fresh. But people forget and become jaded and think about their careers and mobility, and about their retirement, and the thing they work for loses significance because they never built it, but the men who built places like this are making something like it somewhere else, and they do not have careers—they have the work, and that is what they have until they are worn out or die.

Sometimes the stories of the workers span only a few years and are remembered and told for a little bit while their place in the whole tale is ignored. But the small parts are heroic too, because they are the lives of working men, and without them there would be no story to tell. If you think about it, the story of what laboring men have built spans thousands of years. In a sense, workers and their work are inseparable, and it's the things they build that last, and I mean things like the pyramids and the Roman roads and the railroads too, not just the Golden Gate bridges and the Hoover Dams.

That's what we talked about at night when I was twenty and working on the Little Long Rapids because, at times, it was like the projects had a life of their own, and called us up, like recruits, (though we were only boys then) to build them, as though we were incidental, and it was the buildings, the monuments, that called the shots. What we made lasted, and we were forgotten. Weird, I know, and maybe it was the beer, because in that camp of seven hundred men there wasn't much to do besides work and drink and talk and sleep, and the work was hard and men died, so the drinking was hard too. And there's anger in such places. I can still feel it.

Phew!

Now I really will sign off. But I just realized that's when I started waking up in the middle of the night—at Little Long Rapids.

Finn

CHAPTER EIGHTEEN

# Once More to the Islands

August 1990

## The Way Out

He drove through the flat country of southern Ontario to the rolling north that catches the still, small lakes between the hills and hollows. The highway rises over the Barry escarpment, and the broadleaf woods of oak and maple and beech give way to the northern conifers. The country falls away to the basin that cups Lake Nipissing, a remnant of the old Mesozoic rift valley, and it is open all the way to the horizon with stands of black spruce, swamp aspen, birch, and white pine, with the land punctuated by ponds surfaced like smooth obsidian.

As he drove, Finn rehearsed the farms and the stubbled fields he passed, conjuring up their images through the autumn rains when the leaves lace the pungent air, when the snow brings the long winters, and when the colorful little towns spring up through the sagging snowbanks like crocuses along the roads and the acrid tang of bursting tree-buds ride the rain. When he was a boy, it was unspoiled country all the way to the Little Abitibi River, and as a student at Western, he travelled the southern roads from London and the townships with their British names, and, after the war, again with Lara laughing in the seat beside him as they passed the northern places called Temágami and Temískaming and Muskóka, Cree and Anishinabe words from the Nipissing Nation, nine thousand years older than European contact and, for Finn, names that linked the land to the old geologies of father Iapetus and his son Atlas, namesake of the Atlantic Ocean.

And now it is back to Lake Nipissing where the water marries the soft curves of granite islands in very particular ways that make the lake hard for Finn to forget.

It is the middle of August and Finn is glad to be on the lake. He is glad to fish it too, although the rocks are treacherous because the water is low. The red buoys bare their pitted footings and ride the rocks like barnacles. Beds of pike grass wave in the water below, and muskelunge move slowly through the wavering strands, but where the water is deeper and the rocky outcroppings cool the sandy bottom, walleye wait in the shade.

Finn checks his son on the seat beside him, tests the straps on the lifejacket, then pushes the throttle forward.

The boat hits the waves and throws up a spray like fine rain in the morning sun. He lifts his face into it and feels the sting of the water on his skin. The smell of the lake fills his lungs, bringing the rich, pungent smell of life under water.

He glances behind where the sky is bright with the cries of seagulls and the trees on the shore diminish. Ahead, a sun-shower appears brief and quick on the water. The rain catches the sunlight up in a fine net, holding its brilliance, and a sudden gust tosses it over the waves. Finn swerves the boat into the whirlwind, and laughs. The laughter comes from a place that feels at first strange, and Michael looks up as though startled at the sound, then cries out as the prow plunges through the shimmering line. Finn eases the throttle back and lets the boat drift. The fine drops whirl around their heads, beading their hair like summer cobwebs. The wind lifts Michael's curls against Finn's face, and when Finn breathes in through the curls, he thinks of Lara.

"It's a rainbow," Michael says, and Finn laughs again.

"Perhaps it is."

"It is, Dad. It's a rainbow touching the earth."

"It could be," says Finn.

"There's a pot of gold right here," says Michael. He looks over the side of the boat into the lake. "Down there."

"You're very literal," says Finn.

"It's what they say about the end of a rainbow."

"Well, you may be right. We could be as close as you can get." The mist comes down like wet light around them, and Finn squeezes Michael's shoulder. He rests his hand there, and Michael leans into it as Finn opens up the throttle. The prow of the boat lifts clear of the water again as the boat surges ahead, pushing Finn back into the seat. Then the prow settles. The outboard thunders as the wooden hull slaps the waves, and though Finn can't see clearly into the distance, the boat pushes suddenly out of the shower into the clear air, skipping brightly over the water.

"How are you doing, Michael?" he calls over the wind.

"My bum hurts," Michael, yells back. They sit close, shouting over the noise between them.

"Sorry," says Finn. "Here, slide a life vest under and sit on it. Come closer. We'll slow down a bit." He slows the boat and reaches under the seat for the vest and hands it to Michael. "Would you like to help steer?" he asks.

"Sure," says Michael.

"Then hop over and sit on my lap. Bring the vest with you." Finn holds the wheel steady as he reaches over. Michael nestles in against Finn's chest. "This is a better idea," Finn says. Michael reaches for the wheel and Finn slides his own hands down to guide him. "Ready?" he asks.

"Yep."

"Let's go," says Finn, and he opens up the throttle. Michael's hands are firm on the wheel, and Finn covers them with his own. They are cool, and Finn can smell the scent of Lara in his son's hair. "You've got the same little cowlick here that your mom has," he says. Michael nestles closer in to his chest, and Finn looks up into the wind.

"Well," he says, "here we are," and the lake rolls out ahead of them like wavering glass. The Manitou Islands hover in the distance, distorted by the heat waves. It is not at first a shore he recognizes, and above it, the little popcorn clouds of the north catch the sun.

Where the pink granite knolls are bare, spotted with a thin carpet of topsoil, they stop and idle the motor. Pines grow to the edge of the soil and lean out on the lake. Eventually their roots will tear free of the earth and the trees will fall into the water, for the sand beneath the duff is soft and always eroding forming narrow beaches at the base of the rocks that last until the spring melt washes the shores clean, mixing the fine sand of the little strands into the water and carrying away the fallen trees. It is a constant process, and the trees, stripped of bark and foliage, finally wash up on the banks, silvered and dried by the weather, bright as bones, ideal firewood.

Finn watches for the wood as he engages the engine and steers the boat towards the rocky outcroppings and small bays where the round domes of granite rise smoothly out of the lake.

"Let's try it here," he says.

He looks down into the water. The rocks are just below the surface, clear, but wavering as though seen through a sheet of old, imperfect glass. Pike grass sway up from the sand, and at the rock ledges the water darkens quickly to a deep, tea-brown. The pickerel will be in the thickest of the plants with their gills flaring and their ventral fins pulsing slightly to maintain their position until a perch ventures too far from its rocky cover, but the day is too bright for the Walleye to feed and the water is not choppy enough.

Finn reaches for the tackle box, rummages through it, and picks out an old red-and-white float. The paint on the box is flaked and pitted and its trays are loose. Finn is surprised his father has kept it, and grunts as he attaches the float to Michael's line. Then he opens a jar of fish eggs, runs the weighted hook through three of them, and hands the gear to Michael.

"That should be about right," he says. "Try it."

"Thanks." Michael swings the rod back sideways, then forward, sending the float six feet away into the water. Finn nods his satisfaction, then reaches back into the tackle box and selects a thick, nickel lure. The spoon is short, wide, with two faceted eyes cut from red glass, and trails a fine, triple hook that has never caught a fish but had been his father's favorite when they lived on the Abitibi River. The lure is wrong for pickerel in the lake. It was meant for the silt-laden waters of the Abitibi, but this morning, Finn doesn't care about luck. He likes the lure's familiarity and thinks again about the plastic float his father kept and never used. He closes the tackle box, turns in his seat, brings the rod back over his shoulder and casts out to the rocks where the cool holes wait.

"Why can't I cast too?" Michael says.

"You can," says Finn. "I just thought you'd like to take it easy. I used to have good luck with that float."

"I don't use floats. Grandpa taught me how to cast."

"Good," says Finn. "Well then, you must be pretty good. But the boat's small, so how about letting me cast for a while, and then we can switch?"

"You always give me a float," Michael says.

"I like both," says Finn. "I like to sit and think about the fish circling the bait down below trying to decide what to do. It gives me a chance to think."

"But you get to choose." Michael isn't going to let him off so easily, Finn thinks. He likes that.

"Not always. Sometimes you have to do what you don't want to." Finn knows he is folding the meaning back on itself. He recognizes now that it is the same indirect way of getting a complaint out that he disliked in his father.

"Says who?"

Finn laughs. "I guess it's what's expected."

"Why?"

"Probably for no good reason," Finn admits and snaps the rod behind his head and casts again. He focuses on the lure. The line unwinds with a faint, high song, comfortable and good in his ear. The spoon traces a silver arc towards the deep water.

The glass eyes gleam red, and the spoon hits the water with a heavy splash. Finn smiles. He eases the tension and reels the line in, thinking about the fishing lures lost in the lake over the years, hundreds of them, maybe thousands, little ghosts populating the bottom of logs and rocks and weeds and catching sunlit shafts as the lake's silt settled down on them. Each had a fisherman's hope. "Everything has its manitou or spirit, Finn," his father said when Finn was a boy. "Animals, birds, even machines. You can see it in their nature: cat nature, dog nature, the behaviors of a species." Finn wonders if it were true of fishing lures. He shakes off the thought and glances at Michael. Michael meets his eyes, then turns his attention to the red-and-white float bobbing passively alongside the boat.

"I wish Mom were here," he says.

"Well," says Finn, on the verge of conceding defeat. "She can come fishing tomorrow. Today is for you and me."

He thinks back to the night before, fighting the stuffy air of the room at three a.m., wrestling the dreams, until he went to the window to look at the lake. Then he woke Lara to talk.

"I knew you'd wake up," she said. "You always do here. Why is that?"

"I don't know. Something about the lake, I guess."

"It was the first time you really talked about what happened to you, remember?" she said.

"Yeah. I remember. And the next day you fell in the lake," said Finn.

"But it was you who was all wet," she laughed. "And you should have seen your expression as you ran along the rail. I thought you'd trip over your tongue, your mouth had dropped open so much."

Finn looked at her. "You never mentioned that before," he said.

"I have my secrets too," she said.

"I was scared to death, Finn said. "For a minute I thought I was going to freeze up."

"No, you wouldn't. You can't help it–you'll always jump in, Finn. It's who you are."

"You never said that before, either," said Finn. "I didn't know that's how you see me."

"Everyone sees that Finn, God knows," Lara said.

Finn nodded and looked out the window to the lake. The moon was up and a light wind stirred up the surface of the water to a Walleye chop, and he thought about fishing the next day with Michael.

Later, he walked outside down to the shore to forget the old echo in his head:

> *You do this and you do that for people, and people rely on you. Don't you ever need anybody, Finn? You're here, but*

*you're not. You're attentive, but you keep your distance. How*
*do you do that? It's like you're somewhere else, someone else.*

The grass, wet with the dew, cushioned his feet, and the little waves, protected from the open water by the break-wall, called him. Small minnows waited by the shore, Finn knew, and the smell of the water was the smell of home, so he walked into it and stood with his feet among the minnows.

He pulls himself out of his thoughts and looks back to his son.

"Mom likes the lake too," says Michael. "We always visit Grandpa when we come up here, but he doesn't go fishing in the boat." Finn nods. "Will uncle Phil visit us? He likes to fish."

"He's not your uncle," says Finn.

"But Mom calls him that."

"Jesus. How did Grandpa teach you to cast?" Finn asks. "And when?"

"From the dock, last week, when you were gone. Mom too. She wasn't very good, but she laughed a lot."

Now Finn casts again and again into the lake, thinking of Lara's laughter, sending the spoon higher and further, snapping the tip of his rod like a whip for more distance. The spoon is too heavy for the light pole, but he doesn't let up. He looks over the lake toward the far shore home as he reels the lure in.

"Did your mother say Phil was going to visit?" he asks, but Michael just shakes his head and says nothing, so Finn looks to the physical properties of the world around them.

The small islands rise smoothly out of the clear waters of the lake. The water is a placid lie over the fires below. He visualizes the cross section of the lake and the earth like a schematic in his mind. Facts: *water, crust, mantle, core.*

Facts bring order to the world and to life. These are the words of his father. They are dependable and unchangeable. "They keep the mind focused, predictable," Finn. And Finn remembers the facts and visualizes the pages and the words: an old trick. The old trap. He murmurs silently.

"The inner core is the center of the earth and is the hottest part of the planet. It is a solid mass of iron and nickel. The temperature of the core is around 5500°C. It is hotter than the surface of the sun, and its engine is radioactive decay.

"The outer core is the layer around the inner core. It is also made up of iron and nickel though it is liquid.

"The next layer is the mantle. This layer is made up of semi-molten rock known as magma.

"The final layer is the earth's crust. This layer is between 0-60 kilometers thick. It rides the mantle like a raft, except where the mantle breaks through and forms the surface of the planet. It is easily identified because the behavior and nature of this rock is different than the crust.

*"The inner earth is layered,*

*The inner earth is hot,*

*The inner world must flow and churn*

*The outer world must not."*

Finn tugs his line more gently as he reels it in and looks down into the water. Come on, he thinks, bite! He visualizes a fish easing out of the shadows into the light, following the lure up into the clear water. He imagines the fish with its mouth open and gills flared, ready to strike. Come on, he thinks. He clears his throat.

*The inner earth is layered …*

He looks over at his son and stops his thinking. Michael has his mother's eyes and his grandfather's line along the chin, and he does not have Finn's impatience. Finn tugs his line gently as he reels it in and looks down into the water.

"Any bites?" he asks.

"No," says Michael. "Maybe a nibble."

"Fishing is all about patience," says Finn. "The secret is not to fret. Just ease into the rhythm of the fish." Michael nods. Finn thinks about the fish hovering over the sandy bottom, keeping their positions with their fins wavering, feeling the pull of the waves on the surface high above them as they hang in the thick silence. "It's a different sort of time down there," he says. "Under the water." He isn't quite sure what he means by that, and thinks of Vietnam as he looks away to the horizon, casting the lure far out into the lake again. "Do you know what I mean?"

"Sure," says Michael, looking down his line into the water. "But Dad?"

"Yes?"

"They're just not biting."

"You're right," says Finn. "We're not having any luck in this spot. Shall we try over at another island?"

"Sure," says Michael.

"Let's go." Finn reels in the lures. "Sometimes a place will work, and sometimes it won't."

"It's just luck, right?" says Michael.

"Sometimes that's all it is. But sometimes there's more to it."

"You have to trust your instincts, right?"

"Well," says Finn, "yes. You have to go with that."

"Dad?"

"Yes?"

"Doesn't grandpa know that about fishing?"

"Yes. And he knows it about other things," says Finn.

He looks over the lake as he secures the rods and tackle. It is quiet and the morning is still cool. The early, wispy fog dissipated as soon as the sun had risen.

"Why doesn't grandpa ever fish?"

"He fished often, once," says Finn, "but he doesn't enjoy it anymore."

"He fusses too much when he comes in the boat," says Michael.

"Well," says Finn, "he's uneasy in the boat now, and he prefers rivers."

"Why is he uneasy?" asked Michael.

"He wasn't always that way. He was better in the woods, alone. Then he was unhesitating and sure, sure of his footing. When I was your age, he was confident and graceful, and a powerful swimmer. He had wonderful blue eyes and perfect teeth. He seemed fearless to me." Finn pauses. "He was a wonderful shot too, and could keep a can in the air with a lever-action rifle," Finn says.

"Just like the movies. A marksman."

"Yes," says Finn, "he was a marksman."

"Was he a sniper?"

"They didn't call them that, then," says Finn. "They called them Scouts. He was a Marksman in the infantry, then a Scout later in the war, though he never speaks of it," and he thinks of the old Marlin 32-40 his father used. It was a beautiful rifle with a walnut stock dark from years of oiling and use. Even at the time, the model had been discontinued and the Winchester 30-30 had replaced it. His father had the only issue around, and the rifle fired a cartridge filled with black powder. An orange flame leapt from the barrel with each shot. It was considerably different than the smokeless powder of the new Winchesters, and having it had made his father special. Finn thinks of the time he threw a can in the air on a hunting trip and his father shot it the moment it touched the ground. The can spun back into the air as his father worked the lever and chambered another round. He shot the can each time it touched the ground and never missed. Then he looked at Finn and laughed out loud. Finn was amazed at his father's marksmanship and at the rich, easy confidence of that laugh, but his father rarely talked about the shooting or where he'd learned to do it so well.

His shooting and his pleasure in silence were the things he was best at, but in other things he grew clumsy in ways that tormented Finn and contradicted his skills.

"Did he just get old?"

"I think it was more than that," says Finn. "Sometimes you lose your confidence, or something happens to make you stop believing in yourself. It's a funny sort of thing, a sort of sabotage, and then you stop being active. It's hard to explain, Son. It has to do with mastering your own life or retreating from it. Or being forced to give it up, and so you give up a part of who you are. And if it's a big part, it can be fatal to you." The words come out of his mouth and surprise him. "It never happened to your great-grandfather," he said. What he didn't say was that the old man had remained a cantankerous son-of-a-bitch.

"Will it happen to you?" asks Michael.

"We all get old," says Finn.

"I mean the other part," says Michael.

"I hope not," says Finn.

"I'll never let it happen to me," says Michael. Finn chews his lip and looks ahead over the lake.

"Good," he says.

"And if it happens to you, I won't leave you behind. I'll help you and be fearless too."

"You'll be a great help," says Finn. "I can see that even now." But Finn knows suddenly that it wasn't just age. His father had been whittled away by small betrayals until the sureness was gone and what was left was at times unrecognizable. It is something that Finn is consciously afraid of.

"I want to be a rifleman in the infantry like Grandpa," Michael says. "A sniper."

"Let's try the big island," says Finn.

"Why are the islands in a circle?" Michael asks as Finn pulls in the anchor.

"It's an old volcano. A 'volcanic pipe'."

"In the lake?"

"Before the lake. A long time ago."

"I thought volcanoes were mountains."

"Usually. They can get worn down, like a dog's teeth, or ones like this are just eruptions that get backfilled with the lava and dirt. A bit gets left around the opening, little hills that can become islands like these. This is the only big lake around here with two old pipes in it."

"How old?"

"Old. The lakebed here is an old rift valley, part of a failed arm of a prehistoric ocean called the Iapetus Ocean. It was where the Atlantic Ocean is now."

"That's a funny name. Who thought of that?"

Finn tells Michael what he knows. Again, the words appear before him. "The Iapetus Ocean was named for the titan Iapetus, son of Uranus and Gaia, who in Greek mythology was the father of Atlas. The Atlantic Ocean was named after Atlas. He was the Titan of Mortal Life, while his other son, Prometheus, was the creator of mankind. Atlas was condemned by his son Zeus to keep the earth and the sky apart, Gaia and Uranus, to prevent the birth of more titans." Jesus, he thinks. Once a teacher ...

"What about 'Nipissing'?"

"The lake's name means 'Big Water' in the Algonquin language."

The facts. Finn thinks of his father relating these things like orders before a battle. *Lake Nipissing has a surface area of 337.2 square miles, Finn, and is 643 ft above sea level. It's the fifth-largest lake in Ontario, excluding the Great Lakes. It's shallow for a big lake, only 15 feet deep on average. The shallowness makes for many sandbars along the shoreline. The lake has a lot of islands, five of which are the small archipelago of the Manitous. Are you listening to me, Finn?*

*It contains two volcanic pipes, which are the Manitou Islands and Callander Bay. The volcanic pipes were formed by the violent, supersonic eruption of deep-origin volcanoes.*

*There are over forty species of fish in the lake. Know the facts, Finn. Facts can save your life. Finn, are you listening?*

*The rift valley was formed when the Earth's crust moved downward about a mile between two major fault zones known as the Máttawa and Petawáwa faults. It's an old arm of Oepetus Sea. The faults are still active and sometimes cause a quake, like the 1935 Timískaming earthquake. The length of the rift, the old arm of an ancient sea, is about 435 miles. That's why the volcanic pipes are out there in the lake. Know the facts, Finn, and keep them like a map in your head.*

Looking down now, Finn envisions the fish swimming in a shallow basin with two plugged pipes separating the flowing elements of water and lava. The agents of separation, be they Titans or pipes, Finn thinks, are fragile things to hold the worlds apart. He thinks of the fire moving beneath him and hears the names in his mother's language like an evocation on his father's tongue, and the lilting names of the little towns his grandfather drove to in the summer where the Ottawa Valley Irish brogue lay thick and sweet. "Well, I'll be on the road and whistling down to Calabogie for the afternoon," his old man would say, and Finn later would hear the old man in his father's voice.

Finn looks up over the bay as they head for the big island. The water spreads out like puckered flannel as the breeze picks up. He eases up on the throttle to smooth out the ride.

"Why are we going around to this side?" Michael asks.

"You have to keep the sun between you and the fish, or the shadow moves along the bottom in front of you and the fish go for cover," says Finn.

"Why are they afraid of shadows?" asks Michael.

"Because the lake is shallow, and there are a lot of fishermen," says Finn, "so the pickerel are wary and hard to lure back out." Michael becomes still and peers into the water. Finn lets up on the throttle and lets the engine die. He lifts the anchor from the floorboards and lowers it quickly and quietly into the water, careful to avoid knocking the cedar hull. The rope burns his hands slightly.

The old uranium mines keep Finn off the island. "We'll stay in the boat," he says. He's wary of the pits and tailings. Digging down into the plugged pipes that keep the fiery sea contained below seems like folly to him. His mind goes down, and his memory goes back to the surging molten rock in the volcanoes he stared into as a young man in Hawaii. "The fires are ever-present," he thinks, "and strain below the waters we float on, and we are like long-legged flies heedless of the deeps beneath us." In that moment, Finn realizes that one thing that kept him apart from people was his notion that they chose to ignore the fragility of these separations and lived in denial.

He peers down into the water. It pulls at him. Michael is looking down into the water too, leaning over the side of the boat, peering towards the weed-tops just visible six feet below. He puts his hand in the water to the wrist, and moves it slowly back and forth. Finn looks up over the water. The lake is quiet. He hands Michael his rod.

"Okay," says Finn. "Maybe we'll have some luck," and he takes over the float. Michael watches it ride the little waves, but does not pick up the casting rod. Together they watch the old red-and-white bob on the surface of the clear water.

"Try casting," Finn says, handing Michael the rod. Michael takes it, twists in his seat, and brings the rod back over his shoulder, snapping it forward smartly and sending the lure in a high arc.

"Nice," says Finn.

"Too high," says Michael.

"I didn't know you could cast that well." Finn watches him reel in the line.

"I felt a hit."

"Probably just a snag," says Finn.

"No," says Michael.

"There are weeds down there," Finn says.

"There!" says Michael as he pulls the rod up quickly to set the hook.

"Set the hook!" says Finn.

"I already did."

"Bring him in slowly," says Finn.

"I know, Dad. I won't lose him. You get the net."

"All right," says Finn, and he watches Michael bring the fish in, playing him, giving him line when he fights hard, tiring him out. "You're getting good at this," says Finn.

Michael looks at him.

"Well," says Finn. The fish is alongside the boat now, and Finn quickly dips the net down behind it, scooping it up. "It's a beauty. A pickerel." He looks up brightly.

"I know," says Michael. "You can tell by the fight what sort of fish it is."

"Right."

"I'll bet it's ten pounds. You thought it was a snag."

"You were right," says Finn. "Well done."

"Grandpa will be happy," Michael says.

"Yes," says Finn. "He did a good job teaching you," and he sets the fish on the floorboards. He reaches for the pliers to extract the hook.

"I can do that," says Michael. "Grandpa says you should always set up your own lures and unhook your own fish."

"Right," says Finn.

"You've got to finish what you start. That's what he says."

"Right," says Finn, wincing, and hands over the pliers. Then he looks overboard to the red and white float bobbing on the waves. "Watch the dorsal fin," he says.

"Dad!"

"Okay," says Finn. "I'll stop fussing."

"Where's the chain?" says Michael. "We need to get him back in the water and keep him fresh."

"Here," says Finn, and he looks closely.

"You can match me, Dad," says Michael.

"Not a ten-pounder on this little float."

"Well," says Michael, "it's your float."

"Not right here under the boat."

"Not if you keep rocking the boat and talking, Dad. You can have the rod back after I catch another fish."

"No problem," says Finn, and he watches the float quiver once, then twice. Something small has nibbled the bait off the hook, and Finn thinks about leaving it down there, bare. It seems too heavy to bring up, like a sudden and great weight. Then he begins reeling it in.

"Did you lose the bait?" Michael asks.

"No. Something stole it."

"You lost it; you weren't paying attention and didn't set the hook."

"You're a lot like your grandfather," says Finn.

"Thanks," says Michael, and looks at Finn with real appreciation. Finn shakes his head as he brings in the float and sets the empty hook on the floorboards under the seat. It is suddenly clear to him that what he dislikes in his father are the qualities he hates in himself. As long as he does not forgive himself, he will never forgive his father for making him in his image, and he, Finn, could lose his own son because, in spite of what he thinks about taking responsibility for himself, he never really has. Michael is proof of that, and Finn is losing him. Phil! And then he wonders if the things Michael is impatient with in Finn might be the things the boy senses latent within himself.

He watches Michael cast, seeing his father's style in the bent elbow, the short arc of the arm, and the quick snap of the wrist at the end of the cast. The old man may not have liked to fish, but he had always been a graceful technician, Finn thinks. After some time, Michael stops and sets down the rod. He dangles his hand in the water. "No more luck here," he says.

"It's late in the morning for them to be biting now," says Finn. "What do you say we head to a smaller island and have the rest of our sandwiches?"

"Sure."

"Then we can explore a bit and catch the sunset fishing."

Finn wishes then that he'd brought a beer or two to help his day along. "Ready?" he says. Michael pulls his hand out of the water and settles into the seat. Finn secures the tackle, pulls in the anchor, and starts the motor, careful of the slippery floorboards. He looks out over the prow.

"Want to pilot?" he asks.

"Pilot?" says Michael.

"You pilot a boat like you pilot an aircraft," says Finn.

"Okay, Michael says. He pulls his hand out of the water and settles into the seat, takes the wheel from Finn and turns the boat sharply while pulling firmly back on the throttle.

Finn looks out over the prow to the far island. The sun is high and a scattering of small, dark rain clouds pepper the sky. He wants to reach the far shore in plenty of time to leave again before dark. He seldom boats on the lake at night because he worries about what's under the water, but thinking about it now, it seems odd. He has never boated home with his son at night after a long day, yet when he was a boy it had been a frequent occurrence on the Abitibi River. It had been very special to come home like that with his father, and he had never tired of the adventure. Every time had been as good as the first, and he was stunned now that he had never done something like it with Michael.

He thinks about the night rides on the Abitibi River, when he sat on his father's knee in the rear seat beside the old Johnson 25 outboard, and the hot engine had warmed them in the night chill. The water had glimmered with starlight as Finn's mother sat in the front seat.

Perhaps they could return later than he planned.

And then Michael pulls too hard on the steering and spins the boat into a tight wallow. The prow lifts free of the water and Finn is thrown against the gunwale and rises in a crouch to grab the wheel. Then the propeller hits something hard, lifting the motor up on the hinge and Finn is thrown over the side by the the force of the turn. He is aware as he hits the water that the motor has stopped, so the propeller is not an immediate hazard. Then he is under water. "No life jacket," he thinks. "But Michael has his on."

He's surrounded by bubbles and strains to see what is under the boat. He bumps into something large and hard, too yielding to be a rock. A dead-head, he thinks. Wanting to get to the surface quickly to check on Michael, he reaches out to push himself off and up, but something wraps itself around his arm. A sharp pain laces his bicep and he pulls hard to get away from it. The pain gets worse, and he can feel a light filament line in his hand.

He's hooked and tangled by an old fishing line. The bubbles clear and he can see it's a string of small hooks dangling below an old red and white float. It has snagged his arm, and the hooks are sunk deeply into the flesh of his bicep as he tries to tug free. He begins to panic, thinking about Michael, and then the rage kicks in, the lashing out, the sudden numbness and strength, the quick desire to hurt whatever it is that holds him, hits him, startles him. He wraps the line around his forearm and hand and pulls hard, ignoring the pain until the light line snaps.

He breaks the surface and looks around to find Michael. The boy is bobbing in his life jacket beside the boat, looking around with wide eyes.

"Michael!" Are you all right?" Michael nods.

Finn swims to him, ignoring the drag on his arm, and they tread water, checking themselves. Then he helps Michael up and into the boat. He falls back, sees Michael's look of fear. His mother's green eyes. Finn laughs to relive the tension.

"Well," he says, "we were thrown in the drink for sure." Then he swims to the back of the boat to climb in over the stern board.

Once inside, he sees that three small fishhooks are imbedded in his arm, linked by very light filament to a float half-filled with water. The skin is torn and the blood, thinned by the water, covers his bicep.

"Let's get to shore and take care of this," he says. He wraps the arm loosely with a towel.

"They're small perch hooks," says Michael. He looks at Finn's arm with the detachment of a scientist.

"Lucky," says Finn.

The granite knolls of the island roll down into the water for a smooth landing. Finn scans the shoreline for some trees to offer some shade, where he and Michael can set up on the thick duff and dry out.

Finn tries the motor, but the engine revs uselessly. The propeller doesn't spin.

"What happened?" says Michael.

"We hit a dead-head. It looks like we damaged the propeller. I'll take a look." He shuts the engine off.

"We're stuck," says Michael.

"We'll fix it," Finn says.

"How? We can't get home. We'll be lost."

"Let me take a look," Finn says as he scoots Michael aside and moves to the rear of the boat. He tilts the engine on its hinge, exposing the propeller. The blades spin uselessly.

"Is it broken?'

"Nope," says Finn. "The propeller is fine. We just sheared off the cotter pin. Look in the tackle box and see if there's another one. It's a little brass pin."

"What is it?"

"It's soft brass so if you hit a rock the pin will break off before the propeller does. It's an old motor. We just have to fix the thing in place with something else. Look in my book bag there and hand me some paper clips. The big, funny-shaped ones. And some pliers from the box. These old contraptions are easier to fix than the new motors."

"Are we stuck here?"

"Nope. And if we were it wouldn't be a problem. We'd make a fire and camp out."

"Here's a clip."

"Thanks." Finn inserts the soft metal clips and twists them tight, and then he clips them off. "All done."

"How did you know how to do that?" asks Michael.

"Grandpa showed me when I was your age."

"I didn't know you knew stuff like that. I thought you were only a teacher."

Finn laughs. "Right," he says.

"And a pilot," says Michael.

"Grandpa's been around for a while," Finn says. "And I grew up on boats like this." He starts up the motor again and eases the boat into a cove of round granite. There are pine trees and duff on the rocks and shade beneath the trees. He reaches out and grabs the rock, holding the boat steady as he sits and shuts off the motor. "Jump out and tie us down," he says. Michael scrambles over the bow and carries the rope to a stump, pulling it tight and securing it. Finn tightens the towel on his arm, then passes up the tackle and food, and they climb the sloping granite to its crest.

The sparrows clatter beneath dry pines that have dropped their cones on the pungent duff. The shade is cool under the trees, and Finn sits and leans his head back against the earth, tilting his face into the warmth of the sun, and breathes the smell of leaves and loam, and there is the sharp scent of the pine tree in the air and the lingering balm of sweet fern. He roughs up a little of the duff with his fingers and holds it lightly in his hand, and it gives up a clean scent of summer savory. Michael sits down beside him.

"There's Sammy Jay," says Finn, pointing to a blue jay watching them from above.

"Grandpa calls him that too," Michael says. "He has names for all the animals."

"I know," says Finn.

"It's silly."

"Well, there's something in it, too," Finn says. Then he looks at the hooks in his arm. "Here. Rip off a piece of this towel for me." He takes the pliers from the tackle box and snips off the barbs. He backs the small hooks out the entrance wounds, spreads Neosporin over the area, and wraps the portion of towel tightly around his arm. Then he stretches out his legs and looks up through the boughs of the tree. The needles move in the wind, and high above race the small white clouds.

"What else did Grandpa teach you?" Michael asks.

Finn looks at the clouds. "Lots," he says, "and so did the Cree men who worked with him."

"Like what?"

"I had my own trap lines when I was your age," says Finn.

"Up north?"

"Right. In the settlement on the Little Abitibi River."

"Did Grandpa take you out on the lines?"

"No. I went out on my own. All the boys did. It was part of growing up."

"Were you afraid in the woods alone?"

"Once I was out checking my traps. It was January and thirty below. I'd walked about a mile from the settlement when I heard a wolf howl off to my left, then another off to my right. I thought they could be two scouts from a pack, so I turned and hightailed out of there back to the houses. I ran as fast as I could. The howling got louder, and though I thought that wolves made no noise when they were on the run, I was pretty scared. They seemed to be getting close, and when I broke out of the woods and ran across the clearing to the first house, I looked back. Five wolves stood at the tree's edge looking at me."

"Is that true?"

"It was a different time. We used to be on our own for the better part of the day as boys, summer or winter, even at your age."

"I learned at school that wolves don't eat people."

"People from the south never believe these stories. But those people would be dead in a day when it's fifty below, so what they think doesn't matter much. It's like that with what many people think, Michael. About war, about the north, about a lot of things. Believe your own experience and rely on what you learn from it. Keep it quiet inside, like the little animals sleeping under the snow in winter."

Finn looks around, then back at the bandage on his arm. "Whew!" he says. "Let's sit here for a minute and settle down. Then we can make a little fire, have a sandwich, and go for a swim. A real one. While our clothes dry. We'll head back a little later than we planned."

The shade is thick with the smell of needles and loam and the sparrows return in search of seeds as they rest. Finn roughs up a little of the duff with his fingers again.

"Let's make a fire," he says.

"Let's eat now," says Michael.

"Let's make the fire first. It will help us dry out and warm up. Scoot over to the brush and get us some small twigs and branches. I'll get it started here and we'll use what you bring to build it up."

Finn scoops up some dry duff and encircles it with rocks. The fine twigs from the trees are plentiful and close at hand, and the small fire is soon crackling. Michael returns with an armload of kindling.

"Good," says Finn. "Put some of that on the fire, and we'll open the sandwiches."

He thinks back to the morning when he and his father put the food together, standing quietly at the kitchen counter, happy to be packing the food and filling the thermoses with coffee and Kool-Aid.

The smells of toast and eggs filled the room, and the kitchen was warm in the yellow light. At one point, when Michael left to say goodbye to his mother, Finn's father turned and put a hand on Finn's shoulder.

"You seem a little low," he said.

"I gave notice when I left the station last week. No more drops. Just another season or two of recon, assessing recovery rates in the old burns. Very safe. Lara insisted."

"And?"

"It feels like somebody died. And somebody will, without me there."

"Somebody did, and somebody will whether you're there or not. When your life takes on a new direction, Finn, when you decide on a new mission, the old mission is gone. That part of your life is over. But that's what you're feeling: it's a piece of you that's died by giving this up. I've told you this before. It has to be that way, if you're going to live a new life. Who told you the change would be for the worse?"

"I just assumed."

"Exactly, son. You've got to snap out of it."

"Well, it's the end of something, that's for sure," says Finn. "I mean, Jesus, Dad, don't you miss the action? Living your limits? Doing something that really matters? Last year, one of the faculty in the department had a heart attack in his office while talking to a student about a grade. He toppled out of his chair and onto the floor, as dead as a goddam smelt. How pathetic is that? What a way die."

The old man nodded, then said, "Sometimes, when I read about some mission overseas, I wish to God I were there, but I never tell your mother. Can't chance being misquoted or misunderstood. We have to move on. Buck up, Finn. The fish are waiting. And more importantly, so is Michael. We had our time."

"Well, if that's true, why don't those times let us free?" Finn asked.

# The Way Back

Finn shakes off the reverie, and turns to Michael. "How are you doing?" he asks.

"I wish Mom was here."

"So do I," says Finn. "We could all stay here overnight, under the stars. That would have been good."

"She could have come."

"Yes," says Finn, "but maybe it's a good thing she wasn't here to take the spill with us." Finally, Finn reaches into the cooler, pulls out a boloney and mustard sandwich, hands half to Michael, and they eat the sandwich, chewing in silence, watching the small waves move. The sandwiches are thick with slices of meat between layers of lettuce and pickles, and hot mustard on the bread. Finn sucks the bread from his front teeth.

"How's the sandwich?" he says around his tongue.

"Boloney," says Michael. "You always make boloney sandwiches."

Finn stops for a minute and looks at Michael blankly. "What's your favorite?" he says.

"Peanut butter and honey."

Finn looks in the cooler again and rummages through the sandwiches. "Here," he says, pulling out a separate wrapping tacky with honey. "Grandma must have known you'd be wanting one of those and packed it last night. I guess she was looking out for you."

"I thought getting ready was supposed to be for the men only this morning, and that's why she stayed in bed."

"Well, there you are," says Finn. "Whoever said it was a man's world didn't see the whole picture."

Michael shuffles his legs as he sits, stops, and picks up a clean little bird skull, exposed when they roughed up the duff. "Let's take this back for Mom. She likes these things." Finn shudders. The skull is small and beautiful, and Finn looks at Michael's face and ears, and the fine skin there makes him think of porcelain. It reminds him of something.

As Finn eats his sandwich, he looks up over the lake. Being in the stillness with the sounds of the water and the birds is enough, and being alone on the lake with his son makes it better. Finn watches the boy clean the little skull for a few minutes, and then he leans his head back against the tree. Shortly, he hears Michael's breathing slow and deepen.

Finn looks down at the face of his sleeping son. It is calm, and the skin is smooth. His ears and his nose are translucent and very fine. The ears are a copy of his grandfather's and he has his mother's dark eyes. The faces of our children are heartbreaking and perfect, Finn thinks, and suddenly the face of the girl in the jungle is there and he pushes the memory back.

And now, a long time after, as the deep plates of his understanding shift, Finn thinks again about the enemy who died in his war, the boys on the other side who had been younger than he had been, often only nineteen, sometimes only five years older than his son, and they are no longer the enemy. They are sons and brothers who fought for their homes, and he wishes he could see them and be seen by them, that they could see in one another's eyes the looks of understanding and acknowledgement. They played their parts, and in some sense their parts were made for them, and they had no choice in the playing.

He sees again that the world exists outside his preoccupations, even outside time, and he's been lucky enough to simply be here, to experience today's moments. Today is about feeling and sensation, about truth and proximity, and the moments have an honesty that stay with him. The pace of the day was slow and open enough for him be more fully present than usual.

Life on the Little Abitibi River was like that.

He thinks of the long night trips back home in the boat on the river. Who knows now what they had been doing–fishing, picnicking on the Red Sucker–but often the sun had set, and they boated home in the dark.

The stars were bright overhead, and Finn remembers it was by their reflection on the water that his father knew what was river and what was shore. The water shone and the river was a flat black. Navigating like that was a mysterious process, built on a knowledge available to mothers and fathers, and his trust in it was absolute. He felt safe in ways he did not now, and that was something they provided at the time–a belief that the world was a good place. There were instances when Finn sat on the small seat by the motor on those rides, and he hunkered between his father's legs with his hand on the steering stick, his father's hand covering his own, his back warm against the man's chest, their faces close as they looked ahead into the night. Finally, his fingers got numb from the vibrating engine as they steered and he became sleepy. Finn's father scooted him forward and his mother tucked him into bed under the deck. The smoky smell of the boat and blankets calmed, and the slap of the cedar hull on the small waves put him to sleep. It was a good sleep, in a good place: a little family with the stars overhead and mirrored in the waters beneath them, sailing a ribbon between heaven and earth, connected by love and time. Those things never left him.

On more than one occasion, he remained awake long enough to hear his mother say "There are the lights on the dam—we're home!" and the lights beaded the dam ahead and lit the fore bay. When he thinks of those trips home at night, it seems as though that boat is still there with them in it, navigating a river through the stars in the night sky.

That was reality for Finn when he was his son's age.

Once back at the boathouse they tied up, gathered what they could, and walked up the hill to home and bed. The night was cool and happy, napped with security, and he looked forward to his bed and sleep.

And if Finn were to choose a final image to carry him from this world to the next, it would be that small cedar strip boat on the Little Abitibi River with his father at the stern, knowing the waters and the way, and his mother in the boat with room for all of them, and they'd steer that little craft filled along that dark and watery ribbon up into the night sky with the stars like bright wave-tips beneath the boat, bearing them up as they headed for the lights on the headwaters, until he heard his mother's quiet voice saying "Look–we're home."

Stretched out against the tree, Finn dozes and thinks about the morning again.

"How far out are you going?" his father asked when they finished wrapping the food.

"I don't know," Finn said. "Just to the islands."

"The Manitous?"

"Right."

"Have you been to the west shore?"

"No, not in a long time."

"You and I used to boat there."

"Yes," Finn says, "I remember."

"How long will you be gone?"

"Not long. Try not to worry." Finn looked down at Michael. "Ready?" he asked. Then Finn's father walked with them down to the boat.

"Take your time," he said to Finn, and when Finn looked back before disappearing around the point, his father was still standing quietly on the shore. He lifted his arm in a wave, and Finn waved back.

Finally the ground becomes uncomfortable, and Finn realizes he's been thinking for a long time. He looks at Michael, awake and piecing together the tiny skeleton.

"Let's go," Says Finn. "We can try for another fish, then head home. You douse the fire, and I'll load the boat. Make sure it's out."

"Some of the wood just smoldered."

"It was a little too wet. You picked out some sticks with green moss on them."

"But the fire should have dried it out."

"The wood has to be dry before it can burn. And then it needs heat, and water takes away the heat needed for combustion. It lowers the temperature. It can also take away the oxygen and help smother the fire."

"But how does a forest burn if the trees are alive and not dry?"

"Well, it's not just the dry weather that does it. The heat of the forest fire itself can dry the trees at the leading edge of the fire. The trees explode as the water content expands into steam. When the tree blasts apart, it spreads a lot of kindling for the fire to ignite and grow by. And so, the fire feeds itself, in a manner of speaking. If it gets big enough, it pulls in strong winds that feed more oxygen to the flames, and that starts a sequence of higher temperatures and stronger winds. Then you have a firestorm."

"What's that?"

"It's a fire that's very, very hot and big. So big it creates its own weather: lightning and small tornadoes."

Michael is quiet for a moment, "And that's what you do in the summer? Fight those fires?" he asks

"Yes. Well, I fly in the men and women who do the work on the ground, and I pick them up when things get dangerous, or when they need to rest."

"Mom says it's dangerous. That's why she's mad at you."

"Well, there you are," says Finn.

He looks up over the lake. A storm is building in the north-west, and he doesn't want to call it too close. Still, the weather will build and sweep down south-easterly, the direction they will take, and they can run before the wind and make it home. There is time for another round of fishing by the easterly island of the chain, across the bay. He starts the motor.

"Pick up your line," he says. "Let's try the last spot by Rankin Island. It's closest to home, and we'll leave from there." South-south-west and on the way back to base.

"Is there a storm?"

"Yes,' says Finn, "but later. The wind will pick up a little first and that will be our signal to head out. We'll run before the storm and be home before the big waves hit." Finn is thinking ahead to the ride. He is looking forward to it. They will ride the quickening chop with the breeze behind them. The air around them in the boat will be still if they evenly match the speed of the wind. It will be a little like free-fall when his jet hit the ceiling before leveling off after a steep climb. Behind them, the wind will kick up the shallow lake into waves that could make the boat wallow and easily capsize it.

"We'll outrun the storm," he says again. Then he calls out for Michael to come and sit close to him.

Tonight, he thinks, they will ride the boat home in the dark and his father will be standing at the window, watching them ride in. He will wave a flashlight to signal the safe route in when he spots the running lights of the boat, and he will walk down to the shore to meet them, and there will be the silence there is between men when the meeting is good. His father has been waiting a long time, but it is not too late though Finn has only just seen what his father has been waiting for. He knows what he has to do. He is anxious to get back, but he can't rush it now. There is the final round of fishing, and there is still some thinking to do.

The wind is keen over the bow of the boat, as Finn steers southward to the island. After a half-hour and another fish, the sun disappears behind the big anvil heads sailing out over the lake, and Finn gathers in gear.

"Time to go," he says.

"What about the rocks?" Michael says.

"You look for them. Look for the places where the water is flat, calmer than normal." He eases the boat out of the cove, careful of the rocks.

"It's scary," Michael says.

"Look for the little signs. We're going slowly here, and when we're out farther we'll look for the beacons. Keep an eye out for a big rock that shows when the water is low. It should be on the right side."

"Here it is, Dad, but we're on the wrong side. You said right."

"Good," says Finn, "that's fine. We know where we are now." There are rocks all around them. "We're fine. Let's backtrack a little and swing out around the other side of that rock. Then it's straight home." He reaches down and squeezes Michael's shoulder. "Well done," he says. "We're in good shape now. Sit down. How are you doing?"

"Fine," says Michael.

"We're clear now; let's open it up. Ready for a race? Come here beside me and help steer us home." Michael moves over tight against Finn and he pulls the blanket tight around him, holding it firm in the circle of his arm. Then he points the boat towards the lights on the home shore and opens up the throttle.

The sound of the motor envelops them. An anvil-head billows in the southwest. It is too far away to bother them now, and the stars will own their share of the night. Finn is not worried. He knows the lake and keeps the throttle open. The boat cleaves the water, and the small waves hammer brightly on the wooden hull.

He looks up as the boat beats back the lake. The water is vermillion ahead of them with the last of the sun. He eases up on the throttle to even out the ride and match the wind. The wind disappears in the boat as though they ride the eye of a storm, and as he looks to the far shore, Finn blinks as the waves fade and pulls Michael snugly against him.

Then the sun sinks over the waters behind them and the bright skin of the day on the lake rolls back to the horizon.

The water becomes nappy under the stars. Finn opens the throttle to match the quickening wind behind them. The water is black beyond the bow, and he strains to see any hazards.

"How are you doing, Michael?" he says.

"Fine."

"You can see the lights from the city," says Finn, close to Michael's ear. "We'll head in that direction but a little south. We'll keep the lights port-side. See that buoy light blinking starboard? That's the Three Sisters Rocks, and home is right behind that. That's our target."

"I'll bet grandpa is waiting," says Michael.

"No bet," says Finn. "Look how bright the stars are."

Finn is happy to be in the boat at night, and he thinks again about how the day began, about packing the food and filling the thermoses that morning in the kitchen with the lingering smell of toast and eggs and the yellow tungsten light around them. His father looked out to the lake and said that the glassy surface would hold for a few more hours and noted that a thin fog lay on the waters, and decided the mist would clear and by noon a breeze would breathe upon the lake and make the going easier. As Finn stood with his father at the window looking out over the lake, high clouds caught the pink of the rising sun, and the light floated up over the trees, bright and beckoning.

It is late when they pass the last little island to the bay, and Finn's father stands on the lawn holding a lantern high to guide them. His face is clear in the halo of light, and his smile is tight. Finn can see his mother's face in the kitchen window as she watches them come in. Lara is with her. He waves. Lara nods and smiles. Then she gestures to her arm, the place Finn has his bicep bandaged, and shakes her head. Finn knows that when the air becomes still later in the night and the rain pelts down on the waters, he and Lara will sit at the window and talk about the day.

"Grandpa!" Michael shouts. The older man laughs.

"Welcome home!" he says. "You two have been out tomcatting a helluva long time. I hope you brought me some fish!" Finn sees the relief in his father's eyes and the pleasure at their return. "Everything all right?" he calls to Finn.

"Yeah. We took a little longer than we'd planned."

"Good. There's hot coffee inside." Finn watches from the boat as his father wades into the water and grips the towrope. Then he reaches over and tousles Michael's hair. "And a hot berry pie for you," he says, "from Grandma."

Michael reaches down and lifts the string of fish.

"Look," he says, reaching into the boat and pulling up the chain with five fish. He lowers them into the water.

"Did they jump into the boat?"

"No, Grandpa. We caught them."

"Sounds like a fish story to me. There've been reports all day of fish jumping into boats. These look like that kind of fish. Nipissing Boat-Leapers."

Michael laughs. "No, these two are pickerel. We caught them when it was getting dark, didn't we, Dad? At the Manitou Islands. I caught them, and two walleyes, and Dad caught a pike. It'll be too bony to eat, though." He laughs through his small, perfect teeth and says, "Dad can cook it on a wooden board and eat the board." Finn laughs too and steps out of the boat into the water. "Good thing we had the sandwiches," Michael says. "Dad said it was a hell of a fishing trip for five fish," and he pulls the string of fish through the water. The water is warm on Finn's feet as he listens. He stands beside his father and they pull the bow securely up onto the sand.

"Watch your language," says Finn, laughing.

"You all right?" his father says quietly. "Your clothes look wet." He looks at Finn's arm and raises an eyebrow.

"We went into the drink," crows Michael, "and dad was hooked like a fish. Then we broke a cotter pin and dad fixed it. Then we came home and steered by the stars, like he said you did when he was little on the river. Then we raced the storm, and we won," he says.

Finn's father raises an eyebrow.

"We're fine," says Finn. He looks into his father's eyes, and the older man nods quickly at him, then tilts his head towards Michael.

"He all right?"

"He's fine. Gave me no end of instructions on just about everything we did. He's a lot like you."

"Good," Finn's father says again, and squeezes his shoulder. "Smart kid. Reminds me of you at his age. Full of advice. You look a little rough." He turns to Michael. "Come here and let me lift you out." He picks the boy up and holds him for a moment, the old man's arms still gnarled and ropey, before setting him down on the sand. Finn is suddenly happy. He walks back to the stern of the boat, clearing his throat and splashing loudly. His father holds the light high, laughing to relax Michael, joking and teasing, looking up at Finn with quick joy and no embarrassment now, and Finn looks down at the mooring and wonders how long the embarrassment has been absent in his father without him seeing it gone, and he reaches for the rope to keep his head down as he blinks once. The sting is still in his eyes from the wind over the lake. He leans down to the pike trailing in the water, sluggish and torpid and empty of hope, and Finn unfastens the snap, easing the pike off the chain and into the water.

And then it is gone. The big fish wobbles unsteadily and flicks its tail, moving toward the deep water, its flat eye tipping toward the light of the lantern and lifting towards Finn a curious mixture of light at once silver and black and bottomless with the iris ringing the pupil before it vanishes. Finn feels a series of faint bumpings on the tops of his feet. A handful of minnows move in a tiny storm there, nibbling and twisting, throwing the light from the lantern back up at him from their bright flanks. Pinheads, little chips of light in the dark lake, quick and fragile. Finn feels a small thrill as he watches them, grateful for their presence, as ephemeral as the drops of bright rain that fell that afternoon into the lake. They have always been a part of the lake, the rain and the minnows, always in the sky and in the shallows close to the surface, swirling around his head and nibbling at his feet when he was younger than his son beside him is now in his father's boat. It seems suddenly amazing that these things should be so constant, that they were always there and that he forgets, and he pulls his hand from the lake and flicks the water from his fingers and the bright drops fall to the water of the lake above the minnows, lit briefly from the light of his father's lantern and quickly winking out.

Then Finn pulls the boat up onto the beach and looks back over the waters of the lake. He wants to tell Lara about what he learned today. Lightning flashes far out above the Manitous, igniting the clouds against the night sky.

They missed the storm, but it was coming.

CHAPTER NINETEEN

# A Chorus of Voices

December 1990

I t's Christmas, and Finn is trimming the tree with his mother. She is deft as she pins the baubles to the boughs. Her will lays a hard edge on each winking ornament, and she recites its origins with each transfixion. The tree submits to her hands, and the ghosts of the past move over her face.

Finn is restless. The storms are back, and there is no indication when they will leave. He shrinks from the climate outside and the weather within, but his mother's voice binds him to the tree as tightly as the ornaments, so he looks past the glittering spruce through the window to the lake where the snows blanket the world. Smoke floats from the chimneys of the little houses along the street and around the bay as people tend their fires. And here, too, his family is alight as the phosphorus in their bones glows with old memories.

"Inter ego vacua, stella serena nives," Finn murmurs.

"Latin!" his mother says. "What is it? A Christmas carol?" She looks at him. "It sounds lovely. Like 'Adeste Fideles'. We used to sing that in school, in Latin."

"Oh?" says Finn. "No. Something about a star on the snow."

She looks back at the tree and says, "Something from the seminary. I wish you'd come back home when you got back from overseas instead of gallivanting around graduate school. You're still doing it, gone every summer, like you don't belong in any one place."

"Well," says Finn, "I didn't want to become a priest, and if I hadn't done my graduate work I wouldn't have the job I have."

"It's not enough for you, though, is it? You come back here every summer. The north is part of you."

"Maybe it's a push-pull thing, Mother."

"You're equivocating again, Dear. Is that the word? Where's Lara?"

"She's downstairs reading," says Finn.

"It's not what she wants either," she says, "you going off to fly that damned helicopter every summer and fight fires." She shrugs, then says, "But you're here now," and looks straight at him. "For the holiday."

"Yes," says Finn.

"And little Michael," she says. Then she says, "I'm so glad you came early so he could spend more time with his grandfather." She pins another ornament to the tree. "Where are they?"

"Downstairs in the tack room. Dad's cleaning up the fishing gear, and Michael is helping."

"He's not showing little Michael his damned old war medals, is he?" she laughs.

"Just the fishing gear."

"I don't know how they can go out in this cold and sit by a hole in the ice for hours."

"It's not about the fish, Mum," says Finn.

She looks at Finn directly. "That's right, Dear. So why don't you go with them?"

Finn looks away, around the room to the windows where bright crowds of pottery populate the valance, migrants from the old life in Quebec. He reaches down to the storage box at his feet and lifts an ornament. He looks up to see his mother watching him.

She is beautiful to Finn. Her eyes are large and dark, and her spirit, roosting like a small, fierce hawk in her breast, has flown up to them today. A bright bud of color blooms on her cheeks.

"Christmas is a good time, Mum. I'm glad we're together." He squeezes her shoulder, then walks to the kitchen and the window.

The window is cut low into the wall and Finn stoops to look out. Since he's returned, the snow has fallen steadily, and he cracks the window to pull some cold air into his lungs. It carries the sharp edge of promise. Perhaps the weather will break, he hopes. He feels the muscles of his face relax as he thinks of the stars hanging clear and bright over the lake when night comes. But there has been more talk of snow.

"Have you had enough?" his mother asks from the living room. "I can finish this by myself."

"No," he says. "Just moving around a bit." He stretches. "Tea?"

"No, a beer."

"Ah." He walks to the refrigerator, opens the door, and peers inside. Bright packages line the shelves. He rummages to the back and discovers three glass jars, upside down on the top shelf. "Why are these jars upside down?" he asks.

"So they won't go bad," she says. Finn studies the jars.

"What do you mean?"

"If they're upside down they won't spoil."

"Who told you that?" he says.

"Sarah Cohen."

"How does she know that?"

"She read it somewhere."

"Ah. What's in this old mayonnaise jar?"

"Your icing."

"What icing?"

"Icing left over from the cake. I thought we could use it tomorrow. It's cream cheese–your favorite."

"What cake?" Finn asks.

"Well, the last cake I made for you, of course. I only bake when you're here."

"That was last August," he says.

"Time sure flies."

"This is December."

"Yes," she says. Finn counts out the months on his fingers. "It's upside down," she says.

Her logic is a crazy moon sailing through the night of Finn's understanding. "What has being upside down got to do with not spoiling?" he says. "For God's sake."

"If the container is upside down, it forms a vacuum and the food inside won't spoil." She says this slowly, patiently, as though he were slow of learning.

"A vacuum?" Finn peers around at her.

She nods slowly. "Yes, Dear. The food falls to the bottom and forms a vacuum on the top. That's what the space there is now. A vacuum. So it's sealed." Finn imagines the food slipping down the inside of the jar as the burping air relocates itself atop the bolus. He scrutinizes the jars closely for signs of decay. None are visible, but he knows the worst poisons are never seen, and his mouth is suddenly dry.

"I see," he says. He stares at the jars and wonders if it is a joke.

"I'd have thought they taught you something in the military," she says.

"Well, there you are," he says. "Where's the beer? I think I'll have one too."

"Bottom shelf at the back," she says. Finn reaches in and moves a plastic container blocking the bottles behind it. It is a scarred and worn Tupperware relic. As he tugs it out of the way, the bottom drops off with a plop, and the contents spread over the shelf.

"Oh no!" says Finn.

"Be careful," says his mother from behind the tree. "There's an upside down plastic container there that doesn't seal too well."

"What's in it?" he says.

"I think it might be stew."

A whiff of decay snakes unerringly up Finn's nostrils and down into his lungs. "I think I'll have a martini," he says, "instead of a beer. Something more bracing." He pulls a beer from the bottom shelf, opens it, and walks it over to his mother. Then he goes quietly back and mops up the mess in the refrigerator.

"What's that smell?" his mother calls from the living room.

"Nothing," says Finn. "Where did you put the gin and vermouth?"

"In the bottom cupboard by the sink."

Finn finishes his cleanup, then fetches the bottles and walks to the freezer for ice. Reaching in, he gathers a handful for the shaker, but stops with his fingers in the tray. When he lifts his hand enough to see what he holds, he jumps back, flinging the ice into the air.

"Good God!" he cries.

"What's the matter?"

"There are stubby little caterpillars in the ice. Oh Jesus!"

"Corks," she says.

"What?"

"They're corks," she says.

"Corks in the ice?"

"Don't lose them," she says.

"Why?"

"Because I get them from Sarah and I don't have any more."

"No, no," says Finn. "Why are the corks in the ice?"

"To keep it from freezing, of course."

"You don't want the ice to freeze?"

"The corks keep the ice cubes from freezing together."

"How can they do that?" he says.

"They just do," she says.

Finn sets the bottles on the counter and wonders if hosts of little manitous inhabit the refrigerator under his mother's command. Little Oji-Cree spirits meditating intended mischief. He waits for his heart to slow, then kneels to shepherd the cubes into a pile, the corks frozen solidly to them, like small, cold turds. Feeling the need to move very slowly and very quietly, as though the air around him might break, or the ground give way beneath his feet, he places them gently in the sink. He can't tell whose world is unraveling faster: his own slippery grasp on the here and now, or his mother's, sliding down the dark slope of her years. And yet he knows better than to think he understands the indirections of his mother. More than once she has led him down the side-paths to understanding. Hers is a wisdom more hallowed than his.

"Why don't you have your own corks?" he says.

"Only winos have their own corks. What are you making?" she says.

"A martini," says Finn.

"You're drinking martinis?"

"Yes."

"With beer?"

"Without beer. Just gin and vermouth and shake it up, then drop an olive in it."

"Gin," she says.

"I like them that way."

"I haven't made one in years. Your father and Sarah used to like them. They drank and talked about philosophy. About the books they read." Finn hears the boughs on the tree rustle beneath her ministrations. She is a Druid with the tree, he thinks, pre-Christian and pre-rational, combining the old magic of two worlds, and he knows his Anglican defenses are weak proof against her gathered and ancient forces. And the more tentative her grasp on hard rationality seems, the firmer her hold on these primordial strengths. So it seems, he thinks. Or maybe she's just his mother.

Finn shakes the ingredients together, walks out of the kitchen across the grey carpet to the tree with his martini, breathing slowly, and stands close to her. "Dad's close to being a teetotaler," he says. "I didn't know he liked martinis." Her dark eyes flash.

"Only when Sarah visited. When they talked about books. That woman was always reading, and so was your father. Sarah encouraged it. They talked about philosophy and psychology. And geology. Just like you. I'm glad I finally broke him of that psychology habit," she says. "It wasn't easy."

"What about the philosophy?" Finn jokes.

"From books?" she asks. "All you need to know is in the world around you. In the north. Your father used to know that."

"You mean the manitous?" Finn asks.

She ignores him, holds up an ornament and looks at it fiercely. It's an old Santa. The red paint has chipped off the hat and coat, allowing the white porcelain beneath to peer leprously through, and the face is rucked and scarred from decades of poor packing and righteous tree hanging. "Remember this?" she asks. "We got it the Christmas you were born."

The tiny Santa looks cowed in her hands. Then she strokes it gently with her forefinger and her expression softens. "Your father bought it." She looks at Finn. "It's as old as you are, Sweetheart," she says. "All those memories in this little thing."

"Yes, and it looks pretty beat up too," Finn says ruefully. He peers at the little totem closely, but the Santa appears neither animate nor a mirror.

"Well, we all do now, for Heaven's sake," she says, and laughs. "Stop feeling sorry for yourself." She hangs the ornament on the tree and adjusts it carefully. Then she looks at Finn's drink and says, "Your aunt Martha used to drink cheap gin. It must have been the English in her."

"This isn't cheap gin," says Finn. "It's the good stuff."

"Well, I've always liked beer and it's good enough for me." Finn says nothing and hands her an ornament. She purses her lips and looks at the tree.

As he looks around the living room, he notices again the newly covered paneling. "You've done a real makeover," he says. "You painted everything. What's that all about?"

"You know very well what it's about," she says.

"Well," says Finn, and he thinks about the dark, rich wood hidden beneath the paint. "Why did you cover up the wood with paint and then paint wood grain over it? Dad must be fit to be tied."

She looks around. "That damned wood. Since your father retired, he varnishes it every year. The house is a shambles with his projects." She looks at him closely. "Do you know what I mean?" she asks. "He doesn't go to the bush at all any more, and he smokes too much. He needs to get out of the house."

Finn stands up. He knows how this works. This is the shape of their love: at the beginning of their marriage, he was always gone, and now he isn't gone enough. Once, he was too solitary, and now he's too dependent. And while it was her campaigning that made him so, Finn knows what she means: she misses the man she married. Another irony of love and marriage.

"Are you unhappy, Mum?" he asks.

"Oh no!" she says. "That's not what I meant at all. I just meant … " The statement hangs like a poltergeist in the room.

"I know," says Finn. "It's hard. And I didn't mean to criticize what you've done. Dad loves this place, and we love that he loves it. He floats us along on his enthusiasm."

"Floats?" she says. "Aren't you clever. Well, sometimes he needs to 'sail' a sea that's a little bigger than the front yard."

Finn steps back and looks at her. He knows better than to confront her when she's girded for engagement. "Let's think about getting the big meal started," he says, and he turns towards the window. Outside, more snow flurries are beginning.

"He needs to get out more. Now go downstairs and ask Lara to come up here and help me," she says.

"Okay." he says.

"Call your father when you're down there."

"Is that him singing?" asks Finn. "'Christmas in Killarney'?"

"Your father's been singing that damned song over and over again ever since you arrived." She turns and looks at Finn. "He's happy." Then Finn hears his son's voice, high and quavering, join the baritone of his father.

"Oh, God," says Finn's mother, and laughs. "Listen to those two."

"Here, let me pass you some more ornaments," he says.

"No," she says. "Get Lara, and then why don't you go for a walk? It's beautiful outside. I can finish this by myself. Then I'll start the baking."

"No," he says. "It's colder than hell out there. It's snowing."

"It's not that cold," she says. "I love the snow. It's good for you. Go out and enjoy it. There's nothing like a white Christmas."

"I'll go," he says, wondering how she went from her loving the snow to it being good for him.

Finn walks to the mudroom at the back door. He leans on the sill and looks out the window at the little houses hunkered down across the road. The winds have heaped the snow into crazy drifts and softened the clean, rectangular lines of the buildings beneath.

He lifts his father's faded green parka from the closet. "To hell with it," he says. He ties the cincture loosely, pulls the zipper and tugs the hood over his head. The thick, red lining releases a faint but haunting effervescence that he recognizes as his father's, quick and ineffable. He's clothed in his father's scent. As he looks through the glass, thoughts tap at his mind like branches on a windowpane. Finn steps into his father's heavy boots, opens the door, and leans into the wind. Then he turns and looks at the tracks the boots leave in the snow behind him.

Finn is aware that his affect is changing. He's been working at softening it, trying to damp down the "take no prisoners" attitude that Lara hates, but it's hard work and doesn't feel true. Still, it gets better results than the old rage. Tactics, he thinks, to smooth the way. But at what point does the self become lost? Then he thinks of his father, so private and quiet when Finn was young, who learned the difficult business—he refuses to call it an 'art'—of small talk in order to put others at ease, and the more he succeeded, the less Finn recognized him. Now it's happening to him. At times, Finn watches himself perform as though watching someone else, and he observes how those around him react. It's like pulling the strings of a puppet, and people never guess, but the longer it goes on, the tighter the knot gets in his gut and the less he recognizes himself.

It's like the stories brought back from the war, he thinks; most people are more comfortable with the lie, with not knowing, with the easy talk around the issue. And so they refuse to really see those who return by denying the quiet hurt so glaringly obvious to the men and women who have it.

He supposes that much of the avoidance comes from the unacknowledged fact that killing someone changes you, and because you have broken the law of the group, you may be capable of doing it again, and you are, so you are no longer trusted. You become an outlaw in the wordless hearts of men and women who call you hero with their mouths. It's schizophrenic, thinks Finn. No wonder so many of his buddies are fucked up.

He's glad to be out of the house. The mornings always belonged to him, and he usually did not feel right unless he was alone and did not have to talk, but it's been impossible to get away from the houseful of people these mornings, and so Finn is glad his mother sent him outside this afternoon. He fills his lungs with the empty air. Now he can think.

Even now, when he has to talk or listen in the morning, he feels the day leak out of him. It leaves him bare and without resolve. Something numinous evaporates when he listens to the complications of other people's minds in the morning, and he can't define what it is exactly, or why it disappears so readily. The worst is having to listen to other people's dreams before coffee. He thinks it has something to do with the spirit of the day and his growing up close to the voiceless silences in the north. And it has to do with his time alone in the war, when being alive seemed like a dream, but he resists thinking more about that. No good ever comes from his thinking closely about the war.

As his feet lift and fall on the deepening snow, his mind leaves the road and withdraws. He is aware that the mechanics of his movement become automatic as he casts back through the years, as though he is watching his body.

His father likes the silence too, Finn thinks, and he is grateful for having been shown the secret joys of order and quiet. He taught Finn to notice the small things that happen only when you are alone and very still. Then the natural world quickens around you, he told Finn, and you see the small birds and animals that disappear when others are around. You learn the pleasure of seeing the big animals too, the bear and moose that move past when you are noiseless inside but disappear when you are agitated. Even the wind in the trees or the crickets in the night or the leopard frogs in the reeds seem more fully present when you are alone and quiet.

His father showed him how to move with that calmness, not through it. Finn loves him for that, for showing it in walks and hunting, for laughing suddenly after a good wing-shot, and for naming the animals and the birds as though they were people. The crow people. The deer people. With names: Reddy Fox, Buster Bear, Long Legs the Heron, and Chatterer the Red Squirrel. Such tales may move a child into the woods, but the integrity of the old archetypes speak to the dreams of the man.

Now his father is reading those same stories to his grandson, and Finn is aware that his mother watches Finn as he watches his son and father, as though she were waiting for something. That is when he senses the stillness in her.

And then, as he walks, he remembers the moose-hide moccasins and lined mittens with the bright beadwork and puckered seams that he wore on the Little Abitibi. They were gifts from Mrs. Wishee, chewed and cured in the old way so that the comforting smell of woodsmoke never left them. Finn's mother kept them in the bottom of her winter trunk, hidden from the light like buried memories.

Suddenly Finn wants to get back home and take them out of storage.

When he is home again, he kicks off the boots and carefully hangs the parka on its hanger. The house is filled with the rich smells of cooking. As he walks into the living room, he sees his father standing at the window, looking out across the lake.

"Hi, Dad," says Finn, as he walks over to him. He glances around. "Where's Michael?"

"I wore him out getting the tackle ready. We're going out on the ice tomorrow."

"Mother?"

"Putting on her face for this evening," says his father. He looks at Finn. "How was the walk?"

"Good."

"You wore my parka?" asks the old man.

"Yes."

"Warm?"

"Yes."

"Your mother wants to give it away," his father says. "I've had it twenty years. They don't make them like that any more. She's cleaning house."

"I'd like to take that old parka," says Finn.

His father nods. "Good," he says. "It's a good coat, same color as the army issue when I came home, good in the bush. Take care of it." He looks at Finn hard, then says, "How are you, Son?"

"Good," says Finn.

"No bullshit, now. Are you taking care of business?"

Finn feels his eyebrow lift. "I'm trying."

His father chuckles. "I don't mean that. I mean taking care of the wife and kid. Being there."

"I'm trying," Finn says.

His father looks at him. "It's not easy," he says.

"I'm learning that," Finn says.

"You can't bring who you are in the woods or who you were in the war inside your house. It's a different mission."

"I know," says Finn.

"It's just another kind of soldiering," his father says.

"More like undercover work with another kind of casualty."

"Surviving isn't free, Son, and having a family, or not having one, comes at a price. You made the choice and have to define your mission and know what your tactics will be. How you will behave. If you're conscious of those facts, Finn, then your acts are deliberate. They have direction, purpose, and you won't fly off the handle for no apparent reason."

"Thanks."

"There's no goddam excuse for collateral damage in the family, Finn."

"Dad, one way or another, you're gong to screw up."

"You have to minimize it, Finn. That's all you can do."

"I'm trying," says Finn.

"Not hard enough," says his father with the old flash. "Jesus Christ, if you can stay alive for as long as you did in Vietnam, you can be here for your son. And get Phil out of the picture."

"You're right," says Finn.

"Lara's the asset, Finn. If you lose her, you lose your son."

"Christ," says Finn.

"And read your Buddhist stuff about centering yourself. All those damned books that sit on the shelves with the pretty bindings. You talk the talk. Your mother's right. The time comes when you have to live what you believe, not just yap about it."

"Okay."

"All right. Not to be a hard-ass about it." He lifts his chin in the direction of where little Michael is downstairs. "That's our mission," he says. "You don't want him to fall into what we did."

"I know," says Finn.

The older man puts his hand on Finn's shoulder and squeezes. "I wasn't able to protect you from it, Finn. You have to do better."

"Okay, Dad. I know you have my back."

His father nods and says, "Now let's say no more about it and enjoy the holiday."

Finn walks into the kitchen and considers another drink, thinking that, physical or not, his father's presence in the parka is more than a haunting, and he makes a martini with the ice from the freezer. Then he walks back to the living room and sits down. He leans forward.

"I think Mum may be losing it," he says quietly. He sips his martini and picks the small pieces of cork from his tongue.

"Losing what?" asks his father.

"Her mind. I think maybe she's getting a little odd." He looks warily towards the bedroom.

"Oh?" His father lifts his hand from the window sill and turns around.

"What's this upside-down container thing in the refrigerator?" Finn says.

"She's been doing that for years," says his father.

"What about food poisoning?" Finn asks.

"She hasn't died yet," says his father.

"What a concept. Air turning into a vacuum. She said Sarah Cohen told her."

"Yup."

"Sarah's in the advanced stages of dementia, for God's sake. She's in a nursing home."

"Right."

"Why don't you clean it out?"

The older man looks appraisingly at Finn and raises an eyebrow. "It's her refrigerator. She guards it like the arc of the covenant."

"You eat the food she serves out of it."

"Hasn't killed me yet. It's no worse than c-rations."

"What the hell? Why didn't you tell this to me before?"

"Why?" his father asks.

"Before I started eating the food in there."

"Oh."

"Are you trying to be thick?"

The old man turns away and laughs. "I'm pulling your leg," he says. "The food's fine."

Finn breathes deeply, and fingers his drink on the table.

"Where's Lara?" he asks.

"Downstairs getting dressed," says his father.

Then the bedroom door opens and Finn's mother steps out. Her hair is dazzling white. She's highlighted her face with lipstick and rouge and put on a red blouse. Her skirt is black and her shoes are red. "You look great," says Finn, and she does. "Would you like a beer?"

"Sure," she says and sits down opposite them.

Finn stands and walks into the kitchen, filling his lungs as deeply as he can. He retrieves a beer from the refrigerator.

"How do you make your martinis?" his mother calls in to him.

"Just a shot and a half of gin, a half-shot of vermouth, and an olive or two," he says. "I like them wet."

As he opens the beer and pours it into a pilsner glass, he can hear the mutter of talk from the other room and Lara's tread on the basement stairs. There is a question Finn does not hear as she passes through the living room and enters the kitchen. She opens the refrigerator door.

"Did you spill something in here?" she asks. "It smells like an old tomb."

"Oh?" says Finn.

"How has Mother been?" she whispers.

"Fine," says Finn. "Why?"

"We talked while you were out. She said I always have my nose in a book, reading, that it could ruin me."

"Oh?"

"You must have noticed."

"Oh?"

"Don't be obtuse."

"I'm not obtuse," he says.

"You are," she says. "Of course you noticed her watching. She still thinks I'm keeping you from moving back north."

"Yes," says Finn, "that's what she thinks."

"In her mind, I also tempted you from going back into the seminary when you got back from Vietnam. Why is that still coming up after all these years?"

"That's her world view," says Finn. "The vision thing. She's trying to put her ducks in a row."

"And she's all over the manitou thing more and more," Lara goes on, "though she keeps it quiet. Your father goes along with it, too. We've talked about it. He has some books on it. Interesting." She purses her mouth and looks thoughtfully off to the side. Then she looks back to Finn and lifts her chin. "But really, Finn, think about the world filled with little gods waiting to be appeased."

"Maybe that's part of the problem," says Finn. "The appeasement. But Dad thinks of them as a kind of friendly metaphor. Of course, with him, he had a head start with a history of leprechauns. Anyway, I've given up trying to understand her. I love her, but she's totally beyond me. Primordial. Like the manitous she speaks about."

"She sounds a little strange when she does that. It's like chanting."

"Well," says Finn, "some of our best friends are a little strange," suddenly thinking of The Doors. He hums a few bars of their song, "Strange" to her. "Don't let it ruin the party," he says.

Lara looks at him askance, then at the ice tray in front of Finn. "You're turning into quite the comic. And what's that?" she asks.

"Ice," he says.

"What are those things in the ice?"

"Corks," he says.

She looks at them closely. "What are they doing there?"

Finn raises an eyebrow. "They keep the cubes from freezing together, Sweetheart. Didn't you know that?" He swallows a gulp of martini.

She laughs, lifts a large chunk of ice and corks fused together, and holds it out to him. "Would you like this in your martini?" she asks. "Or …" She reaches out and hooks his belt with a finger, then pulls. He laughs.

"What's going on in there?" his mother calls.

"Nothing," he calls back." Then he turns to Lara. "Stop turning me on."

"How about a martini?" she says. "Will you make me one?"

"Yes," says Finn. "Let me take this to Mum." He walks with the beer to the living room and comes back. "Dad wants one too," he says. "What about Michael? A Dr. Pepper?"

"He's napping," says Lara.

Finn takes the drink into the living room, gives it to his father and raises his glass. He looks at his father as he makes the toast. The older man's eyes are large and very fine. Finn looks into them rather than at them and thinks how good they are when they open up and their color lightens with laughter.

Then Lara walks into the room with her martini. Finn feels a little toasted and glances quickly at his mother. He walks to the window and looks over the lake toward the Manitou Islands, hidden in the snow. His father walks over and stands beside him. After a few minutes, Finn turns to him.

"Well?" he says.

His father says, "Bring little Michael up here so I can read *Peter Rabbit* to him."

Finns turns to the room. His mother pats Lara's leg and says to her, "You and Michael talk. I have a few things to take care of."

Finn watches his father walk over and sit beside Lara. He sets his martini down and picks up a book.

"What did you think?" he asks, tapping the cover. Lara brings her hand to her chin and tilts her head as she begins to talk, and Finn is struck with the fact that these two people have such similar gestures. He's never really noticed it before. Peas in a pod, he thinks. His father is looking at her with his own hand on his chin. It's both touching and comical.

Finn looks to his mother and sees she is watching him, gauging. Her smile is ironic and she shakes her head. Finn looks back, and sees the two book lovers talking about philosophy over martinis, looks back to his mother, and laughs. He gets it.

He walks to the head of the stairs. His mother follows and turns into the coat closet. She opens the door and takes out the parka Finn wore earlier.

"What are you doing?" asks Finn.

"Throwing out your father's old coats. He's had them forever and I've wrapped up new ones for him under the tree."

"There's nothing wrong with these," says Finn. "He likes these coats."

"It's time for new ones," says his mother.

"Why?"

"It just is," she says.

Finn looks at her closely. "You're keeping all those old decorations, and all that spoiled food in the refrigerator, but throwing out Dad's parka. What's that all about?" he asks.

"I need the room," she says.

"Well, don't throw them away. I like this parka, and this windbreaker, and I want them."

"Fine," she says, "but don't let your father see until he opens his presents. And clean them before you go."

"Why" Finn asks.

"They smell," she says. Then she looks at him.

"Listen," says Finn, "I was thinking about the moccasins that Mrs. Wishee made for us. Where are they?"

She looks at him suddenly keen, measuring God knows what, thinks Finn. Then she says, "What do you want those old things for?" but Finn gets the sense that what she is really saying is: "Speak to me of these things, and show me who you are."

"Well, they're as old as that little Santa," says Finn, "and I remember wearing them every winter until we moved south. And the moosehide mitts. I was thinking on the walk that they're the clearest things I remember about those times, I mean as far as clothes go."

"Well, that's because I kept them," she says, "and took them out once every winter to remind you. Some things you keep, and some things you don't."

"Those days seems so clear," says Finn. "Uncomplicated, I guess. It must be that way with most people."

"No," she says, "I don't think it is. The things that stay strong in your memory have a special meaning. Good or bad."

"I miss those times," says Finn.

She looks at him, again appraisingly. "You were a very self-sufficient little boy. You had a trap line—that's what you called it—when you were in fourth grade and would be gone for hours at a time in the bush by yourself."

"Dad taught me a lot about being in the bush," Finn says

She looks at Finn and nods. "I miss your father being in the bush," she says. "I miss the camping trips up river. Remember the time at the Red Sucker River when he and the dog got into a hornet's nest, and they both ran back to the river? Your father ran faster than the dog and didn't jump off the rocks—he just kept on running through the air and hit the river running with the cloud of hornets right behind him." She laughs and the tears gather in her eyes. "God, I miss that," she says. "It was beautiful to see him run. And the time he called the moose right to the front door of the cabin, and the moose lay down in front of the steps and wouldn't move until the next morning? And all the times in the boat when he brought us home in the dark, knowing where the rocks were, boating down the river until we could see the lights on the dam, with you asleep on the tarp beside me. It was like the land was part of him then. Before we came south and he started working in an office."

She looks at him closely. "Do you miss hunting?" she asks.

"No," he says. Though he was good with a rifle, Finn had not hunted much even as a boy because of his father's stories on the walks. He'd come to feel personally about the animals, and he had no need to hunt except for food. He'd grown up in the bush and was a good tracker and a fair shot, but he'd never felt hunting was a sport. It was just killing. He'd learned that before the war. He tracked other hunters to test himself then too, and they never knew he was there, so he had no patience for them or what they did. Tracking was easy and there was no need to come home empty-handed when you needed food.

"But I miss the wild food. Remember how the forest was filled with things to eat? Besides the berries in season that everyone knew about, there were Miner's lettuce and wild carrot. Michael doesn't know about these things because he grew up in a city. I feel bad about that."

"He knows other things," his mother says.

"Yes," says Finn, "but not what we needed to know. He doesn't know the green tips and roots of cattails can be cooked and eaten, or that the roots can be dried and ground into flour. He doesn't know that the leaves contain pure water, or that the stuff of ripe cattail tops can be fluffed up and used like down against the cold. He doesn't know that dandelion leaves can be cooked and eaten like spinach, or that the roots can be roasted and steeped to make tea, or that tea from pine needles is rich with Vitamin C, or that the slippery bark of willows contains salicylic acid, like aspirin, and is medicinal. There's Fireweed, fiddleheads, Arrowhead, Goldenrod, Groundnuts, Mallow, Watercress, Thistle, Violet, and Pigweed to be eaten."

Finn's mother laughs. "And the mushrooms were everywhere– Morels, Shaggy Manes, Chicken of the Woods, Horse Mushrooms, and Scaly Hedgehogs. You loved those cooked in butter."

"And most of the meat was brought home by Dad, the grouse and duck and geese, and moose," he says. "I don't miss the hunting," he says again, "but I miss those things. And fishing. The tackle and the peace and the calmness on the water. There's no talking then. Being in the stillness with the water and the sounds of the water and the birds is enough, and being alone in the boat with Michael, who's quiet too. I like that. Michael enjoys the stillness and doesn't have to work at it. He seems to be able to move beyond the quiet into his own solitude."

"He's like you and your father," say Finn's mother. "Of course, your father was different before the war. He was a real doll. Outgoing, and a wonderful voice. He loved to dance. He never sang afterwards, until now, with little Michael."

And Finn thinks of the afternoon his son spent with his grandfather, getting the gear ready for ice-fishing.

He looks up and sees his mother watching him closely. Then she smiles, and Finn has the feeling that on some level, what she's been doing to the ornaments on the tree, she's doing to him, only he doesn't know what she's attaching him to.

"That's our story," she says. "He'll make his own. Times change."

"Those places aren't there any more," says Finn. "The houses are gone and so is the life style."

"The forest is still there," his mother says. "And the things in it. That's something you can show your son."

Finn turns and goes down the stairs and walks into the bedroom. Michael is lying on the bed with his eyes open, watching Finn as he enters. "Let's go up and get ready for supper," says Finn. Grandpa wants to read with you while we set the table."

When they get to the top of the stairs, Finn's mother is still in the closet.

"Michael, run in to Grandpa and let him read. I'll be right there," Finn says. Michael scampers off, and Finn turns to his mother. "Mum?" he says.

"Are you keeping track of things?" she asks.

"Sure," says Finn. He glances across the room to Lara but avoids looking at her too long.

"I have, since before you were born," she says, "and I've saved the little woolen cap and booties I knitted for you while I was waiting for you to come along. Some day, they'll be yours."

Finn doesn't know what to say. He looks at his mother and nods.

"But you're not ready yet," she says. Finn wonders what man is ever ready for the little woolies of his babyhood.

"I couldn't join your father right away before you were born, and I'd sit on the roof of the tenement with the other pregnant women, and we'd knit clothes for when our babies would arrive."

"I didn't know that," Finn says.

He looks across the room to his father, sitting in a chair, with Michael on his lap. The older man is obviously trying hard not to listen to them, squirming a little, and the boy is reading Thornton W. Burgess stories to his grandfather from the same books the old man read to Finn thirty years earlier: Sammy the Blue Jay, Peter Rabbit, Reddy the Fox–all the little manitous of Finn's childhood and woods. Occasionally his father interrupts the reading with a question. "What happens next?" or "Are you sure that's what happens?" The boy is solicitous on his grandfather's knee, as though reading to a child, and the old man is clearly enjoying it.

Then Finn looks at Lara, who looks up from her book and meets his gaze. She looks right into him, raises one eyebrow, and smiles.

He lifts his head slightly and turns towards the kitchen. "The turkey smells done," he says to his mother. "I'll mash the potatoes and set the table. Then we can eat."

"Put it out to set, and your father can carve it," his mother says.

The dinner is a bright oasis. There are the rich colors Finn loves at a meal. There is red wine and white, hot bread and sweet butter. There is turkey and stuffing with cranberry, orange yams in a casserole, baked apples and green beans, mashed potatoes with gravy made from the turkey drippings. There is music and laughter around the table, and with the heapings of food, there are generous portions of understanding. There is communion, thinks Finn, and for the moment, there is only the moment.

When they are done, they sit satiated around the table, an old oak relic his father has sanded and varnished more times than Finn can count.

"I'm going outside for a bit," Finn says, "to look at the snow."

"Go," Lara says. Finn looks at her and nods. Her look is articulate. "We'll talk more later," it says.

"A white Christmas," he says, and he thinks of the northern folk at one with the snows, their buried lives rich and discretely coiled as they drive around with shovels and bags of sand in their cars, waiting for spring.

He walks outside to look at the lake. The world is a white orb. The sky is dark, but the bright snow covers his feet. He pulls the coat tight and looks out to where the Manitous sleep. A flame brightens and fades as the flurries shift, and Finn realizes someone is tending an unexpected fire by a fishing shack far out, looking down a dark hole in the ice. The small figure flickers in front of the fire, and the fish below will be swimming up to the oculus and the light therein.

Finn looks back to the light of the kitchen window. His mother is at the counter, and her shoulders shake slightly.

His father and Lara sit laughing at the table. His mother turns and speaks. Finn reads her lips, and she is saying what she has always said. "Oh, Michael."

She laughs. She speaks. Finn reads her lips, and she is saying his father's name. And then she laughs, and Finn reads the words "You damned fools!" and she laughs again. Then little Michael walks to her and wraps his arms around her waist. She wipes her eyes and looks up and out the window and smiles, and Finn knows they have sailed the frail but serviceable little boats back to one another, back to the country they all know.

At first Finn believes his mother can't see him in the dark, but she waves, and he realizes he is standing in a noose of light falling from her to him through the window. Her eyes are bright, and it thrills him to look at them. Her laughter falls faintly through the glass. She lifts a martini high as though giving a sacrament, gesturing for him to return, and Finn realizes she has been at the counter making the drink for him. It has been a long time since she has mixed a martini. "I'll be right there," he says, but the snow muffles his voice, so he waves and nods and stands looking at her for a minute longer.

The wind picks up on the lake, and Finn thinks of the waters beneath the ice lying thick until the spring.

He looks up into the falling snow but cannot glimpse the hard stars or the seas of the moon. His mother's laughter comes again, and, he thinks of his father and how he must have loved that sound as a young man. What bright stars and moons lit up the skies of his father, he wonders.

He focuses on the snowflakes falling out of the night, slowly at first and then in a dizzying rush as they touch his eyes and melt there, and their cold reaches through the naked white coverings of his eyes to the marrow of his bones, and he thinks that the end may come like this, with a little shiver and surprise and a rush of immediacy.

But then, he thinks, perhaps beginnings start like this too, as he steps out of the light through the darkness and in through the door.

## CHAPTER TWENTY

# The Eggshells of His Mind

June 1991

Though it is spring up on the lake, Finn is down in London wrapping up the term, slogging through the pile of student papers that mark the passing of another academic year. He is more and more aware of the passage of time. He wonders whether he is moving through it, or with it. At any rate, it's accelerating, despite the long, slow toothache of grading themes. Finn looks up from his desk and out through the window to the back yard. The cherry tree is beginning to bloom. Soon, he thinks, he will get away to the woods, wrapping up his years of fighting fires with one last quick trip to evaluate the recovery patterns of a burn three years ago: the Fire Regime. Then this particular tour will be over. He will have to submit to the demands of his wife and son and put aside the old ways.

Years ago, when Michael was born, his father said, "Son, when you have a family, a part of your life is over," and Finn had refused to understand. The idea of giving up flying was impossible, and even now Finn feels the resentment and anger building inside him. A part of himself will disappear, a part that has always been the most private of places, a sanctuary and a way of being in the world, a connection whose immediacy was epiphanic, beyond thought and fear, purely of the moment: satori, the pure joy of flight. Without it, life will be a plodding through time. This will be his sentence: to be partially alive, to be partially Finn, to be a man who dwells in the deep tectonics of memory. Eventually, that hidden land will become formless, and there will be nothing inside him except what was. He will be a hidden man, but now the thought of piloting the Bell 204 into the recovery area and reporting on the land healing itself, the notion of the fresh air and solitude, buoys him.

He bows his head and picks up his pen. Suddenly, while grading these final essays on the lives of the poets, something like a thought strikes him, and he looks up from his desk and out the window to the lawn as a small, grey cloud blooms in the corner of his left eye, moves quickly across the field of his seeing, and leaves him blind. He sits upright, stiff, cautious, observing the gloom, oddly detached though acutely aware that the end, his end, is present, is palpable, a real thing, but before he falls into darkness, the cloud passes and he looks again through the window to the green grass. The grass is clear now, sharp and strange, and sunlight coats the trees in light like an amber honey. He blinks at its beauty. Satori. Found in a new place. Seconds later, a numb tingling drops like a curtain down the left side of his face. This is it, he thinks, dead on a pile of ungraded freshman papers. He takes half a dozen quick steps to the bathroom, swallows three aspirin with a gulp of water, gargles some mouthwash, picks up his keys and phone, and walks out the door. He decides not to call his wife or an ambulance. The ambulance would be too noisy, cause too much fuss, and leave too many questions to answer should he return home still able to speak. Worse if he could not. He imagines his neighbors, strangers really, pained, aghast, staring as his mouth and his lips struggle to form words of conversation from him, a prisoner locked in his mind looking out. He feels small beads of sweat pop from his forehead at the thought, and these sad bubbles are as close as he will ever get to anything like having Athena's springing from the brow of Zeus. Life is so much less than we imagine, he thinks. He watches his mind race, amazed at its racing volubility.

He says, aloud, "Athena" as he approaches his car, and calls up a handful of her forebears' names, Ieptus, Atlas, Mnemosyne, Cronos, Oceanus, but they are pushed aside by the Medusa writhing in his brain, engineering a gestation whose birth will spell his end.

The other options are no better. He opens the door. Lara or the neighbor would be mooing vessels of hysteria, their overweening concern a thin skin over their own panic. Rather than calm, they would heighten his blood pressure and trigger another stroke. His last sensations: a high-pitched lamentation of "Oi vey! Oi vey!" coming from the neighbor, or worse, wails of woe and abandonment from Lara. His exit from the world would be riddled with guilt. Such are his fears, so he grips the steering wheel, dials his doctor, starts the car, pulls into the road, and hits the send button.

"Hello, Doctor Tilley's office." It is the receptionist.

"I'd like to speak to the doctor," says Finn.

"May I take a message?"

"It's an emergency."

"He's not available right now."

"It's important. I need to talk to him."

"He's not available. May I have him call you back?"

"Tell him this is Finn MacBride. I'm having a stroke and driving myself to the hospital. He has my number." There is a small gasp on the other end of the line. Then he hangs up, somehow mollified.

There may be no clean getaway this time, he thinks. Somehow, the thought is calming. As he drives, he looks for likely places to pull over and fade quietly out of the traffic and life should the lightnings come. He's waited too long, he thinks, and has not said to Michael what he needed to hear. What Finn needed to say. Thank God Michael is not at home. No need for him to see this. Better to crawl off into the trees and die alone than have a bunch of family gawk at you while you're croaking.

"Son-of-a-bitch," he mutters. He thought he'd go out in flight. In action.

Outside the car window, bright meadows flash past, small roadside patches of greenery aglow with dappled light. It's beautiful. Finn scans the sky for clouds and sees none.

He is surprised and chagrined that it is happening like this, for he has a fear and loathing of public, messy deaths. He thinks of a friend who died of a heart attack in the middle of an airport while running to catch a flight, her most personal and final moments thrashed out before a thousand gawking strangers, but he realizes now that he may have very little say in the matter. As he drives, he thinks fast and hard because he does not trust the time he has left. He will never trust it again.

Ahead, just around the corner, he can see the hospital set on a rise overlooking the town, and on the building's lower level, facing him as he follows the road's curve through the green grass, he sees the broad, glass doors of the Emergency entrance. He pulls over and parks, keeping the sight-lines clear as he exits the car and stands on the lip of the lawn. The doors ahead are closed and dark. Before him, the world is luminous and lambent. Then Finn steps carefully onto the bright meadow and begins to walk, babying the broken eggshells of his mind.

## Chapter Twenty-One

# Fahrenheit II: the Fire Regime

July 1991

A month later, Finn is alive and feeling like a fool. His stroke turned out to be the onset of silent migraines.

The scene in the emergency room had not been good. The nurse called Lara, and she arrived just in time to hear the prognosis.

"Not a stroke?" she asked.

"No," said the nurse.

Finn said nothing.

"A silent migraine?" asked Lara.

"Yes," said the nurse.

Finn scratched his head.

"But Finn," Lara said, "you thought you were having a stroke and didn't call me? You drove yourself to the hospital without calling me?"

"No time," said Finn, looking at the floor and seeing nothing but his feet. He wanted to say, "SOP, dammit."

"You would have broken my heart," said Lara.

"Sorry," said Finn. "It was a field call."

"That should have included calling me," said Lara. "And anyone else close enough to help."

"To hell with Phil, that son-of-a-bitch. There is no way I was going to have him in on this. I don't trust him." But even as the words spill out, he knows it is Lara he doesn't trust.

"I meant a neighbor," said Lara. "Calm down. I mean, this is not only about you."

"Well, yes it is. Sorry," said Finn. Then he stood up and Lara moved quickly to hold his arm. "Lara," said Finn, "I'm not an invalid." And they left together, his hand in hers.

"You silly ass," she said.

It is a scene that plays itself over and over, and Finn can't make it play right. He behaved selfishly on one hand, but dying had always seemed to him to be a private affair, best done alone under a tree.

Since then, he's had an episode every week, but unlike his father whose headaches kept him in a dark room for two days, Finn learns he has "silent migraines". The only symptoms are the aura: bright little lightnings of blues and violets at the edges of his vision, then a grey curtain of blindness, then finally a world whose light clings to objects like a holy honey. It's wonderful, but it worries him. He doesn't want to think that it's some higher entity calling, because whenever he thinks that way, it's Father Callaghan's long, horsey face he sees.

Right now, as he guides the Bell 204 over the northern knolls of the forest, gliding, soaring, pushing the limits of the little chopper, reveling in the signature *whump-whump-whump* of the blades that can be heard miles away, small lightnings flash out from the corners of his eyes telegraphing the world beyond. These are the scintillating scotoma, he now knows, a flickering alteration in the field of vision. So much of life is about seeing, he thinks. The pages from the medical journal describing the symptoms flash before his eyes. "The scotoma usually start near the center of the field of vision and spread out to the sides with zigzagging lines. Sensory aura are the second most common symptom of migraines, occurring in thirty to forty percent of people. Often a feeling of pins-and-needles begins in the hand and arm on one side and spreads to the nose-mouth area on the same side. Numbness occurs after the tingling has passed." And yet, mystic that he is, he's beginning to relish these episodes, ready for anything from a simple final blackout to a stream of Hebrew flame-script into his third eye.

Finn tears his mind away from the lines of data and focuses on the instrument panel in front of him. The pages on migraines are not a flight plan nor a manual. Still, the old thrill dances in his stomach as he flies the chopper reflexively, like an extension of himself, the controls and panels unchanged since he flew these machines in Vietnam: Helicopter

Utility vehicles, HU-1, with the big Iroquois engines, the first chopper to use a turbine thrust and the model that lasted the longest, out of production for years but still in service. He loves this machine as though it were a living thing.

It is the second summer since the burn, and his last mission. He flies over a land with no roads, above little black lakes cupped in the trees like the deep parts of people that never see the light, little primordial gardens of the self that stay hidden. Finn imagines that such inner places produce the spiritual equivalent of the oxygen we breathe, that perhaps the soul is a little seed in that garden, for the seminary has never left him.

Further north lies Lake Abitibi, headwaters of the Little Abitibi River flowing through the tundra to the Moose River and Hudson Bay and the northern seas. But here and now, the trees are seamless and forever, filling the empty arms of the long-gone seas, covering mountains worn to their roots by the gnawing glaciers, and carpeting the old rift valleys that ruck and line the land. Finn looks out over the taiga, one of the last and largest boreal forests on the planet, a sanctuary for the least compromised and unique ecosystems left. A final refuge. This is the land that seeped its minerals into his bones. It is not only that he loves the land, he thinks, but that he belongs to it. He is made of it, and his brain is formed by its topography, and the deep fissures of his mind mirror its landmarks. The forest is the one place he is never lost.

Now, Finn navigates the chopper through the hills and over the meadows. As he flies, he looks for changes in the land below. A tentative hint of green among the blackened trees marks the spot. The lyricism of the land calls him, familiar and close, and it brings Hopkins' poetry to mind. Every forest has its fire regime, he thinks, 'Where weeds in wheels shoot long and lovely and lush'.

He will meet his father and son the next morning and fly them into this burn area to show them what he sees: the shimmering recovery amidst the ash. But today the copse is his to catalogue and to wander in. He will walk the earth, and the soles of his feet will tread the green path over the shadows of death.

Finn is up and sipping coffee by the canteen window at six a.m. He watches the gravel road stretching from the base into the forest, looking for his father's faded red truck. Finally, he spies a faint dust plume over the trees. It will be the two Michaels, he thinks, so he stands, gulps down the last of the coffee, grimaces, and walks out onto the pavement to wait.

The plume grows closer, and the pickup rounds the last corner out of the forest and makes for the runway. Finn waves and directs them to where he is standing. As the truck gets closer, Finn can pick out the two figures behind the windshield. He blows out hard and walks forward to meet them.

Once the truck stops, the passenger door swings open and Michael jumps out and runs hard. Finn opens his arms wide and scoops the boy high and hugs him. Michael buries his face in Finn's neck, and Finn laughs.

"It's good to see you too," he says. Finn watches his father in the truck, sitting, Finn knows, to give the boy a moment with him. Then the old man slowly opens the door, steps to the tarmac, and walks towards the two of them. Finn puts the boy down, steps to his father and hugs him.

"How was the drive?" Finn asks.

"Beautiful," says his father. "We started in the dark and watched the sunrise." He looks down at Michael. "I had no idea this one was so full of facts."

"Grandpa asked me about fishing Lake Nipissing," says Michael, "and I told him."

Finn laughs. His father looks up and says, "So, what's the plan for today?" Finn looks into his father's eyes, and sees, deep within them, the old warrior now playing the part of the benign grandfather. Jesus Christ, he thinks, the old man is relentless.

"I've secured a couple of bunks for you," he says, "so we can take our time today, have supper, and turn in when we want. We'll have breakfast in the canteen, and I'll introduce you to the mechanics and some of the teams. I'll have to take a crew out tomorrow, but today, you'll be my team. You'll see what we do. Tomorrow, you'll be on your own to explore the base area and talk to the mechanics for a while. We'll pack up when I get back around fifteen hundred, have supper, and turn in. The next morning, we'll head home together. I wanted to wrap this up with you two here. We'll close down the mission together." Finn's father nods slowly and looks towards the trees.

"But we should move out pretty quick this morning while things are cool and calm," Finn goes on. "The target is thirty minutes out. Let's make the pit stops, pick up the packed lunches, and head out." Finn keeps his hand on Michael's shoulder as he talks.

"Good," says his father. "Let's do that. What's the agenda?"

"First, we'll be looking for a particularly green area towards the edge of the burned area. Then, we'll land and walk around to inventory what's growing. That way we can gauge how quickly the forest will recover."

"Fair enough. Let's get the gear and visit the can," says the old man.

"This way," says Finn.

When they return and stow the gear, Finn looks them over. "Ready?" he asks.

"How will we know what we're seeing, Dad?" Michael asks.

"I'll show you along the way."

The old man steps into the helicopter bay. Finn lifts Michael into the seat beside his grandfather.

"Let's strap in," he says.

"Here, let me buckle you up," the old man says. Finn nods and watches. When Michael's straps are fastened, his grandfather secures his own. Finn checks them.

"Good," he says. Then he moves to the front. Seated and secure, he cranes around for a last look at the two behind him.

"All set?" he asks.

"Set," says his father.

Finn sees that Michael has reached out to his grandfather, his little hand cupped in the weathered hand of his namesake. Finn notices their veins, tracking the same path from thumb to forefinger. Then he turns to look ahead and sees his own hand on the steering column, sees the pattern repeated in the map of his veins. He lifts his gaze to the instruments for a final check.

"Mmph," he says.

Once they are aloft and over the burn, the shimmer of new foliage appears like a faint mirage, caught in the corner of his eye as he guides the chopper among the trees. The morning rain has wet the ash on the forest floor enough to keep it down under the downdraft of the blades. The canopy is bare, like the trees in Vietnam stripped by agent. Now, instead of NVA and infantry running over the bare ground, it is the deer that have no place to hide.

He flies the chopper high for reconnaissance. The controls are an extension of his hands and feet and he feels the body of the Huey like his own, feels the sheering forces of the wind, the speed, the weight of the machine and momentum and mass, all in balance and motion, dancing to the notes of lift and weight, pitch and yaw, thrust and drag. Finn and the wind are locked in an embrace, invisible and sustaining, and the dance is the element Finn thinks in, the place his body calls home.

When Finn sees the target ahead, a grove of scorched birch trees, he comes in fast and low, slows the chopper abruptly above the copse, balancing the thrust and drag, the lift and the weight, all going into the reflexes to keep the craft in step with the wind. Finn works the pedals, pushing down hard on the right pedal to increase the yaw and bring the tail around, pointing the craft in the direction they will head home, pulls back on the collective to ramp down the attack pitch on the rotors, twists the throttle and hovers, yaws the tail around and drops fast between the trees to settle on the turf.

Then he throws his head back and laughs. "We're here!" he says.

"Christ!" says his father. "I had no idea you were such a cowboy."

"We're in the woods now, Dad. Not in the home. We don't have to pretend."

Finn turns, and little Michael is looking at him with an expression Finn has not seen before. His eyes are wide with seeing. His father's eyes have the same expression. Finn laughs again. They are seeing him, Finn realizes. A buried land has shifted into the viewing of his father and his son, an island's tip that briefly lifts above the sea into the light of day, for this is the way new countries come, slowly and with false starts.

"Let's see what's here," he says and unbuckles. He steps out, pauses, and looks out to the trees and thinks of the cool sap flowing through the plants in the tight-woven fabric of life that make the taiga. The Holy

Ghost over the bent world broods, he thinks. He misses the forest, but it was coming.

He turns, unbuckles Michael, and lifts him out onto the ground, and begins his cataloguing aloud to Michael and his father.

"Here's what we'll be doing,' he says, "what to look for as we check out the recovery from this fire. We'll use the data to help understand the fire regime."

"The what?"

Finn slows down and looks at Michael. He squats. "The Fire Regime. Every forest has it's own Fire Regime, Michael, a cycle or pattern of the types of fires that occur. It's the order of the burns. The plants in a forest adapt to the fires. They depend on the types and frequencies of them. Some plants can't live without it. The cones on Black Spruce trees only open after there's been a fire, so the seeds couldn't spread without the flames. Once the fire has passed, it leaves behind a number of different habitat patches, or little areas where the plants can grow again. Different plants and animals specialize in thriving in those areas at different stages, and because the different types of fire creates these different types of patches, fires actually allow a greater number of species to exist within a landscape. It's not a matter of rising from the ashes; it's a matter of the fire releasing the potential for growth. In other words …"

"Different strokes for different folks," says Michael. "I get it, Dad. That's why there are blueberries on one patch and strawberries in another patch."

"Something like that," says Finn. "That's what we'll be looking at today. Let's start walking."

"Tell us exactly what we're looking for, Finn," says his father.

Then Finn automatically intones the order of recovery, thinking ahead to what will be happening here now and next year as the grasses and herbaceous plants return.

"*Fireweed, or Great Willow-herb, is among the first flowers to appear in the scorched earth. It is a perennial herbaceous plant in the family Onagraceae, preferring slightly acidic soils of open field. A fire provides both. It is native to the boreal forests of Canada. It is named for its abundance on the burnt lands.*

"*Then come the pioneer species and the secondary succession, the rhizomes buried deep in earth and safe beneath the fires that raged above. Willows and* wild rose and Iris whose green blades push through the ash and erupt in blue and purples.

"After the grasses come the larch, new life sprouting from the burnt trunks, then the aspen and birch whose seeds are winged and the conifers whose seeds are waxed while the fireweed still floats on parachutes of fine fluff.

"Then, the roots and woody rhizomes of Velvet Leaf Blueberry and common raspberries grip the land and sweetening it with fruit and honey. Then Sasparilla and Mayberry.

"Finally, the strawberries creep in, little plants tolerant of the moisture levels unless very wet or dry, that survive mild fires and establish themselves after extreme ones. The diminutive, succulent fruit of the taiga.

"The Fire Regime quickens the lives that depend on it. It opens the hard shells of the spirit. It animates its own ashes."

The sounds he speaks are a sermon that soothes him and takes him away from the thinking. The words he has read become images that move across his vision as though on a celluloid reel. They are the words of a genesis; they are his incantation to resurrection.

He leads his father and his son through the trees.

"The recovery will be slow," he says.

They walk the green meadows and speak of what will come as though their words were a blessing, and each listens, one to the other.

## CHAPTER TWENTY-TWO

# Leveraging

December 1997

It is December in North Bay and twenty below. As hard as Finn tries to move north, the winters beat them back to London and the university. Two weeks at Christmas over the break is as much as Lara can stand.

"Will spring ever come?" she wonders aloud each winter. That it will, is one article of Canadian faith that buoys up his psyche as surely as the granite of the great Shield supports the land.

But Finn is manic. His son drives beside him, steering the Volkswagen Beetle that is his today. Outside the car, lies the frozen country. Behind them, bouncing down the road, rolls the quarrel over breakfast with Lara. *"He's too young for his own car,"* she said. *"Rubbish,"* said Finn. *"He's only sixteen,"* she said. *"Old enough,"* said Finn, *"to drive himself to his own destinations. God knows,"* he said, *"it's a relief to let him pick up his own girlfriend and not me doing it every Saturday night." "You're doing this thing to get at me and your son,"* she said. *And he said, "Damn it Lara, stop nursemaiding the boy and let him go. You've ridden the two of us hard for sixteen years. I had a boat and rifle when I was twelve, and a trap line. The car will be good for him." "Is this just another way to be less involved?"* she asked. *"To leave your son on his own?"* Then she'd carved a silence like a hole in the air and jumped through it, leaving the words to spin round the inside of his head.

Finn recalls a line from seminary: "The silence roared displeasure."

But for now, he's in country, despite the cold. His mother's land, and then his father's, where the summer stars hang over the trees and the little lakes and streams lie tea'd with tannin; where the Little Abitibi, dun brown and gravid with silt, snakes its slow way to a northern sea; where frog eggs loop cat-tailed beaver ponds pin-pricked with stands of tamarack and fed by little brooks quick with trout. Where the light falls like spilt gold over Lara's skin. The soft honey of being alive. That's when Lara loves it best.

But Finn takes a savage delight in the winter when the Aurora Borealis shimmers green and red in the dark heavens and falls like curtains through a cold that splits the skin. Then, the bush is man-deep in drifts, the rivers paved with creaking ice, the air brittle as glass. Trees explode where the silent eye of wolf watches. The bulbs on old alcohol thermometers burst by cabin doors.

Finn scrapes the engine oil from a cuticle with his fingernail. It is six years since he gave up fighting fires. The small Volkswagon engine hums behind them, tuned by Finn this morning in his father's garage. It's not a Bell UH-1N Twin Huey, but fine-tuning the little motor keeps his fingers busy and his mind quiet.

"Michael," he says.

"What?"

"It's slipperier than hell. Slow down. It's what you can't see that can get you."

"It's fine, Dad."

"Don't be reckless." The irony of the warning is not lost on Finn.

"I'm not."

"It's twenty below and the road's a ribbon of ice," Finn says. The snow squeaks under the tires, and Finn sees the steering wheel stiff in his son's hands. He knows the boy has been taking lessons, but he doesn't trust it. Michael lacks the easy fit with the machine.

"Very poetic," says Michael.

"It won't be poetic to land in a ditch with our ass in the air and no help for thirty miles."

Michael meets his gaze briefly, then taps the brake pedal, a conciliatory gesture.

"No problem on the road," he says, but Finn detects the slip of rubber on ice, slight and thrilling. He raises a brow.

"Easy," he says, and looks ahead.

"Why are you so edgy?" Michael asks.

And Finn admits "Because I'm not behind the wheel." He does not say that it's all about being behind the wheel. That when you are, it doesn't matter if you crash and burn, so long as you have the controls and fight to the end. He feels a distant burn of anger in his belly.

The sun ricochets off the white road. Along the ditch, spruce trees edge the meadows, and the little clearings behind them break up and leak into the woods. Finn looks through the trees to the hard, blue sky.

Inside the car, the paint is grey and the air is hot. He tugs the earflaps of his hunter's cap, his father's loaner, and looks across at Michael's hat, a pincushion of red and black squares, senselessly Canadian and akin to no plaid known to man. He pats his own Celtic pattern of black and greens. But even with the flaps up, he sweats. He cranks the window down for a whiff of the cold as the car corners tight and brushes a freighted branch. He is watching himself behave like a fool, watching the words move over the surface of who he is, watching, in fact, the betrayal of self by self.

He's becoming unrecognizable to himself, but words pour out of his mouth in a banal stream. It's noise to still the silence inside and the demands from others. And will the years erode the hard edges of self, and his manner of being in the world change and be shaped by the trivial? he wonders.

Nevertheless, he is feeling freer with his son now that the boy is older, easier to talk to on some levels, easier to poke fun with. It's as though a lighter part of himself is reaching out to the boy, a part that will not reach out to anyone else, not even the boy's mother.

Something hard flies through the open window and onto the seat between his legs. "Jesus!" he says, and frantically brushes it forward onto the floor.

"What's wrong?" says Michael. "What was it?"

"No clue," says Finn, "but if it has teeth or a stinger, I don't want it down there."

Which brings Lara to mind. He thinks of the argument and her morning statement, a statement that bothers him now, speaking as it did to a consensus he does not like to consider: "Think about your responsibility as a father, Finn ..." the father he'd had and the one he'd wanted, put to him in terms of his own son by his wife posturing like a Delphic priestess. He pushes the talk from his mind, leans sideways and looks to the skies, ignoring Michael's laughter beside him.

"A pine cone," says his son. Finn glances at him. Sixteen years ago, and then Michael, and now the two of them here in a sea of snow.

"What goes into the making of a man?" he wonders, watching his son, this boy who was the product of the marriage and the muscling of two hearts. Lara's flesh made strange. Finn leans back, rests his head on the seat, and pushes his thoughts to the winds and the snows of his youth when his grandfather was still alive. The old man guarded his brogue as jealously as a new groom protected his wife. It influenced Finn as a boy, for when the old man spoke it was a spell-binding recitation. Even now, when Finn is in his cups, his grandfather's accent comes out. In fact, Finn was in his cups the previous night, and today the residue of the old man lingers in his mood and on his tongue, he suddenly realizes. Is he becoming garrulous? He paints in his mind a village house of stone and modest measure from whence the old man walked down the rolling roads to pubs set like gems in the green. A low fire there. Finn shuts his eyes to keep out the cold and keep in the scent of peat and past, for he loved the old man and loves the thought of a living line of men gnarled by love and work in the fields when the Church had its own Fathers standing each Sunday by the tall windows that caught the light and lit the saints while the sun hurled its spears into the glooms of the organ pipes.

The old dream takes him to a palace of light where laughter and longing pour in through the doors, but once inside the dream, Finn is looking for a woman who has disappeared with a daughter and he panics. Then he wakes and thinks about Lara.

"Now you're giving him a car and haven't taught him to drive," she said. "Five lessons. And that's your pattern. Never really present, moody, off in your own world—and your need for solitude. You've spent so much time on your own over the years, Finn, in the woods at night and in the early morning, and not enough with your son. With me. Not to mention your month away every summer. We used to talk so much more. The war ruined you." Ironically, Finn remembers his mother saying the same thing about getting an education. Ruined by different things for different people.

"That place ruined you, with all those ideas," his mother said. "You should have stayed home and worked for the Post Office."

But Finn remembers rising before his family even as a boy and making his own breakfast in the quiet of the house. He started this when he was seven; his mother set up the stove and plates for him the night before because he had been too small to reach the cupboards or even the stove top. She set out the heavy cast iron skillet on the front element and pushed a chair to the stove so he could get up to cook his eggs. He scrambled the eggs hard, cooking them like a flapjack, smothering the round disk with ketchup and eating the mess out of the pan. Then he would leave for the schoolyard to have the peace and solitude there before the others arrived to spoil it.

Finn loved the solitude so much then that he'd gone far into the woods for no other reason than to lie down and nap on the pine duff. He stretched his legs and looked up through the boughs while the breeze sang in the needles, and high, high above the small, white clouds raced.

He did this in summer and fall and he listened to life around him as he drifted off. He needed to be filled with something when he was a boy, and as a man he needed to heal, or forget when the times got bad. When he woke, he felt rested, and walked back home.

Since Vietnam, he did it often.

He did not tell anyone what he did because he did not want to explain it. After Michael was born, Finn knew that he would have to explain it one day, but he had never been ready. It would have to wait. He only knew what he felt was all right because his father had felt it too, and Michael was like them, but in ways Finn could not yet fully fathom. He would have to wait and see how things turned out.

"Fine," he said to Lara earlier that morning. "I'll take him out today." He called down the hall, "Michael! Get your coat on. We're going out for a drive."

"Finn," said Lara, "Slow down. Don't lose your temper."

"Fine," said Finn tiredly, watching his own fuse sputtering, and he grabbed his keys and coat on his way to the car. "Michael," he called.

Then he strode through the heaped snow to the car, the snow freshly fallen and the car newly tuned and oiled waiting by the garage door. Finn opened the door, got in the passenger seat to wait, and thought: "Damn the hair-trigger temper, but always the pressure, always the pushing," and the war there in the background, like a voice: *Galileo Galilei comes to knock and knock again, at a small secluded corner/of the ordinary brain.* "Fuck it," he thought.

Now, Finn realizes he is tired of himself and sickened by his counter-punching. He shakes his head clear of the thinking and looks up the barren road. Inside the metal skin of the car, the fogs of sleep cling to him. He blinks, chaffing at the heat pouring from the vent, and rubs his eyes.

Ahead, the road curves, and a light scattering of snow moves over an underlying darkness.

"Black ice," he says. "Son-of-a bitch."

"Where?" says Michael.

"There where the road bends."

"I don't see it."

"That's why it's called black ice. It'll be slicker than hell with that powdering of snow on it. Christ, it'll be a frictionless black hole. Slow down before we're on it."

"No problem," says Michael. He hits the brake pedal and Finn feels the car glide on the road. Free-fall. Then Michael turns the wheel sharply and the car spins like a hockey puck.

"Christ in a kitten!" says Finn. Outside the windows, the word orbits as they float free from the tethers of earth. Finn's stomach clenches.

"Holy shit!" says Michael. His foot slams the gas petal to the floor and the engine screams.

"Mayday!" thinks Finn, and they whirl across the road with life, death, and madness in the back seat.

"Wheee!" Michael shouts. They burst through an exploding snowbank, then rest, as the car gently rocks back and forth. Finn stares at the nappy whiteness through the windshield and wonders if it's a cloud.

"He shoots! He scores!" Michael yells beside him. Then there is silence.

"Are we dead?" Finn asks. He sees between the two surfaces of the glass a distance that could be infinity or could be an inch. The horrors of string theory, he thinks, of transparencies that can never be crossed. The liabilities of knowing. He looks away from that glassy trap to his son and he sees a boy's eyes with Lara's deeps in them. Finn looks back to the surfaces in front of him where vision ends and the unknown begins, seeing the very thickness of transparency in a window. No, he thinks, stay with your son.

He glances round the car, then at the dashboard as though for mileage and speed. The speedometer, chromed and colorless, glares at him like the dead eye of a squid. The needle points to zero. They are at rest.

"I always imagined going alone," he says. Then he pats Michael's knee. He opens his door just enough for a one-eyed squint at whatever fresh hell waits beyond, sees snow and spruce and more snow, the sun sharp on the meadow.

He sucks in the icy air.

"Well?" says Michael.

"We can breathe the air, but there's no sign of intelligent life," Finn quips. "We must still be in Canada. Or heaven. Get the shovel and sand from the trunk. Let's find out."

"We're digging?" asks Michael, something skittering over his words like a bug over a dark pond.

Finn thinks of Seamus Heaney, of fathers digging peat. He can't help it. Once a literature teacher, always chained in the glass cage of metaphor. "Let's get the car back on the road before another bloody ice age sets in," he says.

"Right."

"Get the dirt from the trunk." There is always a shovel and a bag of earth at hand in the north, Finn thinks, and frost in the nose and nose hairs pinched with ice. Shovels carried like rifles over the shoulder.

Finn bends and peers under the car, which rests on a rock, whose high stone point is solid against the car's belly at the balance point, allowing the vehicle to teeter back and forth. Archimedes, he thinks: give me a lever and a fulcrum, and I can move the world.

"A chance in a million," he says, "to have read English at the university, to have flown in a war, and to become a literature teacher stuck in a snow-bank, teeter-tottering on the Canadian Shield."

"What?" says Michael.

"We'll have to winch the car off the rock to get it on the road. I'll cut a couple of poles for leverage. Take the cable and loop that spruce across the road."

"Which one?" Michael looks around.

"The one straight from the car to the road, Pythagoras. It's simple geometry." Finn steps golden-thighed into the snow.

When the job is done, they take up the journey again, Michael at the controls. The engine is no longer tuned and throbs behind them. Finn's head throbs too, and he stares up the road as the car rolls along and Michael morosely clasps the wheel. Finn nurses two knuckles skinned on the winch. His hands burn from thawing and the small bones in his fingers ache. He begins scraping the fresh dirt from under his nails. The hands of a mechanic today, he thinks. He thinks of the clean, strong hands of his father.

"Well, we handled that, Dad. I never doubted you," says the old man's namesake beside him.

Finn snorts and, looks at his son, seeing again the boy's search for completion in another human being, in this case, Finn himself. The coinage of love.

How to see his son, he wonders. Why should a father's challenge be being pleased in his son? And Lara in the middle of it, always. He thinks of yesterday with her friends, one with a two-year-old daughter, talking around the table and the infant uncannily attentive to the women, sucking up God knows what knowledge and all the while the mother's gaze glued to her girl. Naked, mutual admiration. Finn shivers. This timeless adoration of women one to the other, he thinks, seamless, efficient, collaborative, breaching and broaching generations while the men bumble about in cars conveying a whiskered wisdom to their boys, one on one, with crude tools: games, chewing-tobacco and jock itch. Huddled around the internal combustion engine in place of the old fires, in place of the flame in the dark woods, the heat no longer tonguing up into the night.

He thinks of his own power bound to the iron and torque and horsepower of flight, locked like a mage in the stones of ordinary fatherhood and career, bound and raging. A teacher. The impotence of being seen in ways he does not recognize.

He half-hears his son talking beside him in the dusk, as talkative as his mother, the gloaming gathering outside the windows, not yet calling for headlamps, the world quiet but for the faint thudding of the pistons as the words fall from Michael's tongue, something from one of his classes, something he is eager about: "'The unending focus on other people, partners, and miscellaneous other externals can never cure your loneliness, your angst, your impatience, or your longing.' Or words to that effect, Dad, and I thought you'd appreciate them." Finn nods gently as the words greet him, soft as a bruise.

"Oh yes," he says and looks up to a naked and natural moon whose light he had looked for in Lara's gaze long ago. What she had seen in his. The car is quiet as they peak the last rise in the road and the town suddenly lies twinkling in the distance.

The highway slopes to the town, and thickens with traffic. Snow flurries hang in little halos around the streetlights. It's almost Christmas, thinks Finn. Cars slide impatiently between the banks of plowed snow.

"Slippery?" asks Finn.

"A little. Not bad." Then Finn sees the car coming from the right and looks to his son who looks back, and in that instant he sees reflected in his son's eyes himself, still and small and lost.

"Shit! Not again," says Michael. Finn stares at the approaching car and a woman's face at the wheel, her teeth bared in a rictus of fear. She's hit the brakes too late, he sees, driven to fast, and is headed at Finn's door.

"Hang on," says Michael and turns the wheels hard, counter-intuitively, steering the car to meet the other head-on. Finn sees the boy's eyes now, wide and unafraid, sees the hands of his son on the wheel firm and strong, sees them in a detail that surprises him.

And then Finn closes his eyes for the impact. His eyes open on their own accord.

The house-keys lift from the dashboard and float slow and silent past his head, briefly retrograde while maps and manuals lift from the glove box, sail rearward and every edge of them clear, even the print amazing in its detail and precision, small bodies in free fall, tiny planets, celestial in significance and majesty, the heavens enclosed briefly within the car with Finn the astronomer seeing what he cannot comprehend— yet grasping the "thingness" of these marvels, like Rilke's "Dingen", like the "Quiditatis" of Joyce, like the vision of Lazarus Browning wrote of, silent and slow as the world floats lazily past. His head is against the headrest, yet he is aware of a feeling that indicates he has struck his brow in a time too short for his mind to comprehend. "But what *does* the mind know?" he wonders, "of the whatness and the thingness of it all, the world in a grain of sand, the impotence of vision and the power of dreams and who to blame, the strangeness of his own flesh, a son 'full and foreign in the pouch' with a manhood both familiar and unknowable, yet loved through all the days long, the litany of connections, the minting of love."

He sees a ghost in a glass web. Finn peers hard at a horned and ruddy face staring back. The car has stopped, and the windshield is shattered like a cobweb.

"Dead," he says, "and in hell for sure this time." He looks at Michael, who laughs.

"There's a small puncture where your third eye might be, Dad," he says. "How do I look through it?"

"Don't be flippant," laughs Finn. Michael reaches over and pulls the earflaps of Finn's cap.

"Here are earflaps, that were his horns … " he says.

"Don't make me laugh. It hurts," he says. Can he move? He tries to pull himself upright but his legs rebel. He sees in the periphery the shape of Michael's head turning away.

"Son-of-a-bitch," he says. He reaches for the yawning door, feels a stab in the back. He knows he shouldn't move, but his legs are coming alive and there is no way he is going to stay in the car, prisoner to the silver web where his head hit the glass. The glass that held such palpable transparencies earlier in the day, shattered, like the break in the pattern of a Navaho rug letting the spirit out. Better to be on the snow looking up at the sky than to contemplate such things in a metal cage. Above, the sky is lit by the stars, sharp and clear.

"Hold on." Michael is out of the car and moving around the car to the open door.

"Hell," says Finn. His son kneels beside him. "Get me out of this damned thing before it catches fire." *A Volkswagen beetle. The people's car, God help us all.* He sees himself immolated like Sam MaGee, surrounded by the lone and level snows, another Irishman on ice, cremated in a coal boiler, happy at last on the frozen wastes of the Yukon.

"It's not going to catch fire, Dad. Don't be such a baby. It's only a fender-bender. Can you move?"

"No. Yes. Not easily. And aren't you suddenly in command. How do I look?"

"Pissed."

"You knob-head. Am I bleeding?"

"It's stopped. Maybe you should stay still. You look pale."

Finn pulls his legs. They move. "You smart-ass," he says, moving his head: no pain. He grabs the frame and begins pulling himself through the door into the world.

"You can watch me or help me," he says. Michael slips his arms around him and eases him out of the seat. Finn glances at the hands holding him. They are as sharply focused as were the items floating through the air in the cab. Then he is on his legs, his thighs wobbling now, feeble as they push him over the snow. "No problem," he says. "I'll just sit here for a bit." But it is hard to sit, and he feels Michael move close behind to prop him up between his legs, open now like a woman in labor. The child father to the man, thinks Finn. He looks back at the car. Out of one ditch and into another. Not so bad. Water and its own level. His ass is cold. He props his arms on Michael's knees as though in a chair and thinks of the windshield, the ghost in the glass freed at last. He leans his head back onto his son's shoulder.

"Where's the other car?"

"She kept going," says Michael.

"What?" says Finn.

"She missed us. I hit a telephone pole. She went that way." He points into the night.

"Jesus," says Finn. "Is the day over yet? Can we go home?" Across the street a seedy bar flashes a neon invitation for Coors, for Finn the equivalent of a Tombstone City saloon before the advent of running water.

"There's no fight left in me. All this has beaten me down in a way the Viet Cong never could. I don't understand it. Fuck. All the mojo's been pulled out of me like the web pulled out of a spider."

He longs for a pint of ale in the moist, mammalian hug of a country pub. The Irish pap. "Should I take you to Dublin, Son?" he asks. "Would you like that?"

"I don't know, Dad. That's what grandpa asks." The comment startles Finn.

"It's where his dad's from," says Finn.

"Great-grandpa? He never talks about him."

"Well, your great-grandfather, Fred, was the town sheriff in Stanstead and loved a fight. He was Irish and the craziest in the family, but a dapper dresser. It was a hard act to follow, and Dad never tried."

"Fistfights?" Michael asks.

"It was a different time," says Finn. "Hard for you to imagine. A conversation to him was an argument, and to pick an argument with someone was the polite thing to do. It ensured meaningful dialogue and guaranteed the attention of both parties. He never held a grudge, and when he lost an argument he looked forward to its resumption. He told me some of this himself, before we lost him. Arguing with someone was a compliment: it was different than insulting someone, which is what you did when the other person didn't matter and wasn't worth arguing with. It was a simple system and it worked for him, but he was not a simple man." Finn looks briefly at his son. "A simple man with no screw-ups doesn't generally drive his son to the opposite extreme."

"Well, Grandpa is pretty low-key," says Michael.

"He is," says Finn. He looks at Michael, quickly, appraisingly. "The fact that the old man had fistfights with Dad showed that he loved him," he says.

"What?"

"I know," says Finn laughing. "But that's what he told Dad, evidently. And the fact that he engaged the town in arguments and was delighted when others lost their tempers, showed he was a conscientious member of the community with a sense of humor, and didn't hold a grudge. That he smuggled booze and Chinese labour over the border using his badge and jail showed he was compassionate to his fellow man and an entrepreneur. That he single-handedly stopped a lynching by beating back a mob with a buggy whip while escorting a rapist through town in an open carriage showed he was a lawman to be reckoned with. That he thrashed two young hoodlums when he was sixty on the public road for insulting a lady showed why he was loved by women, slandered by doubters, and feared by no-gooders."

"It sounds like a wild west kind of thing," says Michael. "In Quebec. Weird."

"Well, in any event, you look like him," says Finn, "so maybe you should take your granddad up on his offer."

Finn shifts deeper into his son's embrace and hears the faint wail of a siren ride the frost toward them.

"Well, enough of this. Let's call your mother," he says, and thinks— she was right again. "Jesus. Maybe by now she'll be talking to me. She'll have a fit about all this."

He waits, resting his head against his son, cradled by his thighs, and lifts his face to the night. Above him, the stars are unfettered.

"I told her this morning I'm going to apply to officer's school," Michael says. "RMC in Kingston. Like Grandpa did. That's why she's mad. She was taking it out on you."

"Well, it takes something to say that," Finn says. "Thanks."

A shudder sticks its finger in Finn's belly and ripples outward. Spidery legs over a pond. "Ah," he says. He cranes his head to look into his son's eyes and sees the deeps, sees his boy moving through his life to his separate end, sees the years of seeing and being seen. Then he sees the what and the wherefore of Lara's eyes in the boy's.

"A squeaker," he says, squeezing his son's leg. He looks down at Michael's arms cradling him, and then at his hands and the ropey vein standing proud on the flesh from the thumb's base to the index knuckle, like Finn's, like Finn's father's—he's seen this before and how could he have forgotten?—like his father's father, the hands of the dead alive in the hand he holds now, Finn realizes, a long line of men leveraging their boys into the future.

## CHAPTER TWENTY-THREE

# Ritual and Resurrection

January 2002

*Hidden in a dream, the man flashes out like shook foil, tumbles through skies beneath a burning phantom, sees hands through dying eyes as monks reach down to him; he haunts jungles where moons sleep and saps force their noiseless migration through trees, always the dark, always the trees, sensed and unseen, always a forest's wet breath as the waters of the world flow through his nights.*

I t's six a.m., and Finn sits groggily on the edge of the bed watching Lara applying her lipstick. Her face is eight inches from the bathroom mirror. Her lips are parted.

"He was a liar, Finn," she says, "who lied about being born a prince and having thought of Relativity before Einstein."

"Perhaps he meant it with a small 'r'," says Finn.

"Hmph," she says. "His thoughts are not original and his phrasing is the work of a woman he never credited."

"Oh?" says Finn.

She announces this freighted evaluation as she moves to her rouge while he sits groggy and pummeled on the edge of the bed, sullen from the night. He fixes her with what he intends to be a baleful eye and keeps his face expressionless as hers takes on the tones of penciled animation. He is amazed at her artistry but will not admit it. Her transformation in the morning delights him, but since he objects to the process on principle, he pretends to be oblivious. She called him a "lookist" once, and he has never forgotten it.

Thoughts creep from his brain like bears from hibernation–slow, ill tempered, and stumbling. He lives with a woman who, he feels, while making herself beautiful at six in the morning, before he's cubbed the phrases for his nine a.m. literature class, is discrediting Kahlil Gibran as a gigolo who lived on women's money and literary abilities.

She makes herself new every day, but he has unravelled to the point where he's afraid of disintegration. "Who speaks?" he asks himself more and more.

"Have you read him?" says Finn.

"No," she says. "What was the name of his book?"

"There are several. *The Prophet* was one."

"Yes, that's the one the article mentioned," she says. "Have you read anything by him?"

"Yes," says Finn. "*The Prophet* and *Sand and Foam* influenced an entire generation." The words sound like a textbook to him.

"You liked him, then, didn't you?"

"I never met the man. But I read what he wrote and liked what he wrote and the spirit behind it, when I was twenty."

"Well," she says "he was a fake. It was the woman with him who wrote the beautiful phrases and he, *the man*, took credit." She looks at Finn directly. "The woman remains nameless." Then she says, "You were young, and bearded, and no doubt felt like a mystic–Oh, I've seen the pictures of you before the war–so you *would* identify with him."

These salvos carry the freight of marriage, of long love, and Finn is no longer able to parse out the components.

"Well, you'd have to have read his original notes, in Arabic, wouldn't you, to say that, about the phrasing?" Finn feels the latter part of her utterance like a shaft uncomfortably close to a bulls-eye. "The English grows out of the Arabic. It's the thought and sentiment that comes through."

"You don't have to read the original to know what kind of man he was," she says.

"You do," says Finn. "And that's the exactly the point. Literature is not an anthropology. The fact that you know the latter does not make you an expert on the former." For some reason, he sees that Lara is getting enthusiastic about the talk. He used to love these engagements.

But he thinks of his students, gleaning reviews and articles about writers, and then repeating the "facts" of their foibles, their failings, their frailties–in short, their humanity–cheapening the lives of writers and erasing their art. That's what his reaction is about now, not Lara's argument. Never mind that sinners make art and angels do not, he thinks. It's the better part of us that takes wing, but in this age of keeping the bath water and throwing out the baby, no one is safe.

"This, my Beauty, is not intellectual acuity," he continues. "It is not authority and knowledge. It's excavation. You haven't read a word he wrote. You read an article in a magazine, by a woman, and now, this morning, you serve it up as food for thought. It's journalism." Finn knows he is railing about his students and his fatigue and his longing for the lake and time alone. It is not Lara he is addressing at all, though she is taking the brunt of his anger.

But this morning, he wonders, *does* he see it for what it is, this penchant for criticism and bulls-eyes–for more than what it seems? A corrosive in the acid-bath of ordinary life? It etches jagged holes in both his joie de vivre and his drive to live, for he fears, but does not fully admit, that these very criticisms can apply to him, such smears, such flat renditions of his far from exemplary life, his own and oft-forgiven underbelly of mortality, and he further fears that his share of wallowing in weakness is greater than most, that he is a prime target for such mudslinging and sniggering, and he knows that though he considers such parlayers of the snide and superficial to be monkeys in the fun-house, it will, he makes no mistake about it, be him in the cage and the monkeys running the show. Should he ever publish.

He's tired. How is this different than his defensiveness as a veteran?

More importantly, he thinks, he has been taken in, again, by rumor mongering masquerading as critical thought. This does not bode happily for either his abilities to choose wisely or think well. He is no angel and is far from blameless in any scenario in which he discovers himself, and he knows this. He is married to the one person who can tell him he is naked in his own parade and not hate him for it. And, ironically, that's what attracted him to her in the beginning. Is he afraid of it now? What changed?

And underneath it all, he suddenly admits, he is angry at being trapped in the cage of a sedentary career, peering out into freedom. That phrase again. There is no wildness or madness available. But he has not talked about it. It is flying and the thrill of being lit with life he misses, and he blames Lara for it, and it isn't fair. He is a featherless bird. He thinks of the fires of summer, of flying into and over the roar, of the intimate embrace of the flames and those who lit or doused them, a dance on the edge of life. God, I wish I were there, he thinks.

His attention span is growing smaller, he realizes, and his thoughts shorter and more fragmented. Gone are the long, deep excursions into solitude.

He watches her brushing her teeth now, first the incisors, then the molars, building the foam up thickly, and finally, ritualistically, brushing her tongue while Finn waits for the inevitable, the brush too far down the back of the throat, and the reflex. And, yes, yes, now she is barking like an orc over the sink as Finn feels his own gag reflex awaken. His mouth waters. She straightens, spits, and looks at him.

"You're being unrealistic," she says, taking up the thread of conversation. "Respect is not the same thing as denial or cover-up."

You are very beautiful, he thinks, and wants to say that art is the life-giving blood from the wounds of those broken in heart or spirit. It's the blood that nourishes us, and the spirit we should look to, not the wound that lets it out. But he knows that it is a feeble utterance, pathetic and self-serving, and that it will open him up to devastating and deserved salvos of ridicule.

"That sort of criticism is just not helpful," he says, his mouth still watering from the sound of her barks. But he looks into her eyes, the eyes he loves, and wonders what they see. How they see him. Once, when she fell into the lake, he thought for an instant he did see out of them.

"Finn, you use metaphor like a shield–to deflect reality." She looks at his stomach, he sees it, he sees her look and thinks of his inflated waistline, his "belly like a sonorous and hairy pumpkin," a phrase, he knows, he's culled from some forgotten reading.

"I don't want that reality," he says. "That reality is a rich, ugly, old maid courted by incapacity." Here is another stolen aphorism from some unremembered dash through the fields of literature whose gems, he thanks God, stick to him like burrs to a dog. They serve him well when thought fails, but are, alas, a chink in his armor. He looks at his wife, her green eyes unwavering in the morning and very fine, and as he looks into her eyes, she looks back and she sees him sitting on the edge of the bed, his hair bent and airborne from a night fighting the pillow, and he is unkempt, so utterly unkempt in his baggy T-shirt with the holes in the armpits and the collar frayed from his neck whiskers, that she despairs. He teaches literature but still dresses like the carpenter he was when he put himself through school: blue jeans, white sneakers and Tee. He has given up. When did it happen? He is a potted plant, in constant need of trimming and watering and weeding, and she is exhausted. She looks away from him, back to the mirror, then traces the line of her lips with a dark highlight. She glances back at his reflection. He is looking at her bottom, she sees it, she sees him looking, too big for her liking and she imagines his words, "Lara, the biggest part of you is your ego, and after that, your ass." Never spoken but not never thought, she thinks. No, that's not true, she thinks. He loves her ass.

"Go shower," she says. "How can you pretend to think when you look like that?" He groans and rubs the overgrown eyebrows up out of his eyes. "And straighten up," says Lara. "You're slouching."

"I'm carrying a great weight," he says. She hears his grandfather's brogue in the statement, and it indicates Finn is mocking himself.

"Yes," says Lara. "Self-pity," and laughs. She watches him lumber out of the room wearing his character like a rumpled shirt, his belly bare beneath the Tee. She marvels at his pretense to a refined thinking when his appearance is more earthy than soil itself, untended beneath some gardener's cloche, smelling faintly of mushroom and neglect. What's happened to him? She knows he blames her for causing him to be fat and old. She's the reason he had to give up the flying, the risks, the adolescent irresponsibility he called being alive. She made him grow up so that his son could grow up too. But he has never spoken of it, and she has never dared to bring it up.

Lara turns back to the mirror and shakes her head at the image there that acknowledges sadness infinitely reflected. Hers is a nest now empty, a woe with their son gone that the man will not understand, will not pretend to understand, will not pretend to pretend to understand. Nor does he any longer make the effort to hide the amazement on his face as he watches her morning preparations. His judgment and his condemnation. His insufferable superiority. All, all, thinks Lara, thin plating for fears that leak through the joints of his armor despite his best effort at containment and denial. But she married him, loved this man now joined to her in a union more remote in circumstance than tribal tics sung on high and inaccessible hills. The who, what, where, and the why of it all escape her now. Is it, she nods into the mirror, a flaw in her own taxonomy, in her own recounting of the mysterious and incomprehensible, in her own imposition of relationship on time? She seeks the stamp of humanity upon the face of chaos: that is the raft that anthropology has shown her. She knows it. But it is a failed reconfiguration of entropy. How can she expect him to see any of this, she wonders, to understand any of it, wallowing in his own literary perplexities and bad dreams, when even she runs grasping after, and missing, her own understanding of self and science? Her image, bewildered in the mirror, nods back at her.

She envies her husband's show of certainty.

Lara looks beyond the mirror. Over the sink and out the window the sun is rising, brushing the clouds with a pink and painful delicacy. It is the rising of new hope. It is the image of that very hope she builds into her face each morning, a deliberate and constant ceremony, watched but unseen by her husband. The ritual is as predictable as the breaking day, and she looks at the bright orb and back at her flesh now lit by it. She raises her hands to her face. It is the practiced ritual of a priestess. While her fingers trace the delicate lines around her lids and lips, her eyes flicker from sun to mirror as though dipping into pigments of light and relaying them to her face. The sun is paint, the mirror palette, her face the canvass. Her touch upon herself is tender, sensuous. She is aware of this hopeful yet desperate ceremony and marvels at the movement of her fingertips and eyes, knowing they are somehow inseparable, one from the other, and she thinks of Yeats and tries to recall his lines about the dancer and the dance.

"Darling?" calls Lara. Finn, she knows, will know.

She listens for any noises he might make down the hall. Instead, chittering back along the walls and into her head are the echoes of Samuel Johnson's insight into the mechanics of marriage as the triumph of hope over experience, the speaker dead but his truth eternal in each morning's ritual and resurrection.

But she will not accept that. Instead, she walks down to the kitchen and stands in front of Finn, who is looking out the kitchen window towards the little stand of spruce he's planted in the back yard. And suddenly, she sees that without his son and his flying, there is nothing between Finn and his feeling of having been ripped out of the north. He is heartsick.

"Why can't we talk the way we used to?" she asks.

"What do you mean?" Finn asks.

"In graduate school, we talked all night about what mattered to us. Books and ideas."

"Well, yes. That was before Michael was born. There's a lot of water under the bridge, I guess."

"What does that mean?" Lara asks.

Finn looks around as though searching for the facts.

"Grading student papers is getting to be more and more work. We're turning into graders, not instructors. It doesn't leave much time for other things," Finn says.

"It's more than that," says Lara. "With Michael gone to college, I thought we'd have more time for each other. I thought we could get back what we had."

"Well, the empty nest," says Finn. He looks at her. "What the hell," he says. "Let's just deal with it. With Michael gone and the flying finished, there's just not much left, Sweetie. I mean, what's the purpose?"

"What is that supposed to mean?"

"I feel like a nutless bull in the pasture. The thing I loved to do most is gone. My wings are gone. I've lost a part of myself that was most alive. Now I move around the pasture all day, every day, and eat grass. I grade student papers. That's it. I gave up the juice and joy for Michael's sake, and now he's gone too. It's no wonder I'm pissed off a lot of the time. I feel like my life is over."

Lara is stricken, and it's too late for him to take the words back.

"But you don't have the dreams any more, Finn," she says. "I thought that would be worth something. Your demons are gone."

Finn nods at her. "Sweetheart, when you lose your demons, you lose a part of yourself."

"You're saying … " she begins.

"I'm saying that I feel like I'm on tranquilizers all the time. Not here, not fully alive, and mad about it." Lara is already aware of all this, and has been blaming herself. He reaches out and takes her in his arms. "I'm sorry, Sweetheart," he says. "I should have known." He moves a hand down to her bottom, and pats her. "Scoot back and finish up, and I'll bring the paper and breakfast along in a minute. Let's brunch in bed," he says.

Lara nods and walks back to the bathroom and takes up her pencils. She listens for indications of him in the kitchen preparing her morning toast and coffee. And yes, yes, now she hears the front door open, knows he will be stepping out to retrieve the newspaper before bringing all three back to her, back to her as she lies upon the bed she will go to now, where she will wait to solve the morning crossword, where she will wait for him, where she will ready herself for the day. She will wait, and he will wait upon her, an acolyte to their transubstantiation, to their love, she has to admit, and he will bring his offering to her in this morning communion, carried upon a simple wooden board of his own making. He will ask if she wants some coffee, as though for the first time. He makes it new for her every day.

She thinks quickly of their first year together, of the nights looking out over the lake before their move south to London and Finn's teaching job, of the newness then and of the secrets that surfaced and suddenly made the world seem older.

Lara looks through the mirror and into the deeps of her pupils. Then his footsteps are in the hall. She steps into the bedroom and moves quickly to the bed. She wants him to see her as though she'd never left it, fresh and waiting. She thinks of Aphrodite rising from the water every morning, revirginated. That's what she wants. Then Finn enters with the tray, shuffling in like a wounded centaur. He has pulled his hair into a semblance of order, changed his shirt, and the morning air has colored his cheeks. He smiles brightly and pulls his shoulders back. He looks at her and blows noisily. She sees that he is here with her because he wants to be. It is not because he has nowhere else to go.

"Coffee?" he asks.

### Chapter Twenty-Four

# A Prayer for the Dying

Behold, I will tell you a mystery. We shall not all sleep, but we shall all be changed.

~I Corinthians 15:51

April 19, 2002

At noon, the telephone rings. Finn's mother is on the line.

"You need to come home at once," she says.

"What's wrong?" says Finn.

"Your father's in the hospital and he's not expected to leave. He's on oxygen in Emergency."

"I'll drive up right away," he says. He hangs up the phone and walks to the living room where Lara is sitting, working on the crossword.

"Who was that?" she says.

"Mother. I have to go home."

"What's happened?"

"Dad's in the hospital, and he's not coming out."

"Oh my God. What are you going to do?"

"Drive up there now. Call Michael and let him know. Can you pick him up?

"I'll call him at school in Kingston."

"No," says Finn, "he's at Camp Petawawa for a week."

"What?"

"Special training."

"Why didn't I know that?"

"It was need to know."

"There's no 'need to know' at this point, Finn. Stop your bullshitting."

"He didn't want to worry you."

"Now I'm worried."

"It's closer to the lake than Kingston and on the way. Or he can take the bus."

"I want to pick him up," Lara says.

"Across the province and up the Ottawa River to Mattawa and then west. No. It will take too long. It's six hours to Petawawa from here. Have him take the bus. He's less than three hours out, and then you fly up and meet him in North Bay." Finn thinks of flying over the Ottawa graben that cradles the river and the little towns strung out along the shores. Calabogie.

"I know the way Finn," says Lara. "I'll pick him up. It won't take any longer than the flight connections, and I want to stay busy. You go, and we'll join you tomorrow."

"Okay," says Finn. "You pick him up and join me. You'll need time to get him and pack. I'll leave now and you leave as soon as you can." He stands, looking at Lara, feeling as though he is forcibly willing his body to move.

"Go," she says. "I'll pack some food for you."

"Shit," he says. "I don't want to go without you."

"You'll be fine," she says. "We'll try to get there around noon tomorrow."

Finn drives through southern Ontario to the rolling northland where some valleys still hold patches of deep snow. Only the northern conifers are green as the highway falls away to the Nipissing basin, and the road feels hemmed in by the bare branches of birch and maple, and the old geologies are buried in the soggy detritus of the previous fall. After five hours of driving, he pulls into the hospital parking lot and heads to the emergency ward to find his mother.

"Your father's dying," she says. "Where are Lara and Michael?"

"She picking him up at Petawawa and hoping to get here tomorrow."

"It's been a fight," says his mother "and the doctor said earlier he had only two or three hours left, but he was tougher than they thought, or more afraid, and it was probably a little of both because he's hung on."

"Why is he still here by the emergency room," says Finn. He looks around. The beds are lined up against the walls, filled and bewildering in their numbers. The nearest patients stare at the dying man beside them. Not the kind of room-mate you want if you are superstitious, thinks Finn.

"They wanted to move him into the hall because they need the room," she says.

"We're not going to let him die parked in the hallway," says Finn. "What the hell are they thinking? Go tell the nurses to give us a private room for this. I'll stay here with him."

Finn stands at the foot of the bed. When his mother leaves, he looks at his father. Finn always believed an ache in the heart to be a figure of speech, but it becomes very real when his mother leaves. He very nearly can't hold it in, and he can see that it is the same with his father, who looks up at him.

"I'm dying, Finn," he says. "Sweet Jesus."

Finn runs his hand through his hair. He's exhausted. A nurse brings an envelope to the bed, hands it to him and leaves without a word. He takes out his father's wedding ring, and the two men look at each other as Finn slips the ring on his own finger. Then he leaves the room and finds his mother by the elevators.

"I've got a room for him," she says, "at the end of the hall."

"Here's the ring," he says. "Let's get him into his own room."

"We're going to lose Dad," she said. "Keep the ring for a while."

"Let's get him to the room," Finn says again. They enter the emergency room, seize the gurney, and wheel it down the corridor and into a small room in the northwest corner of the building. As they enter, Finn notices the window looks west over the lake. Far away, a beacon light blinks in the darkness.

"When did you get in?" she asks.

"Now."

"How was the drive?"

"Fine. Long."

"I'm so glad you made it," she says. Finn looks out the window and blows an audible sigh.

When night comes, Finn is called to the telephone.

"Where are you?" he says.

"At Petawawa," says Lara. "In a motel. How is he?"

"He's hanging on, but a bit out of it. I don't think he knows where he is, or sometimes who we are. How's Michael?"

"I don't know. He's not here."

"What do you mean?"

"He's out in the field somewhere, doing some damn thing about survival, of all times, and is out of contact."

Finn scratches his head. "Hell," he says. "For how long?"

"Another day," says Lara. "Finn, I can't even begin to tell you how furious I am about this."

"Well, there's nothing you can do here, so relax."

"Relax? If your father hadn't done this sort of macho disappearing act a hundred times, I'd feel sorry about it, but my first thought was that he deserved it. Like father, like son, like grandson. Now I'm stuck here, waiting for this boyhood game to end, and I won't be there to say goodbye."

Finn hears her sob once, then again.

"Mother's holding up," says Finn, "and the important thing is for you two to be safe. Get the best room and come up after Michael gets in. He'll need you."

"I'm going to get drunk and stay drunk until Michael is back."

"That sounds reasonable," Finn says. "I'm sorry about it, Sweetheart."

"I know it's not your fault. I'm just so frustrated. How are you?"

Finn blows hard. "Fine," he says.

"Liar," she says. "I love you."

Afterward, they sit in the half-light listening to the man breathing. Finn becomes aware that he and his mother are saying goodbye to a different man as his father slips in and out of sleep. A thickness in the air fills the room and settles on him, and Finn doesn't know if his father is causing it or if it is his imagination, but it quickly becomes palpable and weighted.

The older man dreams, and Finn watches his father travel those lucid threads and listens to the messages he brings back, but Finn doesn't know whether to discount the visions as delusional or be humbled by his own inability to move with them and know more. The experience is outside his experience, and he feels it changing him. At times, it feels like a conversion. Finn sits quietly, and the sense he has is that he and his mother are protecting a man against something they can not see, prevent, guess at, or understand, but their helplessness is not at issue because it is the vigil that matters.

His father wakes, stares at the ceiling, then looks at them as though he's not really present. But then, thinks Finn, he is himself both in the room and not; he is home, and he is not.

"Where's Dick? Is Dick coming down to visit?"

"Dick who?" says Finn.

"My brother Dick!" his father snaps, irritated. "Where's Dick?"

"Dick had a heart attack and died, twenty years ago, Michael," says Finn's mother.

"Dick's dead? Dick had a heart attack?"

"Yes."

"He's dead?"

"Yes."

"When?"

"A long time ago," she says. "He died in Halifax."

"Dick's dead." He nods in slow comprehension, as though it doesn't fit with the facts. "He had a heart attack. Dick had a heart attack and died in Halifax."

"Yes."

"Well, well, well." And then he lies back and closes his eyes.

Finn ponders this as he sits watching, and then his father speaks out of the dream again.

"Mother and Dad are coming down to visit tonight," he says.

"Are they?" says Finn.

"And Aunt Jean and Lyman."

"Oh?" says Finn. He hasn't mentioned his aunt in twenty years, and she had been the woman who raised him.

"Aren't they coming?"

"Yes" says Finn. "Everyone's coming. There's nothing to worry about, Dad. Everything is going to be all right." And the old man lies back in his bed and fights for breath, and waits.

Later he wakes to speak again.

"George!"

"What?" says Finn.

"There's my brother George. What's George doing there?" the old man demands.

"Where?" Finn's mother asks.

"Dublin. How did George get to Dublin?"

"Did Uncle George ever go to Dublin?" Finn asks. The old man thinks hard for a minute, his face furrowed.

"I don't know," he says, and he doesn't, "but there he is," and Finn is beginning to glimpse the travels of the dead. He thinks of a colleague, a Lakota, who said "The dead are like the Cherokee. They're everywhere."

"Did you ever go to Belfast, Dad?" Finn asks.

"I don't think so," he says. He thinks hard for a moment, but there really is a question whether he did or not.

"Did your Dad ever go back?"

"Christ knows! God only knows!"

"Did Uncle Dick ever go?"

"Who knows where Dick got to!" he says, and shakes his head wearily.

Now he sits up suddenly and looks around.

"How in hell did we get here?" he says.

"Where?"

"In England!"

"We're not in England, Dad. We're in the hospital."

"We're in a private room," he says, looking around. "How did I get here?"

"We got a room for you."

"Well, well, well." Then he dozes fitfully while they watch him.

"Where are we now?" he says later, half-opening his eyes.

"In town, overlooking the lake."

"The lake? The Manitous?"

"Yes." And he nods slowly, taking it in with mild amazement before drifting off again. And Finn can feel his own head nod, and he imagines that he and his father are one and dreaming.

> *It is a quiet summer day and he looks up, suddenly happy and casts the lure far out into the river. Soon he will take the train out to Cochrane and meet his wife. Twiz, he thinks. He will bring her back to their first house. But now, the day is still, and the wind sleeps as he stands on the green bank. His pipe smoke curls in the air, and the water is cool. The jays scold from the trees and swoop down to snatch food, and the squirrels scold the jays, and it is a good day on the Little Abitibi.*

Finn takes the first watch at midnight as his mother goes home for a break.

"Why do it this way?" Finn asks.

"Because," says his mother. "I'll be back at breakfast." Finn looks at her.

"What?" she asks.

"Nothing," says Finn.

At four a.m., the old man wakes, agitated and restless, and insists he get out of bed. Finn lifts him to the chair. He catches sight of the IV unit with the tubes drooping toward him.

"What's that?" he says, alarmed, and Finn tells him.

They sit in the dark for a long while, silent, Finn close to the old man's knees, and they lean towards one another. It is strangely comfortable and wonderful, Finn thinks, and there is no need for speech, and they are happy and comfortable in their silence and their closeness. It is an old space, and a good one.

Then his father reaches out and takes Finn's hand, and he holds it and bows his head.

"You're a good boy," he says softly, and he says it three times, like a benediction. It is the only time he speaks directly to Finn in those final hours, and it is the only time Finn remembers him saying he was something special, and he supposes that this is the father's blessing he's waited forty years to hear.

Finn resolves, when he leaves, to tell Michael as soon as he arrives what has happened and say that he does not want his own son to have to wait through the years. He will give him his blessings as a father now and tell him he loves him and admires him for his efforts at becoming a man. There will be no more waiting.

In the morning, Finn's mother returns. The old man is up and is restless and peevish.

"Where's Lara and the boy?" he asks.

"They're on their way," Finn says.

Finn helps him to the window several times to look out over the bay to the lake. The old man tells Finn about its history again.

Then he sleeps for a while, more and more fitfully as the day goes on, and for a while he is comfortable lying on his back, asleep, and they stand beside him and hold his hand. Suddenly, half awake, he clutches Finn's fingers and pulls at them as though he were trying to pull off a glove.

"Take it off! Take it off!" he says.

"What?"

"Take it off!" and he continues pulling.

"There's nothing to take off," says Finn. His father lapses back into a fitful doze for a few minutes, then begins to wring his hands like Lady Macbeth and pulls at his own fingers.

"Take it off!" he says. "Take it off!"

"Take what off?"

"The ring! Take off the ring!" and Finn knows he is talking about his wedding ring.

"I took it off and gave it to mother last night. She has the ring."

"Good," he says, and drifts away. Goose bumps run down Finn's cold arms.

Finn looks at his mother and thinks that the old man is taking care of more business than they can imagine.

Later in the morning his mother begins to pitch her voice as though she were talking from a great distance.

"John telephoned," she calls across the room.

"Old Donovan," he smiles tenderly.

"And Viv. Do you remember Vivian, Michael?" she asks. He laughs affectionately.

"She's a little squirt," he says.

"And Eileen?"

"She's a little squirt too," he says.

A few of his friends drop in during the morning, as does the Anglican priest, Father Dawn. At first, Finn had thought is was 'Father Don,' and his father laughed. He is asleep when the priest arrives, and when the soothing prayers begin, his father's eyes snap open and he gazes up with such trust and joy and innocence that it shocks Finn to see it. He has never seen such pure emotion in his father's eyes before, and he realizes there is much that the old man has guarded in his life and refused to share, and Finn begins to understand himself.

When Finn's Aunt Mary arrives, she is skittish. She has shared all the things that sixty years bring to a family, including the end, and Finn thinks it must seem huge and unfair that it should all be coming to a close now. Her eyes are wide and she is clearly frightened. It isn't the dying that's the terrible thing, Finn thinks, but the losing of those we suddenly realize are an important part of what we are.

"Drum," the old man says.

"Hello, Michael," she says as she kisses him. He looks at her and thinks for a moment.

"Are we in Dublin?" he asks.

"No, Dad, we're in North Bay," says Finn. But Mary is badly shaken by his confusion, and mumbles a few desperate words before heading for the door. He calls after her.

"Drummer! Drummer! You be good, Drum!" but she doesn't hear him, and they are the last words he says to her.

Later, Finn reminds him that she had been to see him.

"She was?" he asks, delighted. Then he looks down at the floor and smiles and shakes his head and says affectionately "Poor old Drummer," and he chuckles.

Finn asks why his father calls her Drummer. He looks at his son and his eyes shine.

"Well," he says, "she was a beauty when she was young, and she loved to dance, and when there was a man available to dance, she beat her foot on the floor in excitement." He laughed. "She beat her foot like a grouse drumming its feet in mating season, and I teased her about it and called her Drummer. We've called her Drummer for sixty years, and she's liked it. 'There's only one Drum,'" she said to me once, "'and that's me!'"

He's awake most of the night, and asks to get out of bed and sit in the chair. As they sit him up, he looks suddenly at the bedside equipment again.

"What the hell is that?" he asks.

"It's your life support machine."

He shakes his head in disgust. "Christ!" he says with a rueful grin and looks at Finn. "Isn't this a bitch!"

Finn walks to the window. He looks out over the town, past the lights, through the noise of the town, the wet hissing of the tires, to the moon moving over the land. He looks out into the world and sees it, sees the lake which mirrors now not only the images of the present but the scenes of the past–the bright rains on the river, the fishing with his father, boating with Lara, the long nights watching Michael in his crib, riding the boat home at night as a boy, his hand under his father's on the steering handle, the lights from the stars on the Little Abitibi, the ride home under the pure northern sky and the letters to his mother.

Later that night, Father Dawn stops by again. Finn feels the edges of reality rubbering around the room. The wind is howling outside the window, and the priest tells them that her own father is dying in a hospital forty miles away. She says she has to leave in the morning and won't be back to conduct the services, and it breaks her heart because the two of them had been talking about it for several years. Finn thinks it perverse that the priest finds herself in the same situation as they are, but that night nothing seems impossible.

Finn leads her to the bed, and tells her to say the Prayers for the Dying over his father so it will be done and finished. He knows it is what the old man wants, and knows there is a good chance it won't be done if they wait. So they do it, and it is the hardest thing Finn has ever done because he stands there in the presence of life pronouncing his father dead.

After that, there is no sound but the breathing as his father works hard to suck in the air that no longer gives him the oxygen he needs.

The coughs begin deep in his lungs and wrack his weakened frame. He slowly works it up as he fights for the air to fuel the coughs, and they hold him upright to make it easier for him. The spasms exhaust him. Then he shakes his head, a little embarrassed.

"Isn't this a bitch," he says again softly with a tough, little smile.

And it is a bitch, thinks Finn, for this death is a busier place than Finn could have imagined, and his father lies in a room peopled with the dead who call more and more persistently. Though the old man doesn't want to go, the voices are becoming more substantial than his son's and his wife's who wait in the room with him.

"I don't know what to do," he says. "I don't know what to do."

"About what?"

"What else?" he says. "To stay or go."

The wind howls. It pulls at the windows and tears at the bricks of the building. Inside, the three of them sit wordless. At two a.m., they lift him into a chair where he sits with his head back and his eyes closed, resting from the effort of breathing and lying in bed. Finn and his mother sit across from him, memorizing him. Occasionally their gaze meets across the darkened room, but the old man's eyes remain closed. Nothing is said. It is a quiet, dark place with only the wind, and the nurses on their rounds are the only interruption in their watch.

Finn begins to be bothered by the wind. It is eerie, and he resents it because it is taking his father. It is a clichéd and foolish thought, but he believes it and hates the wind because he knows he can not overcome it.

But his father says he's always loved it and it comforts him. He says it's been a wild and natural element that's made him happy and reminds him of the wonderful lonely places where only the wild things live. Finn realizes that this is something else he's pushed away that his father has loved, and he stands and leaves the room and walks down the quiet corridors to the enclosed stairwells. He knows the sound will be louder there, and he stands alone on the stairs and listens to the rise and fall of its song, and it begins to soothe him. In the end, it will come down to losing his father, a man who refused to let himself be known, yet a man he loved and was bound to despite the monstrous heap of secrets that defined their relationship. One thing that was never a secret was their love of the north wind whispering in the summer pines or whistling over the winter snows. The wind binds them now, and in the end, Finn thinks, it is carrying away his father, and it comes down to that, and nothing else.

Then he walks back to the room where they wait, and his father is sitting peacefully in the chair with his eyes closed. Finn looks in from the doorway.

An hour later he leaves to call Lara. She does not pick up, so he passes the nurse's station to the southeast side of the building where it is very quiet and walks the long corridor. There is no sound there. He thinks that it is very odd, and it pleases him, but the quiet becomes unnatural and he approaches a window to look into the night. The window is open wide and the air rushes out of it with a shocking force. He realizes the wind is squeezing its way into the building through his father's room and rushing through to exit here.

He panics and hurries back through the halls to the corner where his father lies, hearing the wind in the room from a long way off. As he approaches the room, the pitch of the wind rises and the noise issues from this particular room and nowhere else. The room feels to Finn like a cauldron of sorrow and death, but he finds his father and mother at peace, waiting. The little room is a space with its scene frozen and still, and he sees himself permanently in a new stillness with them, as though frozen in a drop of amber. A small voice in his brain tells him this is what is meant by the term 'a moment frozen in time,' and Finn thinks perhaps all moments are like this if one has the strength to see them naked and revealed, and for some reason the thought makes him dizzy.

"Take the oxygen away," says the old man finally. "I don't want any oxygen." They remove the mask and put in his nosepiece. He fumbles at it and tears it away.

"Take it away! I don't want any oxygen." And they take it off and remove the nosepiece from the hose and hold the open hose by the side of the bed and point it so the gentle stream wafts toward him.

"No," he croaks peevishly. "Take away the oxygen." And they move the hose out of sight to the head of the bed so the life-giving gas would settle over his face.

"I don't want any oxygen. I don't want any oxygen. Turn it off," he says. They look at each other mutely, and turn it off.

"It's off now, Michael. We turned the oxygen off," says Finn's mother. And he settles back, relieved. Finn walks down to the nurse's station and tells them what is happening, and they nod and say it is fine. It is three a.m. of the second night, and Lara calls to say that Michael is not back and she cannot sleep.

At four a.m., the nurses come in for their rounds and Finn's father is sitting in the chair.

"Who are you?" he asks.

"They're the nurses, Dad. They've been taking good care of you."

"Oh?" and he smiles at them. "I see." They check the charts and vitals quickly and efficiently and keep up a steady banter with him. He rallies enough to charm and tease them. Then they are done and move toward the door.

"So long, Sweetheart!" he says toughly, and he grins his tough little grin and tosses off a wave the way Bogart or Cagney would have. The young women turn, surprised, and their eyes fill with tears and they smile and wave.

"So long, Honey," one of them coos, and he watches them recede from the darkened room into the light, dressed in white. Perhaps he supposes all young women were dressed in white, thinks Finn, that they are all angels or nurses and deserve the cavalier gesture no matter how archaic or forlorn, and so his gift to them is the self-effacing and ironic gallantry that was the trademark of his generation, and with that thought Finn hears a thousand romantic partings rattle in the celluloid corners of the darkened room, archived and evanescent as the dreams that permeate all times and places, carried to him through the years by his father's memories.

Finn sits beside him for long hours in the half-light. His father lies on his side with his right arm stretched out over the bed rail and Finn holds his hand. He pulls it back once to scratch his neck, and then stretches his arm back over the rail and when he didn't find his son's hand he stretches farther until Finn takes it again and only then does he settle back peacefully. It is the only time Finn can recall his father reaching out for his company or comfort.

As Finn sits there he sees, from the corner of his eye, someone enter the room, but when he turns there is no-one there. Later, he stands to stretch and walks away from his chair beside the bed. When he returns, he thinks at first his mother has moved to it, and then he sees her on the other side of the bed. As he steps toward the chair, he hesitates again and the thought comes to him that perhaps he shouldn't sit there for a while, that the old man needs some space to himself. No, he thinks, I'll sit there anyway and takes another step and stops again. He looks at the empty chair and is sure someone is sitting in it. To sit down feels like sitting on top of someone already there, so he backs away and decides it has something to do with his father. As he reaches the foot of the bed, the old man sits bolt upright, suddenly wide awake.

"I want to get up!" he says. "I want to get out of bed."

"Do you just want to sit up in bed?"

"No. I want to get up. I want to get away from the bed."

"Where do you want to go?"

"I don't know."

"There's nowhere to go, dad."

"I want to get up. Get me up." So Finn lifts up his father because his legs no longer obey him, and he walks him to the window where he gazes out over the city lights and into the darkness beyond. They stand looking into the darkness until the dawn breaks and the lake emerges from the night. With his head in his hand, his father looks out the window as Finn steadies him. Through the grey morning and down the empty streets that slope toward the water, they see the lake, and far out the Manitou Islands lying still and flat.

"The Manitous," he says.

"Yes," says Finn.

"Everything has its manitou, Finn, plants, animals, even machines." An old authority creeps into his voice, and he stands straighter.

"I know," say Finn.

"The lake," says his father. "The Big Water."

Finn thinks of the air that had been balanced in the night outside, of its suffocating balance, and he knows that movement only begins when there is no balance. Every night there is a moment that hangs in the heavens and wakes him.

"Do you remember the facts about the lake Finn? The old rift valley it lies in, the graben? The old sea that fathered the Atlantic and reached up here along the Ottawa and Nipissing valleys, when the waters of Nipissing and the sea were the same? The Iapetus Sea." He chuckles. "And the pipes in Callander Bay and the Manitous like two corks in a bottle. How long will they hold, do you imagine? And then what? All that time ago, Finn, and here we are. This is what's left."

"I remember the facts, Dad," Finn says.

"And the naming of things, Son. The names and their meanings are like a landscape you can't be aware of until you know the meanings of the names. This is what we're witnessing."

"Yes," says Finn, thinking that the man was awfully lucid.

"Look, Finn," he says suddenly pointing outside. "What's that? A sparrow hawk?"

Finn sees the little raptor hovering over the field below.

"It's a Kestrel, Dad. A little Windhover. Look at it hovering."

"Well, well, well," the old man says. "Look at it fly. It's a thing of beauty." And then he asks "Where's mother?"

"Right here."

"Oh."

"She's always been here." And his father looks at her and nods. Finn has not realized until these last hours how mobile and expressive is his face. It is the most expressive face he can recall ever seeing.

"The bloody pipes," he says. "God, I miss the pipes."

"What pipes?" asks Finn. "The Manitous?"

"The bagpipes, Finn. You should have heard them in the war, on the foggy mornings." He laughs. "God, they made the Jerries run," he says.

"A big, strapping Scottish piper in a Kilt walking unarmed into the mist at the front of the battalion. It was the eeriest sound you ever heard. I could never listen to a piper without the tears coming to my eyes." He turns and looks out the window. "It was haunting." Finn watches as the old man's hand lifts to his eyes. "And there at Dieppe, and all the boys we lost." He looks back at Finn. "We never talk about our hells, do we? We're as corked up as the fires under the lake out there. Just as well, I guess. God knows what would happen if we weren't, if it all came out."

Then he looks over Finn's shoulder to the door. "Is Michael here yet?" he asks.

"He's on his way with his mother. They'll be here soon." Finn looks past his father to the lake and avoids his gaze.

"Ah. With Lara. She's a beauty, Finn. And your son ... this will be a good lesson for him."

"What does that mean?" Finn asks.

"Who's that?" his father asks rather than answer, and indicates the empty space in the chair. "Who is that?"

Finn's mother looks at the empty chair. "I don't see anyone, Dear," she says.

"Who is that?" and he points to the empty bed he has just left. Again, watching him, Finn sees a movement out of the corner of his eye and turns to see who is in the room, and there is no one there. Finn wonders if he is getting a migraine, scotoma dancing in his vision. Is it an angel or a headache?

But his father is spooked and will not get back into the bed for another hour. Once there he's tired out. From time to time, he opens his eyes to look at them, and his eyes fill before he closes them again. He won't let it out because he can't trust anyone to take it, only the dead. And the priest, because she knows something Finn does not. Finn and his mother watch him travel in and out of his worlds for another hour. Finally, Finn falls asleep in the chair.

> *A man is dying in a bed. He knows this, and closing his eyes, sees the Horsehead nebula, sees big stars, Alnitak, Alnilam, Mintaka, hears around him in the room a faint human rustling. Those who love him. Their sounds fade. He*

*looks into the darkness behind his eyelids. There. In the dark lies the way, the bright stars. There. He floats.*

*And the wind comes out of the north like it always does and it is the same wind that lays down the snow on the hills and whips the icy flakes around the big collar he pulls tighter around his neck. It is the same wind that travels over Europe in the 1940s and earlier and brings the winters to his boyhood and makes the roasted chestnuts delicious. It howls like it howled in the war and kept them inside the bunkers as they dreamt of cherry-red coal fires in Quebec, and it keeps Finn and his mother up all night, the same wind that sings now full of the ghosts who come to see and to be seen by the man preparing to join it as it sweeps over the fields of war and lives and lakes and rivers and trees by the rustling marshes where the crickets and night-birds and all the life of the days fill the wind with their song, and the dawn brings the wind's innumerable imaginings to his bed, an old broken man who understands the song at last and rides it secure and pillowed and sleeping.*

"Oh Michael, do you love me?" *a lovely voice coos once and long ago.*

"You bet," *he answers toughly and looks up into the summer sky and digs his toes in the sand.*

"Do you have to go to war, Michael?" *she asks.*

"You bet," *he says and cocks his head toughly.* "All the boys are going—Poo and John, and George—everybody."

"Look at me when I'm talking to you!" *somebody says once and more than once.*

"C'mon, Michael, let's dance!"

"You're a little squirt, Vivian," *he laughs and they float off into the crowd.*

"Dad, sit up, and let me straighten out the bed."

"Michael. Michael," *Dick says.* "Don't cry. There. You see what you've done, Da. He's only a kid. Leave him alone."

"Dick? Dick? Where's Dick?"

"Dick died of a heart attack, Michael, a long time ago."

"Dick's dead? He had a heart attack?"

"Michael!"

"George? How did you get to Belfast?"

"Was uncle George ever in Belfast, Dad?"

"I don't know. Where are we now?"

"Home."

"Home."

"Sit up for a minute, Mr. MacBride."

"What in hell is that?"

"It's your I.V. unit with a sedative."

"I want to pee."

"You have a catheter. Just relax and don't worry."

"Isn't this a bitch," he says. "My name is Michael MacBride."

"How are you feeling?"

"Okay. I want to pee."

"We're all here."

"Who's that?"

"Who?"

"Mother and Dad will be down to see me tonight."

"Yes."

"And Jean and Lyman."

"Yes. Everyone."

"Is Dick coming too?"

"Yes."

"Who's that? I want to get up. I want to get out of bed."

"Okay. How's this?"

"Good. Good. Where's mother?"

"Right here."

"Oh?" And the wind howls and sings and he supposes it carries him back to his bed and he can feel it blowing on his face cold and steady.

"I don't want any oxygen. Take it away." No, he thinks, he doesn't need it because the wind is bringing him all the air he needs.

*"I'm outperforming the oxygen," he says enigmatically, "I'm outperforming the oxygen." And he is, as the wings grow out of him and lift him and the voices close in and lullaby and call and nothing can stop the wind from entering the room.*

*"Good Morning, Mother," he says brightly.*

*"Michel! Michael!" the voices call.*

*"Hi, Poo!"*

*"Let's go. John's waiting. We'll meet the girls at the dance."*

*"There's John!"*

*"Michael! Let's go. We're late!" And they cock their fedoras the way Cagney does and walk to the dance and stride in together strong in their companionship and youth, and the girls are there for them, Vivian and Twiz and Beulah and Eileen and Margaret.*

*"Look!" cries Vivian, "it's the Three Musketeers!"*

And they dance, long, long before the telephone is built that will ring for the only one left to pick it up and hear the widowed voice on the other end.

"Oh God," says John, "now, I'm the last of the Three Musketeers."

## Chapter Twenty-Five

# The Road Home

T he car traces the road home through the rain. Finn and his mother are quiet as his mind moves over the lake.

He knows his friends will sympathize and inquire after him when he gets back to London, and he will be asked if he feels empty. He could say he doesn't because he lost his father's presence years before. He could say the absence had gradually filled up with other things. It would not be true, for he can feel himself changing, and the intensity of his father's depths over the last two nights has been like peering into a place that was formless and void. He is beginning to feel a deep wound, and though he could deny it, he will not. The fires of loss unfurl around him and his mouth is filled with ash.

As he drives the road with his mother beside him, he remembers the winds in the spruce when he was a boy and the singing of Cree names, Kapuskasing, Temiskaming, Nipissing. The land was vast, without beginning and without end. The snows were long and his father loved them, loved the land emptied of all but itself, and Finn learned to love that too. He told Finn once that the winds in the trees gathered up the secrets of the north and rolled them cleanly through the world. Finn wonders what the winds told his father in the room where he lay dying.

But then, he thinks, understandings, like seeds beneath the snows his father loved, sprout slowly and in their season.

His thoughts move to Lara and Michael who will arrive in the afternoon. He wants to tell his son and his wife that he has learned that the end of the world can come in many ways; that the slow accretion of incremental devastations can bring it, as it did with his father, and as he thought was happening with him, but such an end is different than losing someone you love and cannot imagine being without, the things that you build your life on.

And there are the things that you love and leave you diminished when they go. Finn thinks of the seminary, and flying, and the fires in the earth.

He feels the understanding coming slowly, and he hopes he has the words to tell his wife and his son clearly and without reserve. He knows there are different ways to deal with such sorrow, but mostly they are just ways to blunt it, and that is all that time does, really, and so, he thinks, you have to guard what you have when you have it. Hemingway said this, and said that sorrow can only be cured by death, and if it is cured by anything less than death, the chances are that it was not pure sorrow, and maybe he was right.

Finn is newly afraid of losing Lara and Michael and he is tired of fending them off.

He wants to return to his father's house and look out the window to the lake. He will think of the good things, of Lara and the boat trips, and Michael and the fishing trips, and his times as a boy with his father and mother on the Little Abitibi riding home on the river with only the starlight to guide them. He will walk out into the waters, his feet bare in the sands, holding a lantern aloft to watch the pinheads at his feet, and listen to the lake, and feel the sand in his toes, and watch the red moon plunge like a blade into the waters of the Manitous, for the lake is more home to him than he has admitted.

Finn thinks about the resolutions he is making as he drives, and he wonders why he has not made them earlier. He is no longer afraid to let out his fears in front of Lara. It is no longer better to be misunderstood than to appear weak. He thinks of Father Callaghan, the flinty Jesuit who sowed hardship on an already stony path, and of Father Dawn who spread her arms and took in the griefs of the world.

When Finn pulls into his mother's driveway, he gets out of the car and moves around to the other side to open the door for her. He takes her hand and lifts her to her feet. Her weight is a tentative, birdlike thing, and he thinks of Lara and her love of bones and birds. They are quiet as they glide through the rooms and stand where his father watched the small rains drift in over the water. Finn looks out to the Manitous lying flat in the gloaming.

He thinks of his father's love for the physical world and the world view his mother brought to him, of manitous and reverence. He knows his father worked to meld the two perspectives, and Finn thinks that it is his mission now, to make it coherent and teach it to Michael.

He thinks of Michael training for his own war and tries not to despair.

Out in the lake the volcanic pipes lie dormant, and the buried worlds of his father move into his viewing. The submerged peaks of old lands rise into view and their presence remains.

He reaches out and takes his mother's hand.

"Who are your favorite poets, Finn?" she asks. Finn is startled at the question and looks down at her.

"Jesus, Mother. Well, after Hopkins, probably the English war poets," he says. "Owens and Sassoon. And Rupert Brooke."

"Your father's favorites. He used to read them to you."

"I remember," says Finn.

"And Kipling. 'The Sons of Martha'. He loved that poem."

"I know," says Finn.

"You never recite them," she says.

"No," says Finn. "It hurts to say those particular poems out loud." He looks down and meets her gaze. It is calm and clear. But inside himself, Finn feels a great dissolving. "I don't know what to do, Mum," he says.

"It's time for you to come home, Dear," she says. "Back home."

Finn thinks about the cool sap flowing through the trees and the plants and about the tightly-knit life of the taiga. Less is suddenly more.

A Great Blue Heron sweeps down, coming in slowly, cupping and folding its wide wings with majesty and grace, and lands on the front lawn. It stands motionless before them, and Finn feels his father's love for these birds wash over him. He feels the spirits of small beasts and birds his father spoke of, and a stirring far out over the lake where the old volcanic pipes rest on placid waters. While the heron is poised in the stillness, another glides in and settles beside it. They stroll together out to the rocks and into the water, lifting their long legs reverently in a strange, slow dance, and remain there as the evening deepens and the gloaming all but obscures them. Then, spreading their wings, they rise silently and glide into the darkness.

CHAPTER TWENTY-SIX

# A Company of Men

May, 2002

Exactly one month after his father died, and at the same hour, Finn is claimed by a dream.

He walks down a long hallway to a room where he is expected to give a talk. Approaching the door to the room, he sees, within, a round table, and seated at it is a group of all his father's friends. They are gathered to hear an anecdote Finn is about to recount, and his father is waiting with them, sitting to the right of an empty chair reserved for Finn, a little pale and weak and a little confused. The old man is there to hear the story his son is about to tell. It is the story of his life. Finn somehow knows his father has not heard it before, and does not know it, though the story is his own, but the old man is interested now and earnest, and he wants to hear it spoken and to learn it. While he was living, he was inside his life and could not see his story in its entirety, and so it seems to Finn not at all strange that the tale has not been for his father to tell, nor does it seem presumptuous that it is up to a son to begin it in a way a father can understand, among the company of men he has lived with and loved. Only here can he see what it is for the first time. And so it is for all the men in the room, for only the plurality can explain the singular if it is to be understood, and the story of one man's life is never his own to recount. A life is a tale that takes many tongues in the telling, so Finn leans forward and puts his hand on the back of his father's neck, for he knows that his father is hurting, though he does not know how he knows, and his father nods softly.

The circle of men draw close, shoulder-to-shoulder and lean forward to hear. They are eager to listen and are happy to be a part of the story, to know that each is giving the sharing of their lives as a great gift one to the other, and they are comfortable and happy that Finn's father has shared his life with them, and Finn is thankful. He leans forward.

"I know a man," he says.

# PART THREE

# Interlude: What The Silence Said

## Chapter Twenty-Seven

# What the Words Say

When you come to a fork in the road, take it.

~ Yogi Berra

And then the sons begin to die. Finn's mother conveys the news over the phone.

"When did it happen?" Finn asks.

"Last week. He was so young."

"Jesus. He was only a couple of years older than me. Well, mother, now your sons are dying of natural causes. The husbands are all dead, dammit, except four from the original forty. Three of the wives have died, and now the sons are dying." Resentment balloons in his chest.

"Only three of the women have died?" she asks, surprised. "Oh, yes, that's right."

"That's why Ross broke down and cried over Christmas dinner," Finn says, referring to one of the surviving men. "He was sitting with his wife and four widows of his friends. You were one of them. The man is eighty-two years old and feels like he's in a war. All his mates have been picked off, he's on the front line, and now even the sons are dropping."

"Sweetheart, it's not a contest between men and women," she says. "It's just the way things are."

"It sure as hell feels like it sometimes," he says, "when you profile the casualties."

"Finn," she says, "calm down."

It was worse with the Crees he grew up with, Finn thinks. The fathers of both families were shot, not by women, admittedly. One of the sons, Harry, died in a knife fight, another, Henry, froze to death, both in their twenties. A third died he can't remember how. He believes only one or two of the sons in those families are still alive, but can't be sure. The men didn't last long, he thinks. He tugs his collar, loosening it and wonders if Samson is still alive. The older Cree boy took Finn under his wing when he was eight and they cut their thumbs, mixing the blood into each other's cut to make them blood brothers. It's silly to admit now, but then, as boys, it meant something. More than that, it was formative. He doesn't want to think of Samson not being in the world.

"Tell me more about your trip back to the Canyon," says Finn, breaking away from his thoughts. His mother and four widows returned to the place where the little settlement once stood, and where their lives as brides and new mothers began.

"It was wonderful," she says as Finn sits back to listen. "Edna, Sybil, Marion, Ruth and I took the Polar Bear express as far as Cochrane, and drove the rest of the way in. Marion hasn't been back since she left thirty years ago, and she hated the place then. You know, her husband Bob loved it there, and now she said she was happy to have gone back and make peace with the place. She said she never realized how lovely it was, and wished she could do it all over. Poor Bob missed it so all those years. Ruth of course brought Gord's ashes with her to scatter over the Canyon. We got that out of the way, then enjoyed ourselves. It's so peaceful there now with all the houses gone."

"Yes," says Finn, "now all the little gods of place will return with the absence of the white man."

"Nonsense," she says. "The trees are springing up all through where the houses were," she continues. "Of course, the staff house is still there for the men who come in to do repairs on the dam. And now the Hydro says it was a big mistake tearing down the houses and relocating all the men who worked on the dam. They say it's more expensive running the dam now that it's automated than it was with the families close by. Isn't that something?"

"So there's nothing to show for all that happened there? Fifty years of work and raising families?" Finn asks.

"Like it was never there," she says.

"What about the dam?"

"It's such a shame, it's in such bad shape. The lumber companies have clear-cut everything across the river just over the hill, and there are thousands of square miles without a tree anywhere. The trucks are coming and going day and night, and drive across the poor old dam. They're shaking it apart. And you wouldn't recognize the land where they've cut down the trees; remember how they went for as far as you could see—hundreds of miles–and now those damned lumber companies have cut them all down. God, it makes me so mad!"

"How can they do that?" Finn feels his eyebrows shoot up. "I thought that was all government land?"

"Well, there you are," she says. "It's the government."

Finn snorts; for his mother, there are three hundred years of grievances in that statement. "What about the monument on the dam? The one dedicated to the men who fell into the concrete and were left there?"

"White men," she says.

"I know that," he says. He hears her amusement.

"It's still there," she says.

"Did you write down what was on it? The names?"

"Yes, but when I got back I couldn't read my own writing, so I don't know what it says." Finn is dumbfounded. "But I'll send it to you anyway," she finishes.

"You couldn't read your own writing? When did you discover that?"

"Well, Ruth wrote some of the names too, but a lot of them were Norwegian and she had the same problem," she says. "These things happen to people."

The image of five old women gathered around a weatherbeaten monument to dead men, writing down a record of lives in handwriting that was immediately unreadable confounds him. He summons up an image of the pitted cairn, sees the concrete flaked and cracked by fifty bitter winters. He wants a copy of that record because it helps him think about who was there, and he wanted it in his mother's hand. Ideally, he would like to have a rubbing of the brass plaque with the poem on it, so, like the rubbings of the old tombs in England, it could become a talisman connecting him to a time that is gone. But it is, he realizes on a deeper level, no Rosetta Stone.

"Well, how many men died in the dam?" he says. "Did it say?"

"I don't know," she says. "Some say eight; some say forty."

"Good God. Doesn't anybody know?"

"It was more than fifty years ago."

"Isn't it on the plaque?"

"I couldn't tell. But the poem was written by Kipling."

"Rudyard Kipling. I know that," Finn says.

"Yes," she says.

"It's 'The Sons of Martha'," he says.

"One of your father's favorites," she says.

"I know," says Finn, "and Kipling's other poem 'If'."

"Linda wouldn't come up with Ruth, you know," she says, changing the subject. "She was furious that her father's ashes were going to be scattered there. But Gord loved the place. He said the years there were the happiest time of his life. I think we should go back with the kids."

"Who? What kids?"

"Well, the women, with the grandchildren. They would love it, and the stories we could tell."

"They could see what's in store for them," he says absently.

"What do you mean?"

"Nothing. Did you go upriver to see the Red Sucker River? Or Johnson's cabin?"

"No. None of the men at the Staff House had time to take us up."

"Remember the poplar trees in the summer," Finn says, "with the light tremoring through the pale green leaves along the river, and the spruce trees in the winter, with snow, and the wind whistling through their needles? And the smell of the spring and of the fall, and the fields humming in summer with grasshoppers and the river with the fish and the swimming?"

"Yes," she says.

He thinks of the men who worked hard on the Little Abitibi, now gone and largely forgotten, and the quiet that surrounded them as they moved through the forest, and the love of the woods they taught to their sons.

"Did you get a picture of the monument on the dam?" he asks.

"No," she says, "the damned camera."

"It broke?"

"No, it ran out of film." She speaks as though the camera had suddenly acquired a will of its own, some malevolent little manitou making mischief.

"Didn't you have any extra film?" he asks.

"Of course I did. But I couldn't remember which roll was exposed."

"Good God," he sighs.

"So I put in the wrong roll and all the pictures were all double exposures."

"Spooky," says Finn, trying not to imagine the ghost-like images. "Didn't you get any pictures at all?"

"I threw them all away, I was so damn mad." She is quiet for a moment, then goes on. "You know, all the men who worked down in the operations room were hard of hearing."

"Yes," he says. "Did you do down into the old operations room where Dad worked?"

"Yes," she answers. "Remember how clean it used to be? There wasn't a speck of dust anywhere when the men worked there. Mr. Leblanc kept it so clean and shiny." He recalls the glossy green and grey paint of the pipes and turbines, the spotless terrazzo floors. She goes on. "It would break your heart to see it now. Of course, it isn't used anymore, but it's so dirty and sad there now." She pauses, and he hears himself talking to her, but his mind is back in the operating room when it was filled with working men, clean and confident, a wonder to the small boys who visited. The room gleamed with dials and controls as the water from the river above surged through the pipes and set the turbines spinning with a mighty, low-pitched hum. The sound was always present, and when he had visited his father and the other men working there, his ears carried the deep "o-o-o-m-m-m" long after the visit was over and he was in the sharp, sudden sunlight above.

"What was it like to be back, Mum?" he asks, forcing himself to return to the situation.

"Well, Dear," she says, "it was just the land. Now that your father's gone, you're the only one besides me who remembers the things we did, what it was like for our family. And there's a lot you two did that I don't know about—your time together in the bush. We can't know everything, and there's no use trying. We can't go back, and the Canyon is gone. But the land is still there, and that's what your father loved. You loved it too. He used to say that the land was as close to forever as we can get. People and places come and go."

"I suppose," Finn says.

Did she stand on the bank of the river where Becky Brennan's house used to be, looking to where the wooden docks once harbored the cedar boats, where nothing but memory remained? Had she thought about Johnson's cabin far upriver and the times they spent there camping, picking wild raspberries and telling stories? Her favorite spot was further upriver where the Red Sucker, a small tributary with clear, tea-colored water, flowed into the silt-laden waters of the Abitibi. For years, she wanted her ashes to be scattered at the confluence of the two rivers.

He thinks of the boat-rides with the weathered, green Johnson twenty-five roaring solidly in the back. Sandy cliffs topped by tamaracks lined the river, and hidden bays with clear streams feeding the river nestled between the bluffs. The boat hugged the shores as they sought out secret spots for picnics. His father fished, watching over them from the smooth granite rocks as the sun danced on the river.

At sunset they would start home, loading up the boat and pushing off into the current, riding the river easily in the dusk, and by nightfall they would reach the last bend in the river where the lights strung across the dam called them home.

And he remembers Bear Hill and the blueberries that covered it, across the tracks. He filled the metal honey-tins with the small fruit as he followed his mother, eating more berries than he saved, until the warmth of the sun and his heavy belly put him to sleep, and then she continued to drop the purple berries into the tins with a staccato of tiny thuds. The small sounds lulled him, and the occasional movement of his mother through the low bushes made his sleep happy. She wore a white kerchief knotted at the front to bind her hair, and her white blouse was tied in a single knot at the bottom above her favorite red shorts.

"Oh," she says now, "it was beautiful, the trees and river."

"That part's still there, the things that made the place special," he says.

"Well, we still have you kids" she says.

"I suppose," he says.

"You won't find what you're looking for there, Finn, if you decide to go. It's here now, on the lake. But maybe you should go see for yourself."

"Well, I did go a couple of years ago with Don," says Finn, "but I wanted to hear what it was like for you too."

"You were there as long as your father and I were," she says, "and though you were pretty little, it was your world. That's why you miss it so much. It was everything you knew for a long time."

As he finishes the conversation, he realizes he's not sure what he wanted. He knows his mother is telling him that the place is no longer in the present or the future. It's past. She's saying that the house at the lake is the present and the future. Finn can feel his own resistance.

Perhaps if he calls Eliot Mitchel and gets more details it will help. Eliot was among his favorite people from the old days. He thinks of the dandelion blossoms that Eliot picked to make into wine in the summer. The gold blooms carpeted the grassy knolls of the settlement, and he loved to ride through their rich smell each morning before the hamlet was awake, alone and exuberant in the sunshine. And he loved Eliot's humor and his jokes. Finn's mother spent one hot summer afternoon in 1952 filling bushel baskets with picked dandelion flowers to make wine, and at the end of the day Eliot had seen what she had done and shook his big head sadly. When she asked what the problem was, he told her that she had picked the flowers in the afternoon, and they would be too bitter for wine; she would have to throw them out and pick again in the morning, before the sun got hot. She emptied the baskets into the river, angry, hot, and tired, and began again the following morning. It was nonsense, of course, and Eliot had laughed at the joke later that week and for forty years.

Finn thinks of these things when he hangs the telephone up. He thinks of being happy to leave the house as a boy, of jumping on his bicycle to ride down the grass as the sun warmed him, and he recalls how good it was to reach the school before the others.

Then he thinks about Gord Burroughs and he remembers that the man was laughing and always busy, that his wife packed some of the best picnics in the settlement, and when they went upriver, anyone invited was lucky because it was more like a feast and a party than a picnic. And now here was the last picnic, with Gord himself in the basket.

But something else prods Finn about those men and women. The fathers had been fearsome when they returned from the month-long hunting trips, dirty from the weeks in the forest. Their beards had grown rough and the men had become more like the forest itself, more like the beasts they hunted. They smelled like the trees, like smoke and man-scent and the animals they killed. They had become large and rough and strange, and the birds and animals they brought back in death were strange too. Their rankness lingered and their totem stares came to him in the night. The mothers and wives flew out of the houses when they returned, stepping high and calling to the men in shrill cries. They sang their admiration like strange birds around the circle of men butchering the game in the midst of the little settlement, and the women were wild things too as they helped prepare the meat that would keep them alive when the deep snows came.

These thoughts move through Finn's heart, though he cannot name them. They touch the origins of man and woman, and he can only say that another man moved away and died long after the shelters were leveled. That it was always so. That a man loved a place so much he wanted his ashes scattered where he raised his family, in a human spot where his life was rich with laughter and love, and so he is dispersed where brightness shone for a while before it flickered, a brightness that still shines enough for some to see, and to return to.

## CHAPTER TWENTY-EIGHT

# What the Words Do Not Say

Nevertheless, Finn is shaken. The fortunes of war and the natural span of a life are different things, and luck or skill have nothing to do with the latter. He decides to take a leave of absence from the college and retrace his father's travels in Europe. It feels important that he make that journey part of himself. But his own past is beginning to feel as remote as his father's, so he wants to revisit the places he haunted between his tours in Vietnam: Greece, and specifically Crete, where he spent the better part of a year before re-entering the war. He is convinced that Holland and Greece still beat with a dependable human presence–in Holland, where people live in houses four hundred years old, and Greece, where two-thousand-year old temples stand and the geologies still show the carving of human hands.

A week after his conversation with his mother, he broaches the subject with Lara over breakfast.

"Why?" she asks, setting down her coffee. "What are you looking for?"

"I don't know," says Finn. He looks across the table at her. "Who I was. I don't know, Lara. Something to hold on to."

"More like something to let go of, Finn," she says. She looks down into her coffee, pushes the mug back and forth, then looks up. "You have to get yourself into the present."

"I know, but how?" Finn pushes back in the chair and looks out the window. "Every night I get pulled back, and now it's like some things never existed at all. I mean where I grew up. There's no physical evidence that any of those first decades ever happened. And now, Dad's gone and mum's talking more and more about the spirits."

"You think it's creepy?" she asks. Finn looks back at her and laughs.

"No, but I feel like everything I thought was real is being pulled out of my brain and there's nothing left. Like it was all a dream. Everything. No different than an invention."

"What about moving back to the lake? I thought that was going to help."

"Right, but so much about mother is … I don't know, her mind is in two places: now, and what's gone, and with her, 'what's gone' is more than the 'now'. It's gloomy. Her little manitous are dark. And you know what else? Things don't last in the north—I mean human things."

"You mean buildings," she says. "The land lasts, and that's what your father loved."

"Yeah, I know," says Finn. "But there's no human history. The taiga covers everything up pretty quick. You walk through it and you're still not much different than the paleo hunters moving through the wilderness, leaving no trace. You're a part of the landscape, but in Europe the landscape's been made, it's a part of you."

"It's a blip, Finn."

"But it's a human blip, and we don't see the other side. Here, in the north, the other side is in the present. It's like the world has been humanized in Europe, but not in the north here. You can touch the same pillars that Pericles touched three thousand years ago in Athens. Here, you can't even see where I grew up. It's all trees and scrub and bear scat."

"You're missing your father, Sweetheart. I understand that."

"It's more than just feeling vulnerable, I think," says Finn. "That thing with Mum … her sense of the land and time and the spirits of place—it's always in flux, there's nothing to hold on to."

"Well, it sounds like what you liked about being with the Buddhists, being in the moment, so you're not making a lot of sense. You've been morose since Dad died. You need to get past it. Not bottle it up," she says.

"I know," he says. "I'm bummed." Lara looks at him and narrows her eyes.

"Going to Europe won't help," she says.

"I think it will."

She sighs and leans back, purses her lips, and nods. "Then go for a couple of weeks, Finn, and find what you need to find, and then come back to us, I mean really back to us."

And now he drives east and north from Amsterdam, following the shore of IJssermeer, the old Zuider Zee dyked and silted up to form the largest lake in Europe, and down from Friesland toward the hilly country and the Rhineland's cemeteries, then west again to the lowlands where the country lies lined with canals and the windmills punctuate the fields. The long farms stretch back from the roads that Finn travels, narrow and deep and straight by the little towns, and their tidy pastures unroll behind them.

Finn rehearses his father's stories as he drives, and although his father could never bear visiting the cemeteries of the Canadian dead, it is why Finn is here: to stand where an old man's griefs reside, seeing for himself what his father would not tell: 2,338 buried at the Grosbeak Canadian War Cemetery; the Arnhem Oosterbeek Cemetery with 1,680 Commonwealth dead commemorated; Holten Canadian War Cemetery with 1,393; Jonkerbos War Cemetery with 1,629 Commonwealth dead; Liberation Forest, where the townspeople of Groningen planted a forest of maple trees as a memorial; the Man With Two Hats memorial in Apeldoorn; the Uden War Cemetery with 700 Commonwealth burials. And over the carpets of green, always the groups of schoolchildren tidying the cemeteries, young boys and girls by the white markers. All of it in this country of 41,000 square miles, 1/10th the size of his native Ontario.

And so he travels, stopping in the little towns with their big central squares, through Gouda with its market and the cheese wheels laid out in neat, orange rows on the cobbles, on to Delft where the light fills streets lined with shop windows and their blue ceramics. He visits the Old Church in Delft, the Oude Kerk built in 1246, where Johan Vermeer is buried, the painter who trapped Delft's light on his canvass, and then walks to the Nieuwe Kerk and sits in the shadowed pews, and imagines his father being there as he writes down some thoughts about his passing.

Afterwards, he drives out of the town and stops at the beer gardens and cafés for hot Croques-Monsieurs and puffy little pancakes, poffertjes, and stroopwafels to eat along the way, and he ponders the country as it is, and how it was for his father.

At first, he is caught up in the chimeric nature of time and place until, finally, he drives to The Hague, and as he sits over croquettes and beer in the garden of the Posthoorn Bodega, he sees that the country is much like it was before the war, that the buildings and houses are centuries old, and that his father was caught in one of many fissures of time through which the lavas of war and human nature leak out.

In this wet, flat land married to a cold sea, his father lived with a company of men in quick fires that marked them as surely as time's slow burn erodes mountains and moves seas, for all the works of time are cradled in their own tectonics wherein man and water and rock are moved and shaped, from the early Neanderthal hunters to Finn himself and now his son, and because the cycles seem endless and occasionally marked by small rests in cafés like the one he sits in, Finn orders another beer as the long, soft shadows of evening reach out to him.

That night, he calls Lara.

"How is it?" she asks.

"Good," he says. "Confusing."

"And?"

"The country is amazing. Not what I expected. There's more to what Dad saw when he lived here than I thought.

"What do you mean?"

"Well, there's all this history and beauty, and the food is so distinctive, the place itself, and he was here when it all went to hell. Those guys were over here for years. He lived here and almost never talked about it."

"But it's beautiful again?"

"Yes, like it was before the war."

"The beauty returns Finn. It's a cycle."

"You're right," he says. "But the cemeteries, they were beautiful, but they hurt very much. They're beautifully kept, the white markers on the mowed grass, and the groups of young schoolchildren are there regularly maintaining them. They know more about these soldiers than our own kids back home."

"I wish you were here," Lara says. "There's still a week to go."

"I'm wrapping it up here and going to Greece. Just three or four days there."

"Greece. What happened there, Finn? It's never been clear. You talk less about it than you do the war, which isn't much.

"Just a break between tours. Between the time they pulled me out of the jungle and when I went back to pilot the Hueys. You know that. It's where I made up my mind to come home or go back in. I did a lot of thinking. A lot of it's not clear to me either." Finn hears himself stumbling. "It was a turning point that I don't fully get. I need to be there physically again and see if I can sort things out in my head."

"Sort things out? That doesn't sound good."

"Put things to rest, I mean," Finn says. He listens to the silence in the phone.

"Are you going to come home?" Lara finally asks. "You're not thinking of staying there, of not coming back? My God, Finn, is this what it's about? You're leaving us."

Finn hears the panic in her voice.

"No, no," he laughs. "You little fool," he says, and then his chest convulses in a sob. "Whoa," he says. "That was strange. Lara, there's no way I'm not coming back. You know that."

"But there's more to this trip than I thought," she says.

"Well, there's something I have to say goodbye to. Something in me. Here. Holland was about Dad. This is about me."

"Well," she says, "bring back what will help, and leave behind what won't. Leave it there. With Michael grown, there are no distractions at home. It's just you and me. You can't be spread so thin and get away with it anymore."

## CHAPTER TWENTY-NINE

# What the Silence Says

A nd so he leaves The Hague, rides the train to Amsterdam, then flies to Athens. He stands on the ferry deck as he approaches Crete and watches the dawn break slowly over the water, reluctantly at first, then giving way to a grey and glassy sea sliced by curved ridges of old rock. They look like the spines of sea monsters. As the sky lightens, the profile of Zeus, the god of forked lightnings takes shape on the mountains over Iraklion.

Once in the city, Finn checks into a pension, stows his gear, then retraces his steps downtown. The waiters step up to coax him inside as he walks past the restaurants, and one, wearing a red carnation on his ear, takes his elbow and leads him inside where he orders red wine and moussaka, a side of walnuts and feta, and for dessert a wedge of baklava with a demitasse of thick Turkish coffee.

Finn sips the sweet, muddy brew and thinks about the next day's visit to the ruins at Knossos where the old wars of King Minos brought young men and women from Athens as tribute to leap the bulls in his arena, and because they died quickly and in such numbers, their disappearance gave birth to the legend of the Minotaur, another monster huddled in the fissures of time.

It will be his second visit there, and he will stand on the balcony and look down into the dry riverbed and the old valley where the sea used to be before the volcano at Santorini changed the world in an afternoon.

A day later, he drives the narrow mountain road along the coast, past small shrines that house little lamps marking the perils of journey, and he thinks ahead to Rethymnon, an old fork in the road where a child began a life he now knows nothing about. Whenever he tries to imagine her, he looks out from behind the bars of a bamboo cage, and his mind closes against the thought of another lost girl.

The highway follows the coast leading to the west end of the town, and he drives past the new slips and the beaches to the old harbor whose seawalls cradle the little cafés along the promenade where the fishing boats anchor. He parks, walks the edge of the moorage to the tables at the rear of the restaurants, signals a waiter, and is led to a seat.

He is back at the same café he thought was heaven in an interlude between two acts in the theater of his war, in a country that wouldn't go away.

There is a statue of a warrior by the café entrance and a little green cypress in a terra cotta pot. The handful of colors he remembers are around him, pure and dazzling. There is the unbroken blue of the sky and the gold of the sun, the cobalt sea and the white buildings and the burnt umber of terra cotta tiles and the green cypresses. There is the yellow and orange and red of bananas and tangerines and northern apples in the bowl on the sideboard. There is the white cheese and yoghurt, the amber honey and the red tomatoes with the green basil sprinkled over them, and wine the color of the yellow sun.

Later, he thinks, there will be the sky and the stars and the moon, when the hard memories will nibble at his mind. Finn shifts in his chair inviting them. He looks into the mood of the memories and not at the memories themselves, for he begins to feel that some truths lie not in facts but in their atmospheres, and the moments crowd around him and open into the past.

Decades ago, he came here to think about going back to Vietnam. It took him almost a year to commit, and in that time he met a woman, Melissa, who had left London, travelled through Italy, across to Corfu, and finally to Crete. One evening, as he scanned the menu pinned to the doorframe of this café, she stopped beside him to do the same, and a waiter, mistaking them for a couple, coaxed them inside. They laughed and followed him through the dining room and out onto the patio where the tables were set along the promenade of the old port.

They talked over dinner about the ghosts of the past and the light around them. He said he had come here to determine his life, and her long legs slowly crossed and uncrossed under the table as she listened.

They left the café and strolled along the quay to watch the boats navigate the harbor, then out of the town to the beach. Melissa's eyes caught the sunset and the breeze lifted her hair.

She picked up a small, dried seahorse from the sand.

"Look," she said. "How sad. It's so small and perfect."

"It's still beautiful," Finn said. "Frozen in beauty."

Melissa laughed and took it back to her room.

After a month, they rented a studio together on a rise behind the city. The rooms faced east, and the sun entered the open doors and windows as though the morning came to them like an idea while they slept, and when their eyes opened, the sun filled the room. Then, they walked the streets past the boats, and things were simple and his dreams were quiet.

He liked climbing the narrow, rocky path that led up to their house on the hill where they watched the sea. The walk made life deliberate and gave it meaning. He had come here to think, and the place seemed to have been waiting for him, with just one of all the things that mattered, including Melissa.

At night, they sat in the chairs and gazed up as they talked, and sometimes they fell asleep. Then they rose with the chill of the night on them and entered the rooms and slept again until the sun woke them.

There was only one day at a time, he thinks now, and one night, and that's all there ever was, he thinks, except for memories, and there were plenty of those.

One evening, as she sipped wine over dinner, four mustached men entered the café. They wore the baggy black pants and white shirts of Crete and talked about the Germans and the fascists, about the Turks and the Greek land the Turks held. They walked over to a table, sat, and seethed over the invasions of Greeks by Greeks and by foreigners, and they lamented the wars of attrition through a three-thousand-year-old drama across whose stage even Socrates trudged.

"What are you looking at?" Melissa whispered fiercely. He was jolted back to his own table.

She had become dangerously quiet. He noticed it too late. She knew he was catching war fever, and was appalled.

"You shouldn't go back," she said much later.

"I should," he said.

"Do you want to fight?" She narrowed her eyes.

"I already re-upped," he said.

"Without telling me?" she asked.

Later, he began to see the scorn in her eyes.

"Why?" she finally demanded, but the phosphorous in him had caught fire. He did not babble about the nobility of war and issues of good and evil and the necessity of guarding civilization like he knew his father had, but he was nevertheless a conscript of history and a military family.

He went back to Vietnam, having forgotten the single-mindedness of an enemy who tried to kill him on every occasion. The war was not what he meant it to be, and yet he returned to it for reasons that were far from clear but impossible to resist.

When he returned to Greece after another tour, she was gone.

Finn's mind turns to the night Kostos followed him to this very café and sat down, bringing with him the words that changed his life.

"You're back," Kostos said.

"Where's Melissa?" Finn asked.

"Gone," said Kostos.

"What?" Finn asked, looking hard at the other man.

"She left this note for you," said Kostos. He placed an envelope on the table, sat back, and spread his hands.

Finn opened the envelope and took out the note:

"*Dear Finn,*

*I left this note with Kostos, and if you are reading it, you are alive. Really, Finn? You made no promises, and did not ask me to wait—perhaps you thought you would be killed and did not want to put that on me—waiting—there was no way for us to know, no word from you, so we are returning to England to make a life. Please be well, and let us go our own way."*

He looked up at the older man.

"She was pregnant," Kostos stated flatly. Finn was rocked back on his heels. "Now, she's married."

"What?" Finn said.

"A one-two punch," the other man murmured with amusement.

Finn croaked something about a mistake.

"No mistake about it," Kostos went on. "She wanted a house; he bought her one. Now she's giving him a child."

"Was that what she really wanted?" he asked.

"Yes. She wanted a child."

Why couldn't he be happy about it, he wondered aloud at the time. He wanted to wish her well, and tried hard to wish the husband good luck, but he felt like he had swallowed a stone.

"Well," Kostos said, "it's too late for you. You had your chance—again, apparently. She is showing you that life goes on."

But did she ever really want him? Finn remembers his face being numb at the news. He looked at the other man, and his eyes burned.

"She also left you this," said Kostos as he placed a small box on the table. Finn slid it closer. It was tiny, no more than an inch by three. He lifted the lid, and nestled in a bed of white cotton lay a dried and perfect seahorse, curled up like an embryo.

"My lamentable friend," said Kostos, leaning forward and placing his hand on Finn's. "She had a girl," he went on, "yours, and sends me notes with no return address." He leaned back and looked at Finn, nodding slowly.

"I told you when you first came here," he went on, "that America was a baby nation, not deserving democracy because of the Junta you Americans put in power here, and because of the wars you wage. And your own poor choices, my friend, lead you to be a part of that. Again. You begin to pay the price, personally. You have lost a family, and more of yourself than you care to realize."

Finn mumbled something about time healing all wounds.

"We shall see about that," said Kostos.

The moment closes, and Finn looks over the table to the boats where fishermen unload the catch. A young man, tanned and muscular and wearing only a swimming brief among the others in their dark, loose clothes, laughs as he works, his feet planted wide and firm on the wooden deck. He has the fine bones of the narrow-waisted Minoans in the frescoes of Knossos.

As he sits now, Finn feels captured by all these pasts—his own and others. He was free to sail wherever he wished after his tour was finished and Melissa had gone, but he had not felt free. He felt adrift, and that, he realizes now, is very different.

For three more days, he rises early and navigates the streets to sit in the quiet mornings before the town wakes along the slips of the Old Port where the high prows of newly painted boats throw down their colors on the waters. He has Melissa's note with him. He invites the recollections to wash over him, wondering if she is still alive, wondering about the child and why it was easier to leave then than it is to forget now.

He thinks about his mother and her wish for him to come home to the lake. He understands her call and feels the pull, but it seems like more exile, though he can't explain why.

He wants more evenings with the waiters lingering in the doorways and the diners on the waterfront while the belladonna spills its perfume into memory; more mornings with the smell of new bread threading the streets past minarets and old Phoenician ramparts and little churches with the icons of Christ inside and the humble square homes of the people, all stitched together by the cobble walks. He wants to be able to see the town all at once, with every aspect, every movement, every thought of every inhabitant in one great, completing moment.

And when he is gone, he will picture the men and women by the water as they sit on the metal chairs that are painted blue. He will bring that back with him. The checkered cloths will cover the tables and the town wine that is not very good but an object of pride will capture the candle fire as men and women enter the restaurants to inspect the moussaka and vegetables and joke with the cooks about their choice.

They will find the food simple, the salty olives and cheese filling, and they will laugh and break the white feta as they discuss the things that make life strange and worth talking about. Yes, he thinks, they will talk to one another and learn about themselves and see the world and hear the harkenings of old ghosts.

What business do these elements have with rapture? Finn knows the ruins hold some numenescence, that nowhere are the bones of earth more incandescent with the gleams of meaning than in Greece. It is his geography. It feels, inexplicably, like home.

And finally, he thinks of his son, who travelled here the summer before. Had he heard the distant lightnings of his father? What did they tell him? The boy was eighteen when he came to the islands, and when he left he wrote:

*Dad–*

*—I'm leaving the islands today. They're even more beautiful than you led me to believe.*

*Michael*

Then Finn thinks of the poem his father will never read because the old man has sunk from sight like an island under the sea, but today, today on Crete the morning spreads like honey on the dusty road as he walks to the beach. He strips off his clothes on the sand, wades into the sea, and when the water reaches his waist, he opens his hand to release Melissa's note. As he leans into the water, his feet break free of the sand, and he floats, gazing down at the seahorses hovering below in slow majesty.

# Notes
# Consequential Data

The novel is founded on several contexts whose implications are explored, defined, and analyzed:

- Geology, tectonics, lava/fire/energy, destruction, healing, re-formation.
- Renewal; the buried forces of life:
    1. planetary (physical), geology, continent building
    2. psychological—trauma and character building
    3. mythic: Titans, Atlas, Ieptus: the existential context building of human meaning and its application in names to the planetary features that in turn inform the creation of human minds and values: the inner landscapes inform the outer and the outer in turn inform the inner. We see the world through the lenses we create to define the world: we live behind the barriers of the human mind.

We derive an attribute from an event or feature, give it a name (mythic) and make it a force (a god) then imbue the mythos of the god back into the physical world.

**On Heidegger**: Being-in-the-world.

Heidegger argues that the individual engages in a struggle to discover the self. The struggle consists of separating who one is regarding the individual's potential (the authentic self) from the pull of the masses with their prejudices and values (the inauthentic self). The struggle for authenticity is to discover that each individual is unique and has his/her own destiny in the world–their particular way of inhabiting existence. This is what Finn's struggle consists of. The individual is driven to differentiate himself from the masses to discover who he is.

Kundera suggests that we are connected to the world like a snail is connected to its shell: we are not separate from it, and as the world around us changes, so too does our way of being in the world.

This existential context is the reality with which the characters struggle in the novel.

Moreover, the lens of a single lifetime is linked with the geological: what one character considers his or her own unique behavior reaches back to the neolithic and beyond. The evolution of character includes existential context and is directly linked to the physical world of formative circumstance: it is the shell on the back of every woman and man—or, as *Bones Redux* will explore, the individual may to a degree be the shell on the back of the world.

## Polyphonic aspects of the novel

The polyphonic aspects of the novel: the simultaneous development of two different and emotionally distinct themes, in this case, the contrasting and mutually incompatible states of being—the character's existential context—which in *Bones in the Dam* is meant to illuminate the challenges of trauma: the mode of being (a constellation of behaviors) that ensures survival in war but is designated as anti-social or even criminal in civilian society.

The main characters in the novel, as veterans, have been imbued with self-destructing patterns of seeing and acting in the world. However, the theater in which these patterns operate also allow Finn to experience life with an intensity and intimacy he cannot find in civilian life. For him, it is almost spiritual, and as such feels more real, more true. He feels more alive, more authentic, in these states. This is quite apart from the horrors that the veteran has seen and must deal with on his or her own. Finn is struggling with these two ways of being in the world. Civilian society insists he adhere to the one, but the society of conflict insists on the other. The existential challenge for the character here is to survive—to integrate the personality into a coherent, functioning behavioral set. To survive in war, the warrior may become a monster, sometimes a holy monster, but once the monster is set free, once a warrior becomes addicted to the intense immediacy of such a life with its adrenalin addiction, how long does it take and *what* does it take to become content with the absence of such intensity? Does the self degrade? How does the veteran choose who he or she will be?

What is the self? And what does "authentic" imply?

We trace Finn's struggle to give up who he has come to feel he is in order to be the domesticated worker, father, husband, that he is expected to be, but his fear is that he will not only lose some passionate core of himself, but he will become a hollow man, a hidden man, conforming to a pattern that is forced upon him.

He realizes the desperation of the situation comes in large part from the recognized importance of what he owes to his wife and his son. Can he assume these roles and keep the old one? Can he assume these roles and remain intact? Or must he assume these new roles, this evolved persona in order to keep himself intact?

The struggle is his existential paradox. Who is he, and who must he become in each of these theaters of confrontation if he is to survive?

Hence the "polyphonic" aspects. Again, the underlying metaphor of geologics describe similar dynamics: the slow, incremental movements of the plates that result in sudden and substantial shifts in the crust (personality), the underlying violence of the system (lava/id), the eruptions (vulcanism of the planet and the personality), the embodiment of these forces in the geologic record and in the genetics of humanity— the patterning of behavior repeated in father and son and grandson.

These two engines of change (continent building and character building) and the associated destruction of them (tectonics in the one and the breaking down of the personality through military training in the other) explore the forces of personality and what is involved (the depth, the process, the time) in rebuilding and reintegration. The breaking down in either model is quick and severe; the reassembly is slow and incremental.

## Changes in voice, tempo, and tone

The chapters or sections vary in tone, voice, and temperament (from the omniscient voice that incorporates the language of Genesis to the mundane language and tempo of everyday vernacular), but the thematics mentioned above remain intact—the two forces Finn struggles with, the choice of which world to belong to.

A shift in tempo implies a shift in emotional atmosphere. This is true in music and applies here. When the expectations of consistency in narrative voice override the necessities of tonal and atmospheric variation in the individual movements of the parts, that insistence on convention can be an oppressive stereotype. Variations in tempo and voice indicate what the novel (or section) is attempting on a deeper level. The "textures" of the chapters are deliberately different and reflect the state of being of the character at a specific point of development and are not secondary to an overarching, consistent narrative voice.

These variations in tone and language are commonplace in symphonic composition, but less so in the novel where the expectation of "consistency" in narrative voice can be oppressively rigid. Used here, they are intended to break free from the insistence on narrative homogeneity, which can suppress the spontaneous capabilities of the novel.

## The Poems

THE WINDHOVER
    To Christ our Lord

I CAUGHT this morning morning's minion, kingdom
of daylight's dauphin, dapple-dawn-drawn Falcon, in his riding
Of the rolling level underneath him steady air, and striding
High there, how he rung upon the rein of a wimpling wing
In his ecstasy! then off, off forth on swing,
As a skate's heel sweeps smooth on a bow-bend: the hurl and gliding
Rebuffed the big wind. My heart in hiding
Stirred for a bird,—the achieve of; the mastery of the thing!

Brute beauty and valour and act, oh, air, pride, plume, here
Buckle! AND the fire that breaks from thee then, a billion
Times told lovelier, more dangerous, O my chevalier!

No wonder of it: shéer plód makes plough down sillion
Shine, and blue-bleak embers, ah my dear,
Fall, gall themselves, and gash gold-vermillion.

               ~ Gerard Manley Hopkins, 1877


VIEWSHED
    for my father

The storm drove a heron past the window
as the old man leaned
into the glass and fought the weather.
The bird rowed the wind down
to the lawn, paced to the lake,
and when light thinned
cupped its great wings
around the darkness of the world.

Here,
old incense lingers like a ghost in the nave.
Soft knives of light carve
the church's gloom. Red and yellow columns of it
tilt into the silence where icons
cling to the sun and
air hides in the organ pipes.

Outside, a congregation
rustles in the streets,
winds rush out of the stones
rolling the dead into the loam, grinding
the white fever of my father's years into my own.

~ Finn MacBride, The Hague

## SONS OF MARTHA
~ by Rudyard Kipling, 1907

The Sons of Mary seldom bother, for they have inherited that good part;
But the Sons of Martha favour their Mother of the careful soul and the
troubled heart.
And because she lost her temper once, and because she was rude to the
Lord her Guest,
Her Sons must wait upon Mary's Sons, world without end, reprieve, or rest.

It is their care in all the ages to take the buffet and cushion the shock.
It is their care that the gear engages; it is their care that the switches lock.
It is their care that the wheels run truly; it is their care to embark and entrain,
Tally, transport, and deliver duly the Sons of Mary by land and main.

They say to mountains "Be ye removed." They say to the lesser floods
"Be dry."

Under their rods are the rocks reproved—they are not afraid of that
    which is high.
Then do the hill-tops shake to the summit—then is the bed of the deep
    laid bare,
That the Sons of Mary may overcome it, pleasantly sleeping and unaware.

They finger Death at their gloves' end where they piece and repiece the
    living wires.
He rears against the gates they tend: they feed him hungry behind their fires.
Early at dawn, ere men see clear, they stumble into his terrible stall,
And hale him forth like a haltered steer, and goad and turn him till evenfall.

To these from birth is Belief forbidden; from these till death is Relief afar.
They are concerned with matters hidden—under the earthline their
    altars are—
The secret fountains to follow up, waters withdrawn to restore to the mouth,
And gather the floods as in a cup, and pour them again at a city's drouth.

They do not preach that their God will rouse them a little before the
    nuts work loose.
They do not preach that His Pity allows them to drop their job when
    they damn-well choose.
As in the thronged and the lighted ways, so in the dark and the desert
    they stand,
Wary and watchful all their days that their brethren's ways may be long
    in the land.

Raise ye the stone or cleave the wood to make a path more fair or flat;
Lo, it is black already with the blood some Son of Martha spilled for that!
Not as a ladder from earth to Heaven, not as a witness to any creed,
But simple service simply given to his own kind in their common need.

And the Sons of Mary smile and are blessed—they know the Angels
    are on their side.
They know in them is the Grace confessed, and for them are the Mercies
    multiplied.

They sit at the feet—they hear the Word—they see how truly the Promise
   runs.
They have cast their burden upon the Lord, and—the Lord He lays it
   on Martha's Sons!

(The poem refers to Luke 10:38—42, Revised Standard Version:
   Now as they went on their way, he entered a village; and a woman
named Martha received him into her house. And she had a sister called
Mary, who sat at the Lord's feet and listened to his teaching.
   But Martha was distracted with much serving; and she went to him
and said, "Lord, do you not care that my sister has left me to serve alone?
Tell her then to help me."
   But the Lord answered her, "Martha, Martha, you are anxious and
troubled about many things; one thing is needful. Mary has chosen the
good portion, which shall not be taken away from her.")


## CARILLONS

Antiphonal Melissa, do you know
you sing the song within me, dwindle
and rebuff impingements
of that piece of money given as the fare,
disperse the labeled stacks of attitude,
unwrap a twilight on the grass?

~ Finn MacBride


## CAVAFY

The gentleman who haunts these small cafés
surrounds the tinctures of our fall
with nimble artifice.
Ambiguous as owls', his eyes
research the fissures of the brain.

His poems can uncork the past,
can catch capacities, and cast the parts
we've always played.
They indicate eternity is still the same,
—a sketch in words rehearsing afternoons
some twenty years ago,
an anecdote awakened from three thousand years
made relevant.

~ Finn MacBride


FINN'S DREAM

Who he is will
Flash out *like shining from shook foil* as he dreams, will
Tumble through skies beneath a burning phantom, see
Hands through dying eyes as monks reach out to him, will
Haunt jungles when leaves cradle the moon
And saps flow in noiseless migration
Sensed and unseen, imagined and unheard through all
Forests and in all places he will
Know the trees' wet breath in planetary uplift
As the waters of the world suspire
And flood the music of his nights.

~ Millet

www.ingramcontent.com/pod-product-compliance
Lightning Source LLC
Chambersburg PA
CBHW031104260626
47172CB00001B/209